Charmed, Texas, is a close-knit  **of love can come true. That's n** **waiting, and dreaming . . .**

By day, Allie Greene stays busy with her family diner, and keeping tabs on her teenage daughter. What's really exhausting Allie, however, are the nights. Not that she minds Bash Anderson unbuttoning her naughty desires—if only in her dreams. But what was he doing there at all? He's her best friend, and a father figure to her girl. Talk about awkward. Talk about OMG-heat-and-fireworks that are flipping fifteen years of normal upside down. And now, when Allie needs him as a friend more than ever, logic doesn't stand a chance against his lips and irresistible deep-blue eyes . . .

Sure, Bash has fantasized about Allie, but there's no way he'd act on it. She and her daughter are the closest thing to family he's ever known. With the exception of one drunken moment fifteen years ago, he and Allie have stayed on this side of the line—until that impulsive kiss of hers knocked him on his butt. That's just one hurdle. Not only does Allie need Bash's help to save her diner, but his apiary is in trouble, too. To stir the pot further, they've been roped into vying for the town's Honey King and Queen contest—a sweet event that's making them closer than ever. Something's bound to come undone. Bash just hopes it's not the friendship he's worked so hard to hold on to.

Visit us at www.kensingtonbooks.com

Books by Sharla Lovelace

Charmed in Texas Novels
Charmed Little Lie
Lucky Charmed
Once a Charmer

"Enchanted By You," a novella included in
The Cottage on Pumpkin and Vine

Once a Charmer

Sharla Lovelace

LYRICAL SHINE
Kensington Publishing Corp.
www.kensingtonbooks.com

LYRICAL SHINE BOOKS are published by

Kensington Publishing Corp.
119 West 40th Street
New York, NY 10018

All Kensington titles, imprints, and distributed lines are available at special quantity discounts for bulk purchases for sales promotion, premiums, fundraising, educational, or institutional use.

Special book excerpts or customized printings can also be created to fit specific needs. For details, write or phone the office of the Kensington Sales Manager: Kensington Publishing Corp., 119 West 40th Street, New York, NY 10018. Attn. Sales Department. Phone: 1-800-221-2647.

Lyrical Shine and Lyrical Shine logo Reg. U.S. Pat. & TM Off.

First Electronic Edition: October 2017
eISBN-13: 978-1-5161-0127-6
eISBN-10: 1-5161-0127-8

First Print Edition: October 2017
ISBN-13: 978-1-5161-0128-3
ISBN-10: 1-5161-0128-6

Printed in the United States of America

To my mother-in-law Janell, up there in that fancy book club in the sky...
now you'll always have the first copy. :) Love you.

CHAPTER ONE

"Damn it, Bash, get out of my head."

It wasn't the first time I'd muttered that sentence over my travel mug lately on the way to the diner, but it was the first time it had made me late.

Actually, my teenaged daughter was the culprit on that one, attempting a sick day and dragging the morning out, but the not hearing my alarm part was on me. Or on Bash. My best friend. My really hot best friend that I couldn't quit having very vivid dreams about.

Yes.

Those kinds of dreams.

About Sebastian Anderson doing things to me I had no business thinking about him doing. Thoughts you aren't supposed to have about someone who's been your rock, your buddy, your confidante, and has had your back for everything for fifteen years. Until a few months ago, when I stupidly showed my hand in a moment of weakness. A really old, never-supposed-to-be-seen-again hand that came out waving during a crisis and now spent the twilight hours slapping me silly with fantasies. Before leaving me tossing and turning in frustration until the alarm went off. Too many nights of that, and the alarm ceases to matter.

I rolled my head on my shoulders as I walked through the front doors of the Blue Banana Grille, shaking off all the rest. I couldn't think any more about sex dreams or Bash Anderson. *This* mattered right now, whatever was going on here. My diner. My legacy, passed to me by my father, and maybe one day to my daughter, Angel. After finishing high school, college, medical school, and joining the Peace Corp and saving the world. Maybe. I didn't really see her as wanting to come run a small-town diner in Charmed, Texas, after all that excitement, but stranger things had happened.

Assuming she got out of her phone long enough to finish high school and quit trying to play hooky.

I smiled at Lanie McKane, Nick's wife, who looked up from a crossword puzzle and cup of coffee to wave and mouth a *Hey, Allie!* at me. Nick McKane was my star head chef, and had patrons coming day after day to devour his creations. He was also easy on the eyes for most of the female population, so while his wife was most likely just waiting for him to take a break, I had a feeling that she also liked making an appearance now and then. I didn't blame her. Running a diner, I'd seen almost everything at one time or another, and if there was one thing I knew for sure, it was that women can't be trusted.

No, I wasn't selling out my people. I just called things as I saw them. And most of the women in this town had sold me out a long time ago.

I nodded at a few of my regulars that came several times a week for Nick's breakfast specials, and I picked up old Mr. Wilson's napkin that had fallen from his lap for probably the twelfth time. Our ex-mayor, Dean Crestwell, sat by the window on the far end eating his eggs like he wanted to hide under his jacket and beard. Sully Hart, the owner of the Lucky Charm, sat three tables away facing the other direction reading a newspaper. If I had my guess, one of them faced those directions on purpose to avoid looking at each other. My every-morning-at-the-counter-for-coffee old salts were already perched on their stools, flannel shirts tucked in, and white socks peering out from underneath trousers that were a little too short.

I glanced to my right, and *bam.*

Kick to the belly with all the tingling feels, as a certain pair of major blue eyes looked my way and did a little head nod as Bash sat talking to another man. *Shit!* Instantly, I was transported back a few hours to a particularly lusty dream where those same eyes were heated and dark and looking up at me from—

"Oh my God," I said under my breath, turning away immediately, my hand going directly to my messy bun—for what? To see if I looked okay? "Jesus, I'm pathetic," I added, yanking my hand back down.

I looked back at them sideways after getting behind the bar and tying on my black apron. I didn't recognize the other guy. Not that that was weird. Bash met with many people there at the diner, as plenty of others did. It was a good central location for all kinds of meet-ups, plus the food couldn't be beat. Bash Anderson was a major presence as the owner of the largest bee apiary in the area, and he could easily be talking to a new investor or client. Anderson's Apiary kept the town and probably a quarter of Texas supplied in honey, beeswax products, and beehives for hire. But while not knowing his breakfast partner over there wasn't a standout moment, the guy himself practically glowed with *I'm not from here.*

We were a pretty relaxed lot in Charmed. Casual was the basic dress plan, and stepping up—at least in my opinion—was just nicer jeans and maybe some killer shoes. Guys didn't even need the shoes. In stark contrast, this guy with Bash wore black slacks and a sweater, what appeared to be leather penny loafers on his feet and too much hair gel making his locks shiny. He looked like he belonged in a J. Crew catalog from the nineties. More than that was the leather bag slung over the back of his chair like a purse.

Definitely not from here.

Kerri, a college student I'd hired as a waitress two months ago, who still hadn't learned to memorize orders, came rushing over.

"Miss Greene, Nick said to tell you he needs to talk to you ASAP," she said.

"Okay," I said, glancing through the open window section to the kitchen where Nick was cooking with a scowl on his face.

"Also, that section over there by the Ficus and the bookshelf?" she added, pointing.

"Otherwise known as tables ten through fourteen?" I asked.

Kerri nodded. "Yes. It's leaking over them again. Has been ever since we turned on the heat."

Great. I made a mental note to call someone out to get up on the roof, or maybe Nick would take pity on me and do it later. I nodded toward J. Crew and lowered my voice.

"Who's that with Bash Anderson? Someone about the Lucky Charm?"

Charmed was getting an overhaul in the form of an entertainment complex along our pond. The Lucky Charm was the baby of Sullivan Hart, who came to town a few months back, an ex-carnie from the Lucky Hart carnival that had frequented our town for decades. Restaurants and shopping and rides and a boardwalk—it was already partially underway with a few rides and shops, and the town was in a constant state of chaos. Contractors, investors, businesspeople wanting to expand or kick off startups, they were as stirred up as an ant pile. For the diner, this was a good thing, as most all of them met up under my roof for a good meal.

Kerri followed my look. "No idea, but he was asking for you earlier."

I looked at her with a question. "For me?"

"Right before Mr. Anderson showed up," she said, nodding. "Nick talked to him for a minute, though, so maybe he knows."

I frowned back in the men's direction, where Bash looked to be hanging on every word J. Crew was saying. He did a quick double take my way, which sent the butterflies skittering again until he said something and pointed. The other guy turned toward me with a polite smile.

A smile that didn't quite reach his dark eyes. They remained distracted, and a weird familiar metallic taste filled my mouth as I looked into them. A déjà vu that wasn't pleasant. Which was ludicrous. I'd never seen this man before.

"Good deal," I said, also taking in the manicured hands, the fork in his left hand that was just poking at the food instead of eating it, and the expensive watch on his right wrist. "Get them some more water. Stand toward the new guy's right to fill it."

She frowned, glancing his way. "Why?"

"He's a leftie." She looked at me blankly. "He's new here. He's barely touching his food. So he'll be more approachable, less defensive, and more likely to leave a good tip if you serve him on his weaker side."

Kerri's eyebrows lifted. "Wow."

"Yeah, it's rocket science," I said under my breath as I pushed open the doors to the kitchen. "What's up, Nick? You know Lanie's out there, right?"

He didn't look up, focusing instead on folding some cream into a bowl of sliced strawberries that would go into his famous strawberry cake. That's what I loved about this guy. It was strawberries and cream, and he treated it like it came straight from a cow with a golden udder.

"Yep," he said. "I was just waiting for David to get here so I can run to the bank with her to do some paperwork."

I tilted my head. "She's taking her break from the bank, to come here to get you on your break, to go *back* to the bank?"

"That's what I said, but Lanie said if she waited on me, I'd get caught up in what I was doing and forget." Nick shrugged. "And she's probably right."

"You do get a little tunnel-visioned," I said.

"So did he introduce himself?" he asked, picking up a spatula to turn the strawberries gently.

"Who?"

Dark eyes darted my way. "The guy out there that looks like his mom dressed him to get beat up at school," he said.

I choked back a laugh as I plucked a strawberry slice from the top and popped it into my mouth. "No, he's meeting with Bash about something." I moaned around the berry. "Oh man, I need about forty more of these."

"I have the feeling you might want to double that," he said, frowning as he grabbed another bowl. "This guy—something's up."

I rose from the stool I'd just rested on. "Why?"

"I don't know, he's odd. He only wanted to talk to you, but now he's eating with Bash?" Nick said, shaking his head as he worked.

"What did he say?" I asked.

Nick glanced up. "It has something to do with your dad."

Something that felt like cold little fingers traced a path down my spine. Something old and familiar.

"Wh—why?" I asked, resisting the urge to reach out for the wall, the door, the sink nearby. Anything tangible and touchable that could ground me and yet make me vulnerable at the same time. *Don't show weakness.*

"He said he was here to talk to you on behalf of Oliver Greene."

On behalf of...

I stared at Nick, nodding slowly as I turned for the door. The man's face came into view as I emerged on the other side of it as he shook hands with a smiling Bash and the two men parted ways. J. Crew came up to the counter in front of me and sat on a stool, lacing his fingers. Instantly, I knew what the taste was about, the unpleasant sensation, the déjà vu. I'd never laid eyes on this man before, but I'd seen the others before him. They all had that same useless look about them.

I held out my hand.

"Allie Greene," I said. "What did he lose?"

* * *

My father was a good man. He had a heart of gold with hands of steel that had worked hard his whole life before illness stripped him of that. He also had a weakness. If there was a deal or a sham, a poker table or a get-rich-quick scheme within ten miles, he couldn't resist. If he had five dollars in his pocket, it would burn a hole until he was forced to spend it, and frequently that was aimed at something with chips or a bigger pocket. Especially during stressful times.

I loved my dad with everything I had, but I watched him gamble all our savings away after my mom died. The only new truck he'd ever owned was trailered and gone. Our house—I would never forget the man that came for that. I was seven, and that man's face would forever be etched in my memory as the person that took my room with the purple flowers and sent us to the trailer park.

This man had the same empty eyes.

"I'm Landon Lange," he said, gripping my hand. "I'm an acquaintance of your father's."

A tall woman with big blonde hair came through the door, striding straight up to the counter. "Hi!" she said, her voice perky, teeth flashing. "Can I get a cup of coffee?"

"Sure thing," I said, letting go of the man's hand and reaching for the nearby coffeepot robotically, pouring a cup. "Sugar and creamer are right there," I said, pointing without looking.

"Thanks, hon," she said. "Great place."

I met her eyes. Another stranger. I guessed bringing in a tourist attraction was going to bring that in, too.

"Thanks," I said. "Do you need a table?"

"No ma'am," she said, smiling so warmly I felt it around me like a blanket. "I'm meeting that handsome man over there," she said, pointing at Sully with a wink.

"Enjoy," I said, hoping I came across that welcoming. I felt my eyebrows lift, looking back at Lange as the woman walked away, taking her warmth with her. "So, an acquaintance," I said, smiling. "That's a new one. Although I'm curious how you know him recently since he's been homebound all this last year."

"It's actually been a little while," he said. "I was hoping maybe he'd come through."

"How much?" I asked, closing my eyes.

Landon Lange appeared to study his manicured nails on the countertop, then pulled a piece of paper from his man-purse.

"I own fifty-one percent of this diner," he said.

My eyes popped open. My *everything* popped open.

"What?"

"There's this—" he began, smoothing the paper on the counter. My counter. The counter I'd cleaned 4,394,839,409 times and now held a paper that said—

"No," I said. "That's not—"

"Miss Greene."

"That's not possible," I said, bringing the word down to a whisper. A hiss. An utterance of no-fucking-way. "This is my diner. It's ours. It belongs to my family. It doesn't go on the table—ever."

That was the deal. That was always the deal. *Please God, don't take away the deal.*

"Miss Greene."

"Stop saying my name," I said, hearing my voice rise but unable to control it. It was like someone else held the remote and was watching the show. The blonde lady moved as far over to the right as she could, and

Lanie moved slowly up to take her place as if she might need to vault it to kick somebody's ass.

"Everything okay?" she asked quietly.

"Why don't we go in your office," Nick said, miraculously appearing behind me.

"I have this signed—" Landon began again.

"I don't care what you have," I said. "It's not happening."

"Allie, please," Nick said in a low voice. "Let's take this in the back."

Nick was right. He was being the cool-headed logical one. Acting like management, taking charge of the situation. He was being me. And I was having a mental breakdown next to the coffeepot.

I own fifty-one percent...

Oh my God.

What did you do, Dad?

Walking to my office felt like the walk of doom, as the cold chill of things shifting washed over me. It wasn't my office if this guy owned—

The hell it wasn't. It was my mom and dad's before me and fuck if some man-pursed asshole was going to take it from me.

I spun around.

"Mr. Lange, my father has put a lot of things on the line over the years," I said, focusing on the tone of every word as it left my mouth. He couldn't have really done such a thing. I had to believe that. I had to hold on to that hope. "I've seen too many things lost, including my home, and he made a promise to me after that. The Blue Banana would never be jeopardized."

"Well, I'm sorry," he said, walking in, setting the paper on my desk without hesitation. "It is what it is. Signed and legal. He can verify it."

It is what it is.

Hope left the room. It peeled itself from every surface and floated away. My father did it. He lost it. He lost our everything.

I couldn't breathe.

"He—" I cleared my throat. "My dad can't verify anything. He's got dementia. Some days he isn't sure of his own name."

"Sorry to hear that," Landon said. "He was a nice guy."

"He's still a nice guy," I snapped.

Landon held his palms forward and then picked up the paper, holding it in front of me. "Can you just look at the signature?"

My feet felt rooted to the floor. I shut my eyes, feeling the tightly wound control I valued so much begin to slip away. I didn't have to look. I didn't want to. I'd know my father's writing in a heartbeat, and I knew with just as much conviction that it would be on that paper. Still, my eyes needed the proof. The stinging slap to the face. I felt Lanie's arm link through mine and Nick's hand on the back of my neck, while my eyes fluttered open to a watery image of a yellow form. A deed transfer. Of majority percentage of the Blue Banana Grille to Landon Lange. Signed and dated in a hard right-slanted hand by Oliver Greene, Owner.

I didn't even have a tenth of a percent to my name. I ran it as my own because it was our baby. My mother gave birth to it, my father raised it, and I took it on. Now this stranger that had never set foot in here before today had controlling ownership. Had been in control for a while, and I never knew it.

"This was signed last year," I said, my voice not much more than an exhausted whisper. "Over a year ago, actually. Why are you here now?"

He never changed expression, just set the paper down on my desk when I didn't take it from him.

"Honestly, I liked your father, Miss Greene," he said. "He's straightforward and truthful. I don't see much of that in my line of work."

"I'll bet," I said.

"What exactly is your *line of work*?" Nick asked from behind me.

"He's a bookie," I said.

"I'm a private loan officer," Landon amended.

"He's a bookie," I repeated.

"So," Landon continued. "I didn't want to capitalize on his bad luck. Thought I'd give him a while to straighten his affairs out, but he never contacted me again."

"His *affairs* are about sitting at home watching war movies and sports and taking walks from one end of the trailer park to the other," I said, cutting off the tears that wanted into my words. "Most likely, he doesn't remember any of it."

"That's unfortunate," Landon said, then shrugging. "Or fortunate, perhaps. Spares him the drama."

"What do you want?" I asked, swiping a rogue tear as it fell, letting that one little piece of weakness be my staff. I took a step forward. "You don't strike me as the diner type, Mr. Lange. I don't see you having any interest in a small town like Charmed or any of its establishments."

His lips tugged into an almost-smile. "On the contrary, Miss Greene," he said. "I see a lot of opportunity here. I've recently made a couple of lucrative investments here in Charmed—I figured why not since I own the majority of the most popular eating establishment." He smiled, and my skin prickled. "Give back, is what I always say."

The image of this man sitting across from Bash, shaking his hand, crossed my thoughts.

"What do you want?" I repeated, crossing my arms over my chest.

His smile grew curious. "Are you suggesting that I'm open to a payoff?"

"I'm *suggesting* that anyone able to so glibly take a man's livelihood with a piece of paper is probably just soulless enough to throw something else out there," I said, refusing to blink.

Landon clapped his palms together, rubbing them in a fast motion. "Oooh, an insult and a challenge all in one sentence," he said. "You do make it interesting, Miss Greene."

"How much?" I asked.

"Oliver was in to me for fifty grand," Landon said finally, setting my skin on fire with his oily words. "Not all at one time, mind you. I let him skate by a time or two. But things add up after a while and Oliver—well, he couldn't seem to get on the right side of it."

Fifty grand.

Sweet Jesus.

"But that was before I checked on it," he said. "The Blue Banana appraises for just over a hundred-seventy-five thousand."

I stared at him, not really seeing him anymore. One-seventy-five. Even split in perfect halves, that was over eighty-seven thousand dollars. We were done. I was done. I couldn't get that kind of money if I wanted to. I basically worked for him now.

"You—want Allie to cough up that kind of money to buy her own diner back?" Lanie asked.

Landon shrugged. "Makes no difference to me one way or the other." He turned to go. "But I have to ask—The Blue Banana?" He screwed up his face in dislike. "What's with that?"

My chest squeezed around my heart and I briefly wondered if cardiac arrest might be in my near future.

"It's personal," I pushed out.

He shook his head as if pondering it. "I'll give it some thought. We can do better than that."

And he was gone.

Nick and Lanie were talking to me. I felt hands and hugs, but all I could see were the eyes of another man that took something from me. The sound of his words telling me that my life's plan had just flipped on a dime. The feeling of what had always been solid ground under my feet being wiggled away one tug at a time.

"What are you going to do?" I heard Lanie ask.

"Counters need wiping," I said breathily, forcing myself to walk. "If Dave's back, go do what you have to do, Nick. We'll take care of it."

"Allie."

"Go," I said, looking back but not really focusing. "Business as normal."

Normal.

Whatever that was.

CHAPTER TWO

The next two hours were an out-of-body experience. I saw people talking, I heard the buzz; I even interacted and smiled, nodded and shook hands, and generally breathed in and out as if a universe-sized bomb *hadn't* been dropped on my head.

What was I going to do? What could I do? Go interrogate and rip my dad a new ass for breaking his promise, throwing our lives away again? The bitter anger that raged under the surface of my skin wanted to. With every turn, every pour of a coffee cup, every plate set in front of a customer, I had to grit my teeth together and swallow it back. Because I couldn't do that. I couldn't go off on an old man that did most of his living inside his own head now. Whose biggest joy was when his Dallas Cowboy T-shirt got washed so he could wear it again. He wouldn't remember doing this, and it would be selfish and cruel of me to beat him up with it.

I had to deal with it. I had to find a way to figure this out in what was now a foggy maze with no instructions or directions. Everything that had always been A was now Z. Up was down, green was the new blue, and for the first time in thirty-three years, I wondered what I was going to do with my life. It had never been a question for me. The most college interest I'd ever had was business courses at a nearby community campus, and that was so I could be a better restaurateur.

Now, I had no footholds. Everything was slippery. Everything hung on a sleazeball named Landon Lange. And Bash knew him.

There was another fiery poker.

Bash of the incredibly hot, embarrassing, carnal delight visiting my dreams each night. Bash, of the forever friend category, the man I could normally tell anything. Bash, the honorary uncle to my daughter, the child he delivered in a storeroom during a particularly stressful night when we were seventeen. My closest, dearest friend. Who I had kissed three months ago.

Because—crap.

I'd kissed Bash. And I was pretty sure he'd kissed me back. Everything had been flipped on its awkward ass ever since.

And now I'd seen him sitting buddy-buddy, shaking hands with the asshole out to ruin me. Good times.

My phone buzzed from my pocket. I shook my head free of the crazy and pulled it out. Angel's school. Awesome.

"Mrs. Greene?" a female voice replied to my answer.

"Miss," I said, accustomed to the assumption.

"Oh, sorry," said the young woman, a hint of fluster in her voice, as though she'd practiced a spiel and I'd knocked her off her game.

"Not a problem, can I help you?" I asked. "Is Angel okay?"

"Yes ma'am," she said. "Except she isn't feeling well."

I rubbed my eyes. Today wasn't the day.

"Is that so?" I asked. "Does she have fever?"

"No ma'am," she said. "But Angel said she has a bad stomachache, and there is a bug going around, so—"

"Well, this morning it was a bad headache and her throat hurt," I said. "But her throat was as pretty as can be. Have you asked her about fourth period-itis?"

The woman didn't find me amusing, probably because I questioned her ability to be a school nurse and not spot a fake a mile away. Fifteen minutes later, Angel was in the car, looking appropriately miserable for about thirty seconds before the first question kicked in.

"Can we stop at the Quik-Serve?" she asked, pointing at the convenience store up ahead.

"For?"

"I need to get some random magazines for a project for sociology," she said. And there it was.

"Uh-huh, and when is this due?" I asked.

"Oh, I don't know," she said, shrugging. "Next week sometime. But I'll probably do it today since I'm home."

"Right," I said. "Should I run in and pick them up since you're so ill?"

"Nah, I'm—I'll be okay," she said, placing a hand to her belly. "I'll only be a minute."

I pulled in, handing her a twenty. "Don't move too fast, don't want you puking in there."

Stomachache, my ass. That girl needed to realize who she was talking to, and the level of faking talent she needed to perfect before surpassing me. In my senior year of high school, I was six months pregnant before anyone suspected it. Not my dad, not anyone at school. And that included a month and a half of puking every time I smelled chalk. The only one I told was Bash, and he kept my secret.

I narrowed my eyes, studying her as she returned to the Jeep and got in with a plastic bag full of magazines.

"Are you pregnant?" I asked.

She looked at me like I'd sprouted warts.

"Are you high?"

I turned the key. "Just checking."

"I'd have to have sex first, Mom," she said. "I'm pretty special, but I'm not quite holy enough to pull that off."

And I'm not you.

That's what she had the tact not to say, but I knew ticked across her brain.

I'd never hidden the truth from Angel, she knew how she came to be and what the story was with the boy that knocked me up and bailed. I never wanted her to have the young struggles that I had. The stigmas and social barriers that I had to overcome. I wanted her to enjoy the fun perks in life and be loved and liked for the awesome person she was. I raised her to hold her ground and be her own girl, and not let herself be controlled by someone who got his kicks out of yanking her chains.

When she was younger, I thought I'd succeeded. Now, she was turning into such a *teenager*. Fortunately for her, she wasn't anything like I was. Unfortunately for me, I sometimes had no idea how to decode such a creature.

"Good to know," I said, pulling out. "Have everything you need? What is the project about?"

Angel shrugged and clicked into her seatbelt.

"No idea."

I blew out a breath. I wouldn't be a hypocrite. I was by no means a great student in school, and becoming a single mom at seventeen was certainly no prime example of what to do with your life, but this girl was smart. Like crazy smart. Straight A's without ever cracking a book until the teen years rolled around and she realized that being the class whiz wasn't cool anymore. It punched me in the gut every time I saw her waste her brain.

"Angel, you're better than that," I said, feeling her tune me out without ever looking her way. "I'd be willing to bet you know exactly what the project is, what's required, and five different ideas on how to do it better."

"Think so?" she said in a bored tone, her dark-eyed gaze focused on the small-town streets of Charmed passing outside her window.

"I know so," I said, yawning.

It wasn't even ten o'clock yet, and I felt like I'd lived a week outdoors being stomped by a horse.

"So what's with you not sleeping lately?" Angel asked.

If only that were something I could discuss with a fifteen-year-old. I shook my head.

"Just too much on my mind, I guess," I said.

"Bad dreams?"

I gripped the steering wheel a little tighter. *Lord have mercy.* "Something like that, too."

"About Uncle Bash?"

If I could have yanked my dashboard off and fanned myself with it, I would have. Oh God, what if I'd said something in my sleep and she heard?

"Why?"

"Because you cursed him in the shower this morning," she said. "You were too cranky to ask at the time."

I took a deep breath and let it go. I was cursing him before I even knew I had a legitimate reason. That had to say something.

"Don't say anything to Pop about me having bad dreams," I said. "He worries about stuff like that."

My dad being coherent enough to worry was really a fifty-fifty shot, but when it came to the subject of dreams in our family, he was likely to pull right out of his foggy little world and grill me for hours. He took that crap seriously. Protecting our livelihood—now evidently not so much.

Stop. It would do no good.

"Can we stop for donuts, too?" Angel asked, twisting a strand of dark wavy hair around a finger as we stopped at a red light and a new bakery sat all pretty at the edge of the Lucky Charm.

I stared at her for what I hoped was an uncomfortably long moment.

"For your severe stomach problems?"

She gave me an innocent hurt look. "It's comfort food."

"You are so full of it," I said. "I have to get back to work." *Because...why, exactly?*

"You own the place, Mom," she said.

Oh, just shoot me and throw me in the pond. The stab to my middle was so strong, I had to work for my next breath.

"Pop owns the place," I managed, shoving the words out. I couldn't tell her. Not yet. "I just—"

"Do everything?"

I cut Angel a sideways glance as we started moving. "Run the place," I said. "But yeah, that too." Since my dad's illness kicked in, and before that some back problems that had him down, the list never seemed to end. I'd actually missed the days of coming in to work for someone else who had all the responsibility. The irony of that was brutal and cruel. "Who is going to take care of the diner in my absence?"

"Nick?"

"And if I'm AWOL, what does that tell my employees to do?"

"Take a break because the big bad boss isn't there?" Angel said, tilting her head with a snarky grin.

"You're a piece of work," I said, shaking my head. "There are no breaks in the service industry, baby girl. People never stop eating, boss or not."

She just blinked at me. "So—comfort food?"

A simple little donut *would* rock my world, considering the morning I'd had. I tapped my blinker. "The things I do for you."

"Speaking of people doing things for me," she said, raising an eyebrow my way. "Uncle Bash is supposed to start driving lessons with me tonight, has he called you?"

My tongue stalled as the familiar anxiety washed over my skin. *Has he called you?* No, Bash hadn't called me. Not in the wide awake world of reality. He hadn't come by in his normal drop-by-to-see-my-Angel-girl way or swung by the lunch counter at the Blue Banana to swipe a handful of peanuts from the bowl I had out. He even started having couriers drop off the cases of honey I sold from his apiary instead of delivering them himself. He'd been there as a customer off and on, but always with someone and always engaged in a conversation that didn't look interruptible. Not that I would have, since I was avoiding him like a virus, myself.

"You could call *him*," I said, clearing my throat and my mind as I pointed at her phone. "Text him, message him, Facebook, or Insta-something him. You're the one wanting him to teach you, Angel, and that thing that never leaves your hand has to have some kind of purpose."

"Okay, okay," she said, holding said phone up. "I will. I was just saying that y'all have been weird lately. Normally, you'd have this all arranged and set up and probably giving each other grief about who was doing the teaching, but he hasn't even come over for coffee in forever."

Dryness scratched at my throat. "I know," I said. *Did I know? Did I know anything?* "He's probably just been busy."

She cut her eyes at me in a way that a girl her age shouldn't be savvy enough to do.

"Something happen between y'all to make him be *busy*?" she asked.
My heart skipped ahead. "Why would you ask that?" I said.

"Because you get all—" Angel wiggled her fingers at me as she looked
me up and down. "Like *that* every time his name comes up."

I waved her off and frowned and mentally imagined banging my head
on the steering wheel.

"No, of course not," I said, pushing all thoughts I shouldn't be having
away to pick up one of her new magazines and fan myself. "Life is just—so
why *are* you getting him to teach you to drive?" I asked instead. "When
your mother is right here?"

She turned her head to me in an exaggerated pose. "My *mother*, who's
now famous for riding through town like a crazed hillbilly in the back of Mr.
Hart's pickup truck? Jumping in while it was *moving*, from what I've heard?"

I rubbed at my eyes. "Okay, time to let that horse die, already," I said.
"It's been months—"

"*Oh no*," Angel said. "That little gem will never die. I still hear
about it at school."

"Fabulous," I muttered.

"Truly," she said, a smartass smirk on her face.

"I was grabbing the quickest ride I could," I said. "Bash—was in danger."

I licked my lips as I said it, remembering the absolute terror that had
rocketed through me, and what that had driven me to do.

Don't go there.

"From a flare gun?" she said.

"I didn't know it was a flare gun," I said. "I just—" I just heard *gun*
and all I knew was that I had to get to him. Now, what was he doing to
me? Was he involved? I shook my head. "Anyway, that has nothing to do
with your driving."

"It has everything to do with the jokes I'll have to endure if anyone sees
me driving with you," she said. "So, Uncle Bash please."

"Angel, he's—"

"He makes me laugh, Mom," she said, getting to the real point. "And I
don't get defensive when he tells me I suck." She shrugged. "I miss him."

I flexed my fingers and faced forward, nodding. I'd be lying if I said
that didn't stab me in the gut, because he was the closest thing to a father
that Angel had ever known. He had gone into the Marines when she was a
baby, but had been there for every major moment since. First everything:
softball games, school plays, phone calls when she was mad at me and
needed that dad-like person to rant to.

"Well, who am I to get in the way of someone else telling you that you suck," I said, turning into the bakery parking lot. "Y'all knock yourselves out. Take the Girl Scout cookies you scammed from the neighbors, too. I can't quit eating them."

Angel's eyes lit up as we rounded the menu board like she was six instead of almost sixteen.

"Lemon?" I asked, knowing the answer. "Or something else?"

"Lemon-filled donut, please." She grinned my way all silly. "I looovvvvve you."

"Mm-hmm," I said on a chuckle. "It's your feverish delirium."

"You know, I could get my own donuts if you got me a car," Angel said.

"You don't have your license yet, freak," I said.

"But I will in a few months," she said. "And I could go get lots of things. Groceries. Ice cream. Supplies for school projects."

"Tickets," I responded. "Ten-car pileups."

I drooled looking at the menu, myself. I shouldn't, but I was going to. I could have something ten times more awesome, nutritious, and probably even tastier at the diner. Nick would whip me up anything I wanted, but this morning's lopsided beginning and horrible, terrible, no-good, very bad news had me needing empty calories in the form of thick glazed sugar, creamy sweet filling, and melt-in-your-mouth carb-loaded gooey warm donut.

"Your faith in me is astounding," she said. "Hey speaking of Uncle Bash, isn't that his truck? Is that his new building?"

I had pulled all the way around the building to that point in the drive-thru where a change of heart or conscience is no longer an option because you're trapped within those little curb guides. And there it was with no doubt, the back end of Bash's truck, distinguished by the BEEMAN license plate and a few inches of the Anderson's Apiary logo magnet showing on the door. It was parked in front of the building next door that had been created to look like a woodsman's cottage, and I knew it to be one of the new retail spots he'd snagged as part of the Lucky Charm complex. His apiary was a little off the beaten path, understandably. One doesn't smack a bunch of bees in the middle of a high retail area. So all the products he made from the honey and the wax, he had to cart around to place at other retail sites on commission or whatever that retailer was willing to do in trade for showing his wares. Bash sold online as well, but he had wanted to add a more dedicated local retail presence to his business for a long time. I was happy for him. I hadn't gotten to tell him that, yet, and to be honest I didn't even know it was open, so the shit-friend of the year award was definitely on the table.

"Yep, that's it," I said.

"I could hop out and go run and talk to him real quick," Angel said, reaching for her seat belt fastener.

"Or you could call him later," I said, pulling to the window. "Like when you get home and are lying in bed or doing whatever this project is for *next week*. I have to get to work."

"Killjoy," she muttered.

"Happy morning to you!" a lady chirped from the window, making us both jump at the loud.

"Oh, wow."

"Jesus," Angel said under her breath.

Okay, a little too bouncy for that time of the morning. Even for a service industry. If I was that singsongy at the diner first thing in the morning, somebody would slap me with a pancake.

"What can I get for you?" she said robustly.

"One Bavarian cream filled, please," I said, purposely using my inside voice as a hint. "And one lemon filled."

"Awesome blossom," she sang. Literally sang. Her nametag had smiley emoji stickers on it and read *Hi! I'm Maxie!* "One mo-ment-o."

"Good grief," I muttered, rubbing my eyes as Maxie nearly skipped away.

"That's so not normal," Angel whispered.

"Yeah, I don't know if it's worth it."

"Allie Greene Bean!" said a male voice that both startled me for the second time and made me want to dive into the back seat.

I head-jerked around to see a guy in a red apron and a black collared shirt, strawberry-blond hair slicked and spiked up, and way-too-white teeth.

"Alan!" I said in a pretend excited tone. "Why—are you in the bakery window?"

Alan Bowman. Town narcissist. Asshole. Blowhard. Graduated with me, and probably never knew it until I took over the diner from my dad.

He tugged on his collar as if that was supposed to tell me something.

"I'm the manager," he said proudly. "And the owner."

"Of the—" I shook my head before I said something offensive. There was nothing wrong with managing a food establishment. I'd done it most of my adult life. But Alan Bowman was not someone I'd ever imagine stooping to do such menial work. He dabbled in beekeeping for a time, or so I'd heard, but mostly he made his money in investments. Above and below the table. He tried to swindle Nick's wife out of her inheritance over the summer and had laid low ever since. "I didn't realize you were a baker."

"Oh, I'm not," Alan said, laughing.

"So—what made you decide to—get in the bakery business?" I asked, my fingers pulling up the neckline of my shirt as his eyes fell there.

"Well, with all the flashy new businesses going up down here, it would be dumb *not* to grab a piece of the pie," he said, flashing teeth. "So to speak. Anything up on Main is yesterday's news now."

On Main. Where my diner was. Nice. "Really?"

"Not talking about your little place, of course," he amended with a wink.

I smiled. "Of course."

"How's your dad doing?" he asked, for one split second appearing to care. "Last time I talked to him—damn it must have been almost a year ago. You know, when he was having those *financial issues*," he said in a lowered voice.

I held my smile perfectly, thanks to a lifetime of practice. Tried not to think too hard on just what *financial issues* Alan Bowman assisted my dad with.

"He's fine," I lied. What did it matter? "How's your buddy, the ex-mayor?" I asked. "You know, since he went all rogue on Bash's bees?"

Alan's expression tightened a little. "I think he's good," he said, glancing around as if the next topic—any topic—could be floating by to grab. "He's kind of kept to himself."

"Oh really?" I said. "I see Dean in the diner all the time looking like Grizzly Adams and talking to himself. But I guess stealing your friend's livelihood and then pulling a flare gun on him can send you a little over the edge."

Alan was nodding and smiling which was really just a show of teeth.

"And you?" he said, tilting his head. "I heard—"

"Angel is about to start driving," I interjected, grabbing her hand and yanking her closer.

"Oh wow, seriously," Angel said under her breath.

Alan leaned down to see Angel. "Sweet little Angel Food Cake is old enough to drive?"

Angel's pretty little lined eyes said so many not sweet, crass, and rude things he'd never know about before she gave a snarky smile.

"Hi," she said, lifting her hand in a limp wave.

"My goodness," he said. "I remember when your mother was pregnant with you. Has it been that many years?"

I narrowed my eyes at him, thinking *bullshit* as loudly as my thoughts would manage. If it weren't for Bash and I being friends and my running the diner, Alan Bowman wouldn't even know my name.

"Oh, hey Bash."

My head jerked back to the right as dark hair and striking blue eyes were suddenly filling the passenger window. The same eyes I'd seen in my dream last night. That had burned right through me as I'd rushed into a room three months ago not knowing what to expect and flung myself into his arms in eternal relief that he wasn't shot. Or flared. The same eyes that went impossibly dark as I'd pulled back and—kissed him. That had closed as he kissed me back and—

The same eyes that had looked at me earlier this morning right before he possibly screwed me over.

I swallowed hard over the flips my stomach was doing and held my chin up as Angel lowered the window and they did their finger-knuckle-knock-front-back goofy little hand jive thing they'd done since she was six.

"Allie," he said, a hint of a kind-of-sad, kind-of-amused smile in his expression.

"Bash."

My heart broke a little more.

CHAPTER THREE

"Um, Mom?"

I blinked away and cleared my throat.

"Sorry I startled y'all," Bash said. "I know better than to just walk up to someone's window like that." He leaned his forearms on the top of the window. *Oh God, those arms. The things he'd done that he wasn't even aware of.*

Stop.

"No kidding," Angel said. "I could have stabbed you with—" She stopped to look around and he chuckled. "This pen!"

Bash had a long sleeved black T-shirt on with his logo in gold over the pocket. He threw a quick polite glance my way before looking playfully at Angel. I wanted to punch him.

Polite?

God, it was revolting. We didn't do nice and polite. Bash and I were always without boundaries. Inappropriate. Laughing and joking and finishing each other's thoughts. We were easy. Now, because he was somehow involved with the dickhead bookie railroading me out of my diner, and because I was an emotionally reactive idiot, we were hard. We were polite.

That was really irritating.

"True," he said. "I'll be smarter next time. Why aren't you at school?"

"I'm sick," she said, tilting her head to sell it.

"And you want to go driving with me tonight?" he said.

"I'll be better by then," she said.

I scoffed. "Shocking." At his locked in gaze, I panicked. "So, that's—congrats on the new building," I said, gesturing that way. Good God, that was lame.

"Thanks," he said, not blinking.

Awkward. Awesome.

"Hey, we still on for driving lessons tonight?" Angel asked, tugging on a thumb that hung down.

I saw the flash go through his eyes that said he either forgot or had a conflict of some sort. Probably a date. Or maybe he didn't want to risk lip molestation again.

"Sure thing," he said.

"You don't have to," I said, making Angel give me a look.

"Mom!"

"I'm just saying, it's my responsibility. I can do this, you don't—"

"I've got it," Bash said, settling his gaze on me and making mine fall to his lips, which sent me reeling into every hot microsecond of that brief oh-my-God-heat-and-fireworks that flipped fifteen years of normal upside down. At least for me. "But can we use this?" he was saying, tapping on the Jeep.

I raised an eyebrow and blinked away.

"What, you afraid to use your truck?" I asked.

"Little bit."

"Hey!" Angel said, swinging a fist sideways and missing him.

"You still seeing that little carnie chick?" Alan asked, nodding through my windows at Bash and reminding us he was there with all the tact of a bulldozer.

The expression on Bash's face said that if he could have reached Alan he would have slapped him upside the head. Which at least was a tiny sliver of something, saying either one, he recognized that talking about another woman in front of the woman that laid a big kiss on him was uncool or two, he was still ignoring that and just pissed off that Alan reduced her to *that little carnie chick.*

"Her name is Kia, you imbecile," Bash said. *Well, that answered that question.* "And not that it's your business, but no, we were never dating."

"Really?" Alan said, making a face. "What would you call it?"

"I called it sex," Bash said, covering Angel's ears while she rolled her eyes. "I didn't realize that was confusing."

"I'm not five," Angel said.

Kia had been with the Lucky Hart carnival when it came through our little town over the summer, and stayed behind with Sully Hart to work on the new project. She and Bash worked on each other a bit, as well, not that anyone could blame them. Kia was stunning, and Bash was a major catch. Gorgeous, funny, with the body of an ex-marine and the confidence of one of the most successful business owners in town. He was a hot commodity, and it was nothing new to see females on his arm or in his wake.

I never had a problem with that. Even with someone who'd been here all of two minutes and had every man in town panting and every woman wanting to be her.

"Kia," Alan said, snapping his fingers. "That's right. Hey, no offense, I just didn't know what she'd think about the King and Queen nomination. Not that you'll win," he added quickly. "Because Katrina and I will totally kill it."

I peered up at him questioningly, but that didn't make his babble any more logical. Glancing back at Bash told me he was just as in the dark.

"What?" I asked.

"The King and Queen Bee inauguration to kick off opening the park," Alan said, gesturing out the window. "You got the nomination cards in the mail."

"Uh—yeah?" I said. "For about five minutes till they went in the trash."

"Ditto," Bash said.

Embossed cards went out to every business owner last month, asking for nominations for a new Charmed tradition. Two people to be chosen each year as the face and representatives of Charmed. King Bee and Queen Bee.

Yes.

I know.

Welcome to small-town hell.

"I know, it was kind of cheesy," Alan said.

"Cheesy?" I said. "It's ridiculous. Who came up with such a thing?"

"The Chamber of Commerce," Alan said, pointing. "You've—missed a few breakfasts."

"I've missed where *you* became a member," Bash said, moving his arms down to rest on the bottom of Angel's window. *Thank you, I appreciate that.*

"A few months back," he said, nodding. "When the Lucky Charm sale went down and I knew I'd be doing this, I registered. Katrina did, too."

I frowned. "Katrina? What business does she have?"

"Oh, she does nails now," Alan said. "She filed for a business permit, and has the mother-in-law room smelling of that acrylic powder stuff." He wiggled his fingers at me like I'd get it.

I wiggled my nubby non-acrylic'd fingers back at him since we were bonding.

"Can you check on our donuts?" I asked. "We're kinda late."

"Maxie!" he turned and yelled. "Are you making them from scratch?" He turned back and sighed as if the enormity of his world was too heavy. "So, they've hired a PR firm and everything to handle all the promotion," Alan said. "The Sharp Group. It's to coincide with the grand opening of the complex in a few weeks."

"I thought that was a soft opening," Bash said. "There's only six stores right now. One full restaurant and a handful of rides. The Ferris wheel's the only major thing and the other stuff won't even be done till spring. Why is Sully pushing so hard for full steam ahead?"

"You're all buddy-buddy with him, so you ask him," Alan said. "But I don't think it's Sully, I think it's town leadership."

It was the stupidest thing I'd ever heard. King and Queen Bee. To do what? Parade waves from the podium?

Alan moved aside as Maxie filled the window with her smile.

"I'm sorry," she said, head tilted with a lower lip pout. "We're all out of Bavarian. The car before you took the last one. Would you like a super-duper-yummy strawberry or another lemon? I think there's even a chocolate."

I stared at her. "It took you all this time to tell me you *don't* have it?"

Maxie's happy face faltered a bit around the eyes. "Well…"

I shook my head, turning my gaze back frontward as Bash chuckled to my right. He knew I wasn't made of patience. Or he used to know. Before I kissed him and killed us.

Okay maybe that was sulky.

"They do have the super-duper-yummy strawberry," Angel said, her tone full of mock innocence with a pinch of maybe-I-should-duck.

I blew out a breath and smiled. "Blueberry cake?" My tone was sour, but Maxie wouldn't know that.

I got the pout again. She had to be kidding me. "Out of those, too."

I shook my head in awe. "Just the lemon."

"Two?" Maxie perked up.

"One."

"Gotcha," Maxie said. "Want some donut holes?" I looked at her without blinking till she averted her eyes. "Gotcha," she repeated, turning to bag Angel's donut.

"Beat me with a stick," I whispered, rubbing my forehead as though the dull throb behind it might somehow be massaged.

"Rough morning?" Bash asked.

I met his eyes. I couldn't say anything about any of it in front of Angel, but I willed him to absorb it through my retinas. "You could say that."

"She's not sleeping," Angel said. "Bad dreams."

I fixed a what-the-fuck look on her. "Angel."

"What?" she asked. "You said don't tell Pop, not—oh!" she continued with an epiphany, filling me with dread. Kind of like when you see someone about to fall off a cliff and you can't get there fast enough. "They're about you!"

I felt my jaw drop, and all the heat of the universe rushed to my head like Mount Vesuvius. *No, no, no...*

"Bad dreams about me?" Bash asked, sending my mind skipping past the pissed off stuff and straight to every naughty, lust-driven taste, touch, and moan that had plagued my nights. Especially the past few. "How bad?"

Bad, so very, very bad.

I licked my suddenly dry lips. "Bad. You know—blood and gore." *Find something!* "Jumping out of a helicopter and getting chewed up by the blades."

Bash lifted an eyebrow. "Did I bounce?"

My head exploded. "What?"

Did he bounce? Fuck yes, he bounced, and so did I. On every piece of furniture I owned. Was it getting warmer? I fanned myself with my shirt.

"The blades are overhead," he said, twirling a finger over his head. "So if I jumped down—"

"I have no idea," I said weakly, not giving a flying fig which way he jumped in my fake story when visions of him nailing me on the kitchen table were so much more vibrant. "Maybe the helicopter fell. You know how dreams are."

He smirked, looking at me all clear of mind, free of stress and Landon Lange and apparently any memory of our embrace (tackle) and lip-lock.

"I know if your dad heard about this dream, he'd tell me I was about to die," Bash said. "Should I be worried?"

Only if he was worried that falling into naked aerobics and fucking me senseless every night might come true. Whew...where was the cold on that AC?

Alan ducked back through the window, holding Angel's bag.

"Oh, thank God," I said under my breath as I grabbed it, tossed it to Angel, and slapped the Jeep into gear. "It's been fun, guys, but we need to get going."

"So, if y'all threw your cards away, who nominated you?" Alan said.

"Who—who did what?" I asked.

Alan reached behind him and pulled up a laminated card with lots of scrolled fonts, pointing at two names.

"Right there below me and Katrina," he said. "The two of you together."

Together.

"What—" My brain cut off the thought, and I just blinked as I put the Jeep back in park. "What?"

Alan handed the card over, and Amber took it from me so Bash and I could both read it. At the top was a bunch of scrolled lettering with bees flying around them, and underneath was a list of paired names that owned or ran local businesses. The first pair was Mr. Masoneaux from the candy store and Mrs. Boudreaux from the feed store. I could see that. Several of the names made sense. Alan and Katrina Bowman. Not a shocker. They kissed ass everywhere. The last one was the mindblower.

SEBASTIAN ANDERSON, ANDERSON APIARY ~ ALLIE GREENE, BLUE BANANA GRILLE

"Oh dear God," I said in barely a whisper.

I turned to meet his eyes, but he wasn't looking at me. He was staring at the card, the unaffected thing leaving his expression, replaced with displeasure.

Okay. Yeah, I wasn't excited about it either, but he looked like someone shit in his cereal.

"Why would someone nominate us and not tell us?" Bash asked.

"And why me?" I asked, hearing the pissy enter my tone as I watched his face. *Dial it back.* "I mean, I understand *him*, he's like Rambo Ken, but I'm—Diner Barbie." I shook my head. "Nobody wants Diner Barbie."

"Rambo Ken?" Bash echoed.

"Aaron told me about the prizes," Angel chimed in.

I looked at her. "What prizes?"

"Who's Aaron?" Bash asked at the same time, and we met gazes for a second.

Yeah, I probably should have asked that one.

"Aaron Sharp," she said, holding up palms at both of us. "He's new at school and—we talk." I noted the shrug that I didn't buy for a millisecond. "His mom is in charge of that Sharp Group you were talking about."

Fabulous. "And?"

"He said all the businesses donate stuff and the winners get cash and scholarships and all kinds of things," she finished.

"Do they give away eighty-seven-thousand dollars?" I asked.

Her eyes got all squinty. "What?"

"Nothing." Hey, it was worth a shot.

"There is a formal event," Alan said. "An essay, and maybe a talent thing, I can't remember if that was approved—"

"That's a pageant, Alan," Bash said.

"Kind of, but it's done in pairs," Alan said. "You work together with someone to win, like you'd work together to benefit Charmed."

I was going to throw up. Right there. Bash and I—we—oh my God, there just weren't words. And where was I supposed to find time for all this shit, around trying to oust Lange and keep him from turning my eclectic little diner into something I wouldn't recognize?

"They suggested that we come up with off-the-wall creative things to do to make it different," Alan said. "I was thinking grand entrances for each couple to the bandstand, like maybe get a crane to lower us from up high."

"Yeah, that's not happening," I said, finding my voice.

"Why not?" he said, looking disappointed that I'd shot down his idea.

"Because it's ridiculous," Bash said.

"Because she's afraid of heights," my daughter added helpfully.

"Because *no*," I said, my tone flat as I fixed another look on her. I didn't advertise my weaknesses to the world. Especially that one.

"Omigod," Angel said, clapping her hands together in oblivion to my evil stare.

"What?"

I started to sweat. It was fifty degrees out, and I had half a mind to climb out the window.

"A formal event? You have to dress up!" she said. "I've never even seen you in a skirt."

"I don't think I have either," Bash said.

I don't think I have, either? Okay, this was insulting. He couldn't continue to flip between acting like nothing ever happened, or acting like I was a pariah. Or—he could. But I didn't have to be okay with it.

"I want to dress you!" Angel said.

"You people need a life," I said. "And we have to go." I yanked the Jeep back into drive and slow-rolled through.

"Text me when you're coming tonight!" Angel called back to Bash, and he waved.

"You'll get e-mails telling you what to do," I heard Alan calling on my side. *Don't look. Don't look.*

I looked back in my rearview mirror and saw Bash slow-walking back over the curb to his truck, *not* watching us drive away. Ugh. Of course he wasn't. He had no damn issues.

"I think it'll be cool," Angel said. "And something fun. You're always working, you never do anything fun."

I frowned. "I have plenty of fun."

Angel slid a narrow-eyed look my way. "Lies."

"Mommy never lies," I said, pulling out onto the street. I hit the air one more notch.

"Any sentence that begins with *Mommy* is going to be a lie," she countered. "And what about men?"

"Men always lie," I said, pointing.

She rolled her eyes. "I mean *you* and men, Mom. You never date anymore."

With my nightly activity in my dreams lately, who needed to date? I exhaled loudly.

"Well, maybe no one is ever worth my time, baby girl," I said. "And I'm not talking about dating with you. Unless it's about you." I pointed. "And then you're too young, so who's this Aaron?"

"And back to you," she said.

"Cute."

"This will be a good thing," she said. "Social." She looked my way as I started to laugh. "Why is that funny?"

"Because *social* and *good thing* don't play in the same sandbox," I said. "At least, not for me."

"I know," she said. "But I'll help you out with that. You know, studies show—"

"What studies?"

She blinked and held up a finger. "*Studies* show that reconnecting with old friends and peers in a social setting clicks off endorphins and positive neurons in the brain. It's actually *healthy* for you."

Another laugh bubbled up as I patted her cheek and she ducked my hand. "Oh, my naïve girl."

"Why is it naïve?" she asked.

"Because you think those people are my friends," I said, the funny still tickling me.

"They are, Mom," she said. "Everyone likes you."

Oh, the simple thoughts of a fifteen-year-old girl with no social problems and not a care in the world. How I wished my teenaged life could have been like hers.

"I'm social enough every day at work without making it an extracurricular activity," I said, sighing. "I ought to be as healthy as a horse. But yes, if I have to get dressed up for this freak show, you can dress me. We'll go shopping."

Angel laughed. "You should see the face you just made."

I nodded, patting my chest. "I feel like I need to spit."

CHAPTER FOUR

It was late. It was way late. The diner had long since closed and I would normally have been home two hours earlier, but instead of letting the closers clean/shut down/lock up like I normally did, I let them all off early and did it myself.

It was easier to deal with all the thoughts buzzing through my brain when my hands were busy.

Diner…contest…Bash…diner…Lange…Lange and Bash… Oh, and I never did anything fun or dated anyone. All I did was work.

Well, maybe so, but that's how the bills got paid and the diner stayed afloat. That's how I paid myself and my employees, how Angel got those cute clothes and the phone that never left her hand. How I was saving for her college and paying for the home health nurse that I'd recently hired to help with my dad.

Who the hell had time for fun?

Plus—Charmed had never really been my biggest ally. Teenage pregnancy might slide under the radar and be forgotten in bigger cities, but little towns like mine had big memories and bigger hypocrites. Everyone *liked* me? Not quite. I'd gained *respect* through my management of the Blue Banana Grille, but somehow that managed to fade once I stepped outside those doors. Like once I walked into a club somewhere or went on those few and far between loser dates or just ran into someone I knew at the grocery store, I became that girl again. Allie Greene, Tainted One.

Dating was complicated. Girlfriends were sometimes even more so. It was easier to be sexless Allie Greene, the tough trailer-park girl that rose above and ran the Blue Banana. I didn't need to find a man to validate me or go out with friends or do any of those things single women were expected to do. I just needed to keep doing what I'd always done. Run my business. Raise my daughter. Make sure my dad was okay. That was enough.

Straightening a napkin holder, I closed my eyes for one second of quiet, of peace—or no, probably not that. Not today. I lowered slowly into the chair as my brain went back to the rotating door.

Not my diner. Not my chair.

That damn contest.

With Bash as a partner.

Someone shoot me.

Once upon a time, every girl in school had a crush on Bash Anderson. He was the hottest thing on legs, with a smile to knock you on your ass and eyes that would go ahead and melt you right into the ground while you were down there. Kind of like now but with homework.

I wasn't someone that Bash would give a second look back then, but in addition to helping his dad with one single beehive, he worked as a busboy at the diner when my dad was running things and I waited tables. We became friends in that way that people do when they can't be in real life. When shallow social circles don't allow the golden boy and the trailer-park girl to hang out in public or have lunch together in the school cafeteria. But at work, closing up late at night, those silly walls faded away. Words came easy to us, snarky personalities melded, dreams were confessed, and secrets unveiled. We both had mothers that had passed away when we were young, leaving big holes behind. Things weren't all that golden over in the Anderson household, and where my home life was fine, the guy I was seeing from nearby Denning was a neurotic, controlling prick. I didn't see that yet but Bash did. He became my secret best friend. My ally.

Then the stick turned blue, and my entire senior year became a blur of oh-my-god's and tears and learning how to hurl quietly so my dad wouldn't know. Then it was learning how to dress baggy so the school wouldn't know. Then it was wanting to disappear completely when everyone knew, when my boyfriend decided to bail, and the only person to shoulder my tears was Bash. Through thick and thin and so much drama, he was the one constant that never wavered.

Now we were dancing all around each other because I was a fool. And he was wavering because...

Why the hell was he meeting with Landon Lange?

So, there I was. The boss, cleaning tables and washing dishes and mopping and prepping for the morning. That was something I hadn't done in probably six or seven years. Even when my dad was there, I'd been managing the place since I was twenty-six, and hadn't palmed a mop in years, but tonight was different. Tonight, I needed to do more than close the register and sit at my desk doing the paperwork. I needed to get my hands in the weeds of it. Get gritty. Get sweaty. Feel the work that built this place; that kept it going, that kept the people of Charmed coming day after day.

I ran my fingers along the scarred and dented table. If it could talk—if they all could talk, my God, the conversations they'd overheard. The secrets they could divulge. It was a friggin thought-gasm to even consider. The Blue Banana had been serving patrons since before I was born, all under the umbrella of the Greenes. Oliver and Maggie Greene, then he and I, and then just me. I hoped one day Angel, although she'd never shown interest in it. Honestly, that was okay; I just figured I'd lead the ship until I was too old and then pass it on to a deserving soul of my choosing.

This wasn't my choosing.

This—I gripped the napkin holder until it felt like it had finger holds, and forced myself to let it go before the urge to hurl it across the room took over. This was unbelievable.

The dementia was a blessing right now. It kept me from marching over to that pathetic little trailer and telling my dad off in an enraged fit. I couldn't be mad at the man he was now, sitting blissfully watching television, unaware and unaffected by anything going on around him. It would do no good to bring it up or ask him about it. He wouldn't remember it, and if he tried to he'd just get confused and upset and it wasn't worth all of that.

This was on me to figure out. A stain on the ceiling above table eleven caught my attention and told me that it was on me, too. I needed to call a maintenance guy out, but I had no idea what to say was going on. I'd been so distracted, I'd forgotten to ask Nick to go up on the roof and check it out before he left.

This morning, my biggest headache was worrying about Bash. That feeling of loss, that I was missing something necessary. Bash, my rock, the only one I could talk to about all this crap, who I was suddenly stumbling around like a silly school girl. Now, more than ever, I needed us to be normal again and I didn't know how to get that.

He'd always been there for me. Nearly sixteen years ago, he was my miracle the night I went into labor a month early, alone in the storeroom, doubled up on the floor and screaming as a tiny human was demanding her way into the world. Bash was my angel as he delivered Angel Elizabeth Greene before the paramedics and my dad could get there.

No one else ever knew that. No one at school. Not Carmen, my only other friend from the park. Not anyone. Nobody knew that Bash Anderson had probably saved both our lives, then held my hand all the way to the hospital saying, "I've got you, Al." And he did. He argued with the nurses when they only let family see the baby, telling them he *was* family.

He didn't tell, and neither did I. I just became the girl who had a baby in high school, who got knocked up by some loser who left us behind. Bash became Uncle Bash, he loved my daughter fiercely, and all was good.

Then there was *the night*. It seemed a million years ago now, but lately it had become like a source document in my head. Angel was almost one, and we were living in a tiny little apartment my dad made for us over the garage. I'd just put her to bed when Bash came over with a fifth of whiskey, two paper cups, and some news. He'd signed up for the marines. He was leaving.

He had to go, he had to get out of Charmed and get away from his dad, and while I understood that, all I could see was no Bash in our lives. I was crushed, we killed the bottle, ended up in a three-minute wild thing on my couch, and then he was gone with an awkward goodbye.

That was fifteen years ago, before he left for six years and I became jaded, before he came back a little less lighthearted, a lot more guarded. Before we both grew up and never spoke of that drunken night again, deciding without words that we were what we were: friends. Family of a sort. Something much more important that neither of us could afford to lose.

It worked for us. All these years, it was good and it worked, and then I went and stirred that shit up.

Damn it.

Now, I needed him. Nobody understood my ties to this place like he did. No one else could understand the need to hold on to something that houses your soul. Bash did. And now—now we were awkward and weird and he was consorting with the damn enemy.

I looked up at the ceiling again, at the spreading stain, and forced my anger to spread throughout my body. I was no weakling. I knew where the ladder was, and I could get on the roof and take care of my own business. I didn't need a man to do it for me. It was still my damn diner—sort of. Forty-nine percent of it, anyway, belonged to my father. I went to the storeroom, grabbed a flashlight, and headed out the back door to where an aluminum ladder lay horizontal against the building on two hooks. I hoisted it and trekked around to the side of the building, leaning it up against the roofline and peering up into the darkness.

The shakes began.

No. Screw that. I took three deep breaths and shook out my hands.

I'd managed most of my life to be pretty tough, but anything requiring me to leave the ground for more than a few feet stripped me of the role.

My irrational fear of heights could be pretty inconvenient when trying to do normal things like jumping off the high dive or riding a Ferris wheel. Not to mention stupid things like—oh—climbing up on the diner roof to prove a point.

I could put on a badass front, but the trembling of the anxiety attack always gave me away. I was too pissed off tonight to let that win, however. Shakes or no shakes, I was getting up on my roof.

The squeak of the rungs as I made it up each step echoed in my head. No big thing. I glanced down and shut my eyes immediately, gripping the ladder tighter with clammy hands.

Don't look down, idiot.

It was dark, and it was only maybe sixteen feet or so, but looking down for me was always the game changer. Didn't matter if it was six feet or sixty, up went down, right went left, and panic took over.

"Keep going," I whispered, feeling the cold sweat break out over my body. "People do this shit all the time. It's not climbing Mount Everest."

And yet, reaching the roofline sure as hell felt that way. My breathing grew shallower, and it felt like there was nothing underneath my feet as I looked out over the flat concrete top of the diner. Or at least about five feet of it before it disappeared into shadow. The flashlight hung around my neck, but I'd have to let go of the ladder to mess with that and my hands weren't having it.

"How the hell do I get from here to there?" I asked the air.

I'd never been up there. My dad certainly knew better than to ever deal with me having a nervous breakdown on top of the diner, so I'd never had to contemplate the logistics of ladder to roof. Did I assume that handles magically sprung from the top? Rails morphed on either side so that one could just keep walking up and traverse the space without fear?

I don't know what or how I thought it was going to happen up there, but standing at the top hyperventilating on trembling legs I could no longer feel probably wasn't the best time to figure it out.

"Okay," I breathed, sliding my hands one at a time from the ladder to the rough concrete of the roof's surface without ever breaking contact because empty air would send me plummeting to my death. I pictured normal people doing this. Roofers did this all the time and didn't die. Contractors did this. Maintenance guys like the one I should have called did this. "Okay. You can do this, too."

I took one more step up, putting more than half my body above the roofline and forcing confidence through my blood—when my equilibrium shifted. And so did the ladder.

It was just a little shift. Metal scraping against concrete. To me, however, it felt like the entire world came out from under me, and all the panic I was trying to tamp down came rushing up in a tsunami-sized wave.

"Shit!" I yelped, lunging forward as the ladder wiggled again.

The flashlight banged against the roof and broke from the lanyard around my neck, clattering off into the dark. Half of me sprawled over the concrete and brick, while everything from my ass down hung off the building. Okay, really, I was hanging over the ladder, but to truly go with the deep-seated terror coursing through my veins, I was hanging off the building by an invisible thread, like something in the movies. Probably ten stories up instead of one.

"Fuck!" I screamed, reaching out at a snail's pace to find something to grab onto. I didn't want to move too quickly. Plummeting, and all that. My phone was in my pocket, but there was no way I could get my hand down there. Tears sprang to my eyes as the anxiety-ridden paralysis washed over me. "Oh my God, please get me off this building. I promise I won't ever touch this ladder again, just—" There was a click from below.

"Who's up there?"

Relief mixed with mortification flooded my brain.

"You like messing with me, don't you God?" I whispered through my tears.

"I see you," Bash said, his voice harsh. "Identify."

"It's me," I said, my forehead pressed against the rough cold of the concrete. "Allie."

There was a pause and another click as what was likely a nine-millimeter un-chambering a bullet.

"What the hell?" Bash said. "What are you doing?"

"Laying here trying not to die," I said. "You?"

"Jesus," I heard him mutter, just before the ladder moved again and rapid creaks sounded as he sprinted up.

I felt the jolts as the ladder bumped me, and I sucked in a breath.

"Don't!" I yelled in a cracked voice. "It'll pull me down!"

"You aren't going anywhere," he said, suddenly right below me. "I've got you."

I've got you.

He had no idea how good those words were.

"I can't move," I said, my eyes filling with hot tears of frustration and embarrassment.

His hands on my ankles startled me, but the slow movements as they moved to my calves quickly calmed my blood.

"I'm putting your feet back on the rungs, Allie," Bash said. "Do you feel that?" His hands moved back down to my feet, pushing down on my toes, shoving the balls of my feet against the metal.

"Yes."

"Okay, just stay like that," he said. "I'm coming up higher behind you."

Like I had a choice. I felt the ladder move a little as he came up another rung and his hands slid slowly up my jeans to just above the backs of my knees. If I weren't so terrified, or mortified beyond measure, I might have been turned on.

"Take one more step down," he said. "I'm right here."

I shut my eyes. "So my ass is basically in your face."

I felt him laugh. "Yeah, it's rough to be me." He reached up slowly and took hold of my hips. "Come on, I've got you."

"Yeah, so you keep saying," I said, trying to calm my trembling hands and stem back the tears. "But who has you?"

"Come on," he repeated. "You just need to stop thinking about where you are, and concentrate on feeling the rungs under your feet. Just get standing upright again and get off the building, then it's a piece of cake."

"Oh hell, that's all?" I said under my breath. "Damn, you're a genius."

"Hey, I can leave—"

"No!" I yelped. "Just—it's just not that simple. It's—"

"I get it, Allie," Bash said, letting the pause that followed fill the space. "But you're going to have to trust me. I've got you. I won't let you fall."

I blew out a breath and flexed my fingers. "Shit, shit, shit."

"I'll count to three."

"Do you have insurance?"

"Medical or life?" he asked.

"Both?"

"We aren't falling off this ladder," Bash said. "We're adults and we know how to use our feet."

My eyes popped open. Was that a slam? I was pretty sure that was a slam.

"You—you think I'm just being a wuss here?" I kicked at where I felt he was, but then panicked when I couldn't find the rung again.

"You're trying to kick me off the ladder?" he asked, shoving my foot back into place.

"Just—" I swallowed hard. "Just get down and hold it still so it doesn't move," I said. "I'll make it down."

He did. Thank God. Sort of—because now I was up there by myself again, and that hadn't worked so well the last time. Hell if I was going to cave this time, however. Not with his cocky-assed smart- (and sexy) mouth patronizing me with *we know how to use our feet.*

It was chilly out and I hadn't worn a jacket over my jeans and T-shirt, but I was sweating from head to toe and my heart was about to come bouncing right up my throat. What the hell was I thinking?

One inch at a time, I thought. Slowly, methodically, I pushed back in tiny increments until I could theoretically stand up on the ladder, and then I inched some more till I was sliding my body down to the next rung like a sloth.

"There's a technique I've never seen," Bash said, closer than I thought he was.

"I thought you were on the ground," I said, finding a foothold.

"Just keep going," he said. "Don't worry about me."

Sliding was working. I could not explain why slithering down slightly spread-eagled with no real grip to speak of was less scary than stepping the traditional way, but it was. It was faster. More productive. Until—

"Oh!" I screamed as my grip-that-really-wasn't slid off track and my calm sliding concept turned into a spasmic moment of grope and flail. Landing hard and ungraceful, straddling Bash's torso.

CHAPTER FIVE

Strong hands clamped down on my thighs and lowered me to a position sandwiched tightly between Bash's body and the ladder. Even in my terror-riddled state, I was aware of everything I moved against, as well as the arm held tightly around my middle.

"Put your feet down," he said, his mouth just above my right ear. "Open your eyes and breathe. It's all about perspective. You'll see where you are."

My eyes fluttered open, but breathing was a challenge with him pressed against me like that. There had been whole dreams with similar—

"You okay?" he asked. "You're all sweaty."

And that killed it.

"I'm fine," I said, looking down. We were halfway. I could see the ground. "You can—you can go."

Bash let go of me and stepped down, and I pushed my disgusting sweaty, shaky self down the rest of the way.

Concrete never felt so sweet. I sank to my knees and pressed my palms to the cold surface, letting that sink in.

"Allie."

"I'm good."

I tucked damp tendrils of hair behind my ears, realizing my standard messy bun was now probably a hot mess.

"The hell you are," he said. "What were you doing up there?"

"There's a leak," I said, standing carefully.

One eyebrow rose in question. "And you decided to take that on by yourself at eight-thirty at night?"

"It's eight-thirty?" My head was still spinning and I reached out for the brick and mortar wall. "Crap, y'all's driving practice."

"Already done," he said. "We took my truck. But when we got back and you still weren't home, I got worried."

A little tingle went through my belly, but I quickly wrote it off to post-anxiety nausea.

"Well, you didn't need to," I said, one hand on my hip. I was desperately seeking my bad-assness and it had clearly stayed up on that roof. "I've been a big girl for some time now."

"I didn't need to?" Bash laughed. He headed three rungs back up the ladder before I could process it.

"What are you doing?"

"Cleaning out your grates," he said, nearly to the top.

"My—my what?" I asked, peering up from the bottom. "Bash, you don't have to do this—whatever you're doing."

"I don't suppose there was a flashlight in this scenario?" he called down.

"There was," I said indignantly. "I wasn't going to climb around up there in the dark. It's probably—still up there, though."

My voice trailed off as he disappeared over the top like those imaginary rails showed up for him.

"God help me," I muttered under my breath, leaning back against the brick.

After tonight, there was no reason for sex dreams to continue plaguing my nights. Except for his hands gripping my thighs as I straddled him, and then pinning me to a ladder, I had probably killed any sexual fantasy between us. Nothing screams *hot* like dangling off a building like a sweaty defeated rag doll.

I didn't have long to ponder that, however, as a sudden rain of something gooey and slimy began to fall on me.

"Shit!" I yelped, recoiling in horror, batting at the foul-smelling, nasty-textured crap that was oozing down my neckline. "Ew!" I pushed off the wall and attacked my neck and hair like I was being invaded by snails. "Get it off me!"

"It's leaves, Allie."

I stopped and looked up toward the voice I couldn't see.

"You threw this on me?"

"I'm sweeping leaves out of the grates," he said.

"Grates."

"Around the drains."

I took a couple of breaths. "Drains."

"This is a flat roof," he said. "So there are drains in place to divert water to the gutters."

I pulled a section of rotted goo out of my hair.

"Uh-huh."

"When the drains and gutters get blocked up with leaves and shit, the water has nowhere to go but sit at the joints, and it being an old building, there are probably cracks letting it into the structure."

Great.

"When's the last time this was cleaned?" he asked.

I shook my head at no one and stared at the ground. It was like the day was hell bent on kicking my ass.

"Well, since I'm just hearing about it," I said, letting that speak for itself.

"Probably your dad," he surmised.

"Yeah."

"Over a year ago," he added.

"Most likely," I said. "Where did you get a broom? And how did you know what it was?"

"Because he used to send me up here to do it when I worked here," Bash said. "And we left the broom so we wouldn't have to drag it up and down. I figured he might still do that."

I nodded, although he couldn't see it.

"So you might want to move," Bash said. "There's more."

"Jesus," I muttered. "Thank you, Bash. You didn't have to do all this."

Ten minutes later, we were standing in front of the door, the roof de-leaved and the ladder re-hooked. I was past the mortification of my behavior and the highly sexy look I had going on. He'd seen me worse. Bash once pulled a human out of my hoo-hah while I was contorted in pain and covered in more sweat and blood than should be possible. This was nothing.

"Get someone out to do that once a month and you'll be good," he said. "And you probably want to get your ceiling joists checked for damage. Just in case."

Yeah. Someone like Landon Lange. Let *him* climb up in the attic and check that. *He* could get up on the roof and sweep rotted leaves. He owned more, it was his right.

The thought gave me a screaming headache, and I covered my eyes with my hands.

"That's not that big of a deal, Al," he said.

That wasn't. But something else was.

"What were you doing with Landon Lange this morning?" I asked, dropping my hands and forcing my gaze to stay on his. I needed to see his eyes.

Surprise crossed his expression. "You know him?"

"You pointed me out to him," I said. "I saw."

"Yeah," Bash said. "He asked me who owned the place, and I told him."

"What else did he say?" I asked, crossing my arms over my chest.

Bash's brow furrowed. "About you?" He shook his head. "What's going on?"

Distrust flooded my body, and that very fact made my heart hurt. There was no one on this earth that I trusted more than Bash, and to question that—

"Why were you having breakfast with him?" I asked, swallowing that thought down.

Bash studied me for another couple of seconds. "He's investing in the apiary."

I've recently made a couple of lucrative investments here in Charmed...

Nausea swirled in my gut.

Lange had done his homework. Bash's business had taken a financial hit since the great summer bee heist, when a third of his bees didn't reorient. His honey production fell in a big way. With a contract for the new building in the Lucky Charm complex already signed and new customers in the books, the timing could not be worse. I knew Bash had been looking for investors to help out with costs, or even a partner if it got bad enough, but—how did this bottom-feeder find that out?

"I'm excited about it," he said. "I've been bleeding money for months. Lange's willing to pour that money back in for a percentage without owning anything?" Bash held out his arms. "It's a win-win."

"Or too good to be true," I said.

Bash dropped his arms with a frustrated breath. "Damn it, what's going on, Allie?"

I opened my mouth to tell him, but then shook my head slowly. Bash wasn't plotting against me, and he evidently didn't know what Lange was up to, so why steal his hope?

Because his hope was a slimy crook. And Bash was still my friend, even if it didn't totally feel like it right now.

"Just watch your back," I said, brushing leaves off my clothes. "He's not a nice guy."

"Watch—" he laughed. "You're telling me to watch my back."

"Yes," I said, holding up my chin. "You aren't so badass that someone can't fool you."

"I don't need a nice guy, Allie," Bash said, leaning forward. "I don't care if he kisses babies or pets dogs. I care if he's ruthless with money."

I scoffed. "That, he is."

"How do you know this guy all of a sudden?" Bash said, crossing his arms.

Why couldn't I tell him? Why couldn't I say the words?

Because the words were horrible, and I couldn't stand the taste of them in my mouth. And because I hadn't actually said them out loud yet. Voicing them somehow made it all real and solid and I wasn't ready for either.

"How did Angel do?" I asked, in the world's most unsubtle changes of subject. Luckily it was dark, and he wouldn't be able to see the fear and panic living in my eyes.

"Seriously?"

"Roll with it."

Bash ran hands over his face and sighed with irritation. "Okay, in the spirit of that, is Angel allowed to have people over when you aren't there?"

I blinked at the flip. "No, why?"

"Because there were two Coke cans on the bar," he said. "On either side."

I chuckled. "That's your proof? Coke cans?"

"Well that," he said. "And her saying 'Be cool, Uncle Bash. Don't tell Mom' when I asked her about it."

I hung my head. "That little shit."

"Roll with it," he said, patting my shoulder in passing.

Cute.

"Bash," I said, cringing as I turned slowly.

"Yeah?"

"Thank you," I said, gesturing upward. "For rescuing me tonight. Being there for Angel."

Bash walked a few steps back to me, and my heart skittered in my chest when he reached out and pulled a moldy leaf from my hair. That move probably wouldn't make the naughty dream files, but it warmed my skin anyway.

"I told you a long time ago, Al," he said. "You and Angel are family. I'll always be there."

CHAPTER SIX

I was shopping.

Shopping.

An activity just short of visiting hell in my book. I know most women were somehow predisposed with the shopping gene, but it missed me.

Carmen had heard through Lanie—who'd promised Nick she wouldn't tell, but it was *Carmen* so that didn't count—about the man-purse guy steamrolling the Blue Banana. Which is exactly how she said it when she called, and I decided from that moment on that Landon Lange would forevermore be referred to as Man Purse Guy. It just seemed right.

Talking about MPG led to the King and Queen contest disclosure, something Carmen didn't know about either, and being a proponent of anything that would promote Sully's project, she was all excited about this. And decided that I needed to take Saturday off and do a little retail therapy.

I tried to argue that I was supposed to go see my dad that day, but Carmen pointed out that he wouldn't know what day it was so it could wait. I then countered that shopping was the opposite of therapeutic to me, but she claimed that having girlfriends do it with you trumped that.

Even Angel opted out, claiming she needed to study. On a Saturday. Which brought me around to Bash's line about Angel asking him not to tell she had someone over. Angel wouldn't pick studying over shopping if she had a test in the next two hours and a gun was pointed at her head. Something was up.

But I went, reluctantly.

Because—*girlfriends.* Either Carmen was just really smart, or was incredibly plugged in to exactly what I needed to hear, but I'd never had girlfriends. Ever. Not in more than an acquaintance capacity, anyway. And the thought of a day of that was just enough to make me skip the dad debacle and shake off my dread and see what it was about. Especially if I could maybe pick the brains of two women who may have no kids but had been very active, very sneaky teenagers once. I wasn't. I was quiet. I wasn't Angel.

Two shoe stores and three dress places in, my eyes were crossing and I still hadn't gotten around to Angel. We'd talked about the contest and how to dress for it and how cute Bash and I would look together until I thought I might implode. I knew how Bash and I would look together in every way. I saw us every night. How we dressed was irrelevant.

A teenage girl and her boyfriend passed us as we made our way down a sidewalk to a "boutiquey" formal place (Lanie's word) off the beaten path. The girl had nose rings, the boy had gauges, and both had visible tattoos. Already. They couldn't have been out of high school yet.

"So at what age did you start sneaking around?" I asked as Lanie opened the door.

"I didn't really sneak till I met Sully," Carmen said. "And that was seventeen. Granted, I made up for lost time."

"And I couldn't really sneak much in a house with a—with an Aunt Ruby," Lanie said, referring to her rumored-to-be-psychic late aunt. "I had to be creative."

"Why?" Carmen asked. "Is Angel fluffing her feathers a little?"

"Oh man," I said as we entered, glancing around the place that was divided equally into men's and women's sections with little staging areas that were surrounded by mirrors like tiny amphitheaters. "Fluffing, plucking, grooming, stroking. Mouthing," I added. "You name the button, she's pushing it. I was the boring teenager who didn't push anything, so I'm on foreign territory with her right now."

"Um, pregnant isn't boring, chica," Carmen said, going straight to a rack of sleek and shiny dresses. "You were doing something."

I shook my head. "I had my first boyfriend, and let him in my pants. Nothing sneaky about that, and until then I was squeaky clean. After that—I was suddenly the class whore, like no one else had sex but me."

A couple of quiet moments passed, and I guessed they were pondering that. Carmen and I had been friends only in the sense that we both came from the trailer park. She managed to rise above it a little, whereas I always felt that I had one foot stuck in the muck. And she always had Lanie. I never had a friend like that. Not a girlfriend, anyway. I just had Bash, and that was kind of under the radar.

"Hi," said a redheaded lady as she approached us.

"She's in the Honey Queen contest," Lanie said, pointing at me. "And needs a dress to stop time."

Red nodded, assessing me from head to toe so thoroughly I could see the math figures whizzing by. "I'm thinking a size five, maybe a seven if it runs small?"

"Mostly," I said.

"Red would be a good color on you," she said. "Blue. Any deep color would look fabulous with your coloring."

"Ooooh, blue," Lanie said. "You'd look gorgeous in like a deep royal blue."

"Black will be fine," I said. "I like blue, too, but let's keep this simple. Shoes will be easier that way."

"Speaking of shoes," Red said. "How good are you with heels?"

"I'm fine," I said.

Her gaze fell to my sneakered feet. "Would you rate that as fine with four inches, or fine with one?"

I cocked an eyebrow at this lofty chick. "I'm fine with all of it. I do have some girly genes even if I don't advertise them."

Red held out a palm. "Understand."

"I'd rather not go too high though," I said. "Something midway and comfortable."

"Comfortable has nothing to do with formal," Lanie said.

"Comfortable has nothing to do with this entire fiasco," I said. "But if the rest of me has to be trotted out like a show monkey, I'm treating my feet to a little love."

We were invited to browse as Red zeroed in on a few racks, but my head wasn't in it.

"Are there any boys on her horizon?" Carmen asked, smiling knowingly as if she saw my thoughts.

"Normally I'd say no," I said, halfheartedly thumbing through dresses that looked like they were made for movie stars. "But I'm hearing of some boy named Aaron Sharp—"

"Sharp," Carmen asked, looking up from a rack of purses. "As in Vonda?"

"What's a Vonda?" I asked.

"Vonda Sharp," she said. "She's over the promotion for the Lucky Charm. You've probably seen her in the diner. Big blonde hair and lots of teeth."

"Ah," I said, pointing. "I have. Can't miss her. And Angel did say this boy's mom was in charge of that. She's the one that came up with this whole crazy King and Queen thing."

"So Angel is hanging out with him?" Carmen asked.

Something in her tone rang a tiny bell of alarm in the back of my mind. "From the two sentences I've gleaned, I think so." I didn't add the thing about the Coke cans and Angel asking Bash not to tell. Nothing proved that it was a boy there. It could have been a girlfriend. "Why?"

Carmen's eyes said that she was weighing her words carefully, and that tiny bell became something Liberty-sized.

"Carmen," I said. "What do you know?"

"Well, I don't really *know* anything," she said. "It's just an impression I get."

"Of?"

"Of a seventeen—eighteen-year-old kid hitting on grown women like a player," she said.

My mind heard the *player* comment but it put that on hold and hit long loop on—

"He's *eighteen*?" Lanie said, voicing my concern. I was thinking *boy*, and eighteen was no boy.

"Well, he's a senior," Carmen said. "So he could be. But Angel's a sophomore so that's not all that out of line."

In theory. It was done all the time. But somehow, from a parental perspective, it sounded like a ten-year gap. A senior was likely to have a lot more experience than a fifteen-year-old girl. Speaking of...

"Okay, tell me about the player thing," I said, rubbing at my face.

Carmen pulled a dress from a rack and draped it over her arm. "I don't know, it's just kind of creepy. He's a good looking guy, and evidently knows it, and he knows how to turn on the charm way past his years. I see some of the women on the design committee turn goofy when he flirts with them at meetings—which is another thing. Why is this kid coming to promotional meetings with his mother? What teenager does that?"

"One that likes the attention of older women," Lanie said, pulling a red strapless out and holding it up for me to see.

I shook my head no. "So what is he doing messing with a fifteen-year-old?" I stopped moving and held up a hand. "Not messing. I didn't mean messing."

"No, I'm sure they aren't," Carmen said, grabbing my extended hand and squeezing it to pull me back down to earth.

"Dear God, she's not that stupid, is she?" I asked. Really, I was asking God, but I was looking at Carmen. "I know I was. But she's smarter than me. She's—"

"Allie, breathe," she said. "Don't go panicking before you know anything."

All I could think of was the gut-wrenching despair that had ripped through me when I'd peed on that stick and reality came crashing in. I wouldn't change having Angel for anything in the world, she was my everything, but she didn't need an everything right now. I didn't wish that kind of jolting start to adulthood on her.

Should I not have left her alone at home? Jesus, if I had to start thinking like that…

"Allie," Lanie said, pulling me off the crazy train.

"Yeah," I said.

"Back it up," she said. "I can see the wheels turning from here."

"One issue at a time. Let's find you a dress," Carmen said, handing one over to our saleslady. "Get you ready to blow everyone away for the stupidest contest in history. Then we tackle teenage hormones and man purses."

I shook off the worry weighing heavy on my skin.

"So it's not just me then, right?" I asked, giving a black halter dress a second look. "That contest is over the top, even for Charmed?"

"Please," Lanie said. "It's so cutesy-corny it makes my teeth hurt. Like we don't have enough with the Honey Wars and the games and the festival dance."

"I don't understand why there's such a dog and pony show over it anyway," I said. "Even with the silly contest, why not just vote by mail or online and voila! We have a king and queen."

"With little *I Voted* stickers," Carmen said.

"Exactly," I said. "What's with this pageanty crap? That's what Bash called it the other day."

"And who ever heard of a pageant by-the-couple?" Lanie asked, holding up a palm.

"Which means that you and Bash will need to up the chemistry," Carmen said, putting a dress she was holding back, and picking up another with much less material. "You need sexy."

Sweet God, no we didn't.

"No—no sexy," I said. "We don't—we're not like that. We don't have chemistry like that." I cleared my throat as last night's dream came to mind. The one where I was blowing him and having an orgasm at the same time while he stared down into my eyes. Yeah, no chemistry at all. No imagination, either.

Carmen and Lanie both laughed and exchanged a knowing look.

"What?" I asked.

"The hell you don't," Carmen said. "You two ought to arc electricity when you pass each other."

I waved a dismissive hand at her. "Come on."

"Seriously!" Lanie said. "You already have it, you have to know that. Nothing's ever gone down between you?"

I opened my mouth and then focused really intently on a silver dress that would look hideous on me.

"Nope."

"Bullshit," Carmen said giving me a side-eye.

"What?" I asked, wondering in a rush how she would have found out about our quickie sexcapade all those years ago.

"Let's talk about that kiss," she said.

Heat flooded my body and floated on top of my skin as the memory of being lips to lips with him as he caught me and held me tightly against him washed over me in a rush. I'd forgotten that Carmen was there for the whole thing.

"So—" I subconsciously ran my fingers over my lips in memoriam. "So there was a little panic or something in the chaos and fear," I said. "He's my best friend, I was terrified for him when I heard about the gun—"

"Oh yes, the flare that my ex-husband shot at my head," Carmen said snidely.

"And I might have been extraordinarily relieved to see he was okay," I said, blinking away. "You know, the emotional comedown."

"Or the emotional hurdle into a lover's arms, getting lost in the moment, lost in the embrace," Lanie said.

"What she said," Carmen thumbed behind her. "As cheesy as that sounded, add *lost in each other's lips* to that."

It *was* an incredible kiss. Not even a passionate or intimate one, no tongue, no heavy breathing. Just a meeting of mouths that might have been intended to be a quick chaste thing but once it was there, I couldn't pull away. I melted into him as that arc that Carmen mentioned cemented us together for not just one, but two long and tender kisses before our eyes met and the *oh... wait a minute...* set in.

It didn't have to be passionate. The dreams it kicked off ever since made up for that.

"I didn't even see that go down," Lanie said. "But I've never bought the innocent best friend thing. He's too damn hot to just be any woman's friend—unless said woman has an equally hot man."

Carmen gave a half shrug. "Yes and no. I was friends with him for a long time and even when I didn't have a man, and we were just friends, but he also never made a play for me, either."

I laughed through the need to fan my face. All this Bash talk was making my blood hot.

"You're saying if he *had* made a play for you—" I prompted.

"I'd have jumped him like a monkey in heat," she said cooly, talking to the dress she was holding up.

I snorted so loud, I had to clap a hand over my mouth as the redheaded lady came back.

"Are we ready?" Red cooed.

Lanie laughed harder, turning around to hide the shaking.

"I think I have a few to start with," I said, swiping the tears under my eyes and snatching the dress from Carmen's hand. It was the halter one, and after that comment how could I resist?

"I have a dressing room set up for you," Red said as I plucked whatever Lanie had draped over her arm and followed her.

Three minutes later, shoveled into a "boutique" dressing room, I held up something that looked like a bunch of black rubber bands attached on the sides.

"No."

I opened the door and hung that one on the outside.

"Didn't fit?" I heard Red say in a melodic tone.

I closed the door and studied the others, hung side by side in front of me. A deep blue strapless with tiny rhinestones at the waist. A black sheath dress that was super-simple. And the black halter-style dress with no back.

The sheath dress was probably the most me out of the three. It was conservative and covered everything, sexy in its sleevelessness but covered all the way to the neck. I went with that one first, wrangled myself into it, and walked out tugging at the hem.

"Wow," Carmen said. "I've never seen you look like that."

Yes, yes, yes I know. I dress like a unich.

"Beautiful," Lanie said. "What do you think?"

"I think it's short," I said, pulling at the bottom that was resting happily at what felt like the curve of my ass. "I have underwear longer than this."

"That may be the next shopping need then," Lanie said.

"That is the style," Red said, all her teeth gleaming.

"I'm good," I said, already unzipping it.

I went for the blue one. I was pretty sure it wasn't for me, it being of the strapless variety, but it *was* beautiful and I was curious.

"Holy shit," I said, looking at myself in the mirror.

"Good?" Carmen called. "Or bad?"

I came out and she whistled. "Damn, girl. I never knew you had a rack that good."

"That is a gorgeous color on you," Red said. "Definitely a contender."

"Definitely not," I said, preening in front of the three-way mirror.

"Why?" she asked.

"Because it looks like she's going to prom," Lanie said.

"Exactly," I said. "It's hot, but I feel like I'm going to get laid in someone's back seat later." Carmen snickered. "Not that I would know, since I was way too pregnant to make it to prom."

"You're right, though," Carmen said. "It's really pretty, but not the look you want for this."

Whatever the hell that was.

I sighed. "Next."

The other one took a little more time to get right, since the plunging open back meant no bra, and that meant some adjusting up front. I heard a man's voice muffled out there, which was no big deal. Half the store was for guys coming to rent or buy suits or tuxes. Lanie and Carmen's laughter, however, told me it was someone they knew. Maybe Nick or Sully came for bow ties to play out Chippendale fantasies for their women.

Damn, now that thought was going to work its way into my naughty Bash dreams. That would be a good one.

I got everything in its place and turned from side to side, oddly hit with a wave of warmth. This dress had it going on. Seriously. The halter style held the girls snug but also pulled them up into some kickass cleavage. The bare back was majorly hot and tease-worthy without looking like I was working a corner, and the length was perfect. I bent over, and yep. Long enough to cover my ass, and yet short enough to flirt with my legs. The right shoes, and this would actually work.

Another round of female and male laughter reached my ears. Lanie catcalling and Carmen clapping as some poor sap was modeling something on the other side, and I figured what the hell. Great time to step out of my box and test this out on a male perspective.

"Okay," I said, breezing out of the dressing room and twirling with a rare female-empowerment as I pretended the man's residual chuckle was male appreciation for me and I soaked it in. I laughed too as I stopped in front of the three-way mirror, and I heard the quick inhales and whoa's from all three of the women. "What do we think?"

"I think I could almost change teams looking at you in that thing," Lanie said, making a show of fanning herself.

"Hell on wheels, Allie," Carmen said, eyes wide. "You're gonna stop hearts, all right. But the true test is did you stop his?"

Blushing from the thought, I grinned as I turned around with my hands on my hips, and nearly swallowed my tongue at the creature on the other staging area with a black-on-black action going on and the shirt completely unbuttoned.

Bash.

Staring at me with his hands frozen mid-reach to his buttons.

CHAPTER SEVEN

"Sweet—J—" I breathed, as my words left me.

My mouth went as dry as sand as Bash stared back at me with blue eyes gone almost black and the hint of a smile still pulling at his lips. I may as well have been totally naked. His gaze slid from my face to my neck, to land and linger in more cleavage than he'd ever seen from me. Well, except for that one time. A hundred million years ago. And even then I wasn't sure all our clothes made it off. It might have just been the important ones.

Suddenly it was like one of my dreams, and we were the only people in the room. Bash, looking messy and rumpled like someone had unbuttoned him that way, had me lightheaded. I could imagine his lips on every inch his eyes trailed over. My nipples hardened at the thought, and I watched his eyes notice that. I saw the fire in them dance, before it jumped the space between us and shot right through my belly.

Shit, shit, shit.

I crossed my arms nervously, the movement making him blink back up to my eyes.

"Don't—"

"I—" I shook my head and covered my mouth, all while trying to cover my boobs unsuccessfully.

"Don't hide," he said, chuckling, his eyes dropping again. He moved his head back and forth slowly and let out a breath. "Don't ever hide."

I couldn't breathe, couldn't move, couldn't speak as his eyes moved down the rest of my body. My hips. Where the skirt played with my thighs, all the way down to my naked unpainted toes. It was only a few seconds, and yet it could have been all friggin day.

"Allie, you look—"

"See?" a shrill voice said from somewhere, breaking the moment. "It's split in half. Something for both—"

"Whoa."

Bash turned instantly at the word, which was intoned just this side of a lusty catcall, coming face to face with a surprised Alan and Katrina Bowman. Alan had stopped cold to gape at me like I was a giant steak.

"Keep walking," Bash said to him.

"What?" Alan said, glancing back at me. "I just—I mean, damn, who knew?"

I narrowed my eyes in repulsion. "Really?"

"Oh my God, I need a dress like that," Katrina gushed, walking around Alan in apparent oblivion or disinterest with her husband's gawking over me.

"Go change," Bash said over his shoulder, his tone changed.

"Crap, she's the competition," Carmen said, grabbing my hand. "Come on."

"What, she's going to buy the same dress?" I said. "I don't care."

Bash whipped his suit jacket off and wrapped it around my shoulders, holding on to the lapels that covered my cleavage for a lingering moment that seemed to just float between us. Or maybe that was just me, confusing my nighttime activity with the fact that his chest was still bare and just inches from my reach. And maybe that his thumbs were nearly touching my boobies.

"Please go change," he said softly. "Before I have to deck him."

A surprised chuckle escaped my throat before Carmen pulled me toward the dressing room, Bash's gaze heavy on me as the suit coat fell open.

"Sir?" a salesgirl called behind him. "Mr. Anderson? I need to finish measuring you."

He blinked away. Away from me, away from Alan, and toward the woman calling his name, raking fingers through his hair. Messing it up. Squeezing my chest with that just-fucked-on-a-boardroom-table look.

I clapped a hand over my mouth to make sure I didn't say that out loud. But oh my God, I just thought it. And worse. I wanted it.

"You don't want her getting the same dress," Carmen was saying, although her words just bounced off my brain. "She'll find some way to upstage you."

I found myself suddenly back in the dressing room, standing in front of the mirror, looking like an orphan with Bash's suit jacket hanging on me. His behavior had my head spinning. Was he saying this dress wasn't appropriate? Or was he jealous? *Don't ever hide.* My eyes filled as I pulled it tighter around me and brought a section to my nose. Oh God, it smelled like him. Four minutes on his body and it already smelled like him, full of his warmth and his—

"Stop," I whispered, dropping the fabric and bringing both hands to my face as two tears trickled over my fingers. "You can't do this."

Silly fantasies were one thing. This was getting too—too much like something neither of us messed with. Something we'd decided against a long time ago—sort of.

I took the coat off and hung it up, and my skin felt hot as I unhooked the clasp behind my neck and pulled the dress off. I sank onto a chair with the fabric wadded in my lap, staring back into the mirror. What was I doing? What was I playing with? Yes, I'd kissed him. Yes, I'd been having sex dreams about him. But none of that meant anything. Bash was my closest, most important friend. Why was I getting emotional over this shit? And what the hell just happened out there? I stood up quickly, as the memory set my whole body thrumming again. Since when did my crazy dream content move into real life, and more than that, when did *he* actively join that party?

Because it hadn't just been me. The way Bash had looked at me. Oh my God. He'd never looked at me that way. No one had ever looked at me that way. I'd had serious boyfriends that never did that. I grabbed a promotional sign telling dressing room patrons to keep their underwear on, and fanned myself with it, trying to cool my face.

"Okay," I whispered finally, putting down the sign to put my bra and T-shirt and jeans back on. There. I looked like boring me, again. No one would stop breathing or make lewd comments over this version. "Stop being an idiot," I muttered. "This is silly. Stop acting like a brainless twit and go take care of business."

I took a deep breath as I draped the dress over my arm and grabbed his suit jacket and walked out, holding my chin up. Alan was nowhere to be seen, thank God. Katrina already had a load of dresses hanging on her arm, and Bash was over on his side with his arms stretched out as a young girl measured him and tried not to blush as he talked to her.

"Well, I think that answered that question," Carmen said, pulling my attention back.

"I think that's the dress," Lanie said with a knowing look. "Fix your hair down, maybe over one shoulder. Very sexy. What do you think, Bash?" she called out with a chuckle and making me want to duck back into the safe haven of the dressing room. "Is this the dress?"

I looked back to where he had just turned to face us, arms still outstretched and grinning lazily like the world hadn't just been rocked. How was that? How did he do that? Ugh—men!

He cleared his throat and chuckled, smiling his trademark woman-killer smile at Lanie. *At Lanie. Not the woman wearing the damn dress. For him.* That thought slapped me around a little. It was true. The second his eyes were on me, looking at me like that, I'd known without a doubt that I wanted that dress for him.

"I think so," he said, sliding his gaze to me as I walked up holding out the jacket. "Is this the suit?"

Fuck, yes. *Please wear it twenty-four hours a day, seven days a week.* "I think it works," I said.

He looked at me for a long moment before blinking and changing course.

"I got an e-mail about essays," he said.

"Essays?"

"We have to write one," he said. "One, not two."

"Oh, good lord," I said.

"Can we work on that?" he asked. "I kind of need us to win this thing."

I backed up a step, his adamant tone taking me off guard. "Okay, when's the next time you and Angel are driving?"

"Tomorrow," he said. "So after that?"

I shrugged. "That's fine."

"It's a date, then," he said as I turned to go.

I stopped in my tracks and looked over my shoulder, hating myself for doing that. Four months ago, I would have rolled with that without another thought, and now every word was under scrutiny.

"Yeah, okay," I said.

"I mean—" he said awkwardly.

"No, it's all good," I said, holding up a hand and smiling as I walked back to the girls, but closing my eyes and shaking my head by the time I reached them. "Please shoot me now and put me out of my misery."

"You're getting that, right?" Red said, morphing at my side.

I nodded. "I am."

"What about some accessories?" she asked, pointing toward the purses.

"I'm good," I said. "We aren't going on a date." Nope. No fucking date. "We're just strutting around a stage like prize cattle."

Carmen held up a brochure with bright and glossy pictures of the town. Our town.

"What is that?" I asked.

"Something I picked up on a rack by the door," Lanie said. "As they were setting up the rack by the door."

"Why is there—oh," I said. "Please tell me it's not about this silly contest."

"Not per se," Carmen said, flipping through hers. "But it is mentioned as one of the *Make a Charming Charmed* new events." She turned it around so I could see the list and the glossy photos of the pond front and gazebo built a few months ago.

I took the brochure from her and looked at all the photos, from the front picture of the Ferris wheel at the Lucky Charm, to pictures of jars of honey on a table. Not Bash's honey—just random generic jars. It sported a photo of one of the Honey Wars from this past summer, with Katrina Bowman and Lanie's husband Nick climbing a knotted rope. She was climbing him like a tree. I showed her.

"Yeah," she said, her voice sounding sour. "Just what I wanted saved for posterity. Of course they didn't get one of me stepping on her husband's face or Nick punching him."

"Well, you know, that wouldn't have shown a *charming Charmed*," I said, turning the rest of the pages. "They didn't get Bash's apiary either, or the Blue Banana. What the hell?"

Anderson's Apiary was the driving source of Charmed's wax and honey supply, and my diner—my family's diner—what *used* to be my family's diner—it was the centerpiece of town.

"What a crock of shit," I said, flipping to the back, where a piece of colored paper was stapled.

"It's advertising the Honey King and Queen competition with all the sponsors and the prizes," Carmen read. "Oh wow."

I read what she was wow'ing. Almost twenty grand in cash prizes. Ten apiece. Bash's comment about needing to win made a little more sense.

Once upon a time, that would have sounded motivating. Ten thousand dollars could help us out tremendously. Pay for a couple of semesters of college or get Angel a good used car. Now all I could see was that it wasn't eighty-seven grand.

Still. Who was I to thumb my nose up at free money? Or who was I kidding—after today, none of it felt anything close to free. And the grin Lanie was giving me told me that was just about to get worse.

"What?" I asked.

"Did you feel that chemistry?" Lanie asked, brows lifted high.

"Did you notice he stopped breathing?" Carmen added, looking up.

Did *they* notice that neither of us appeared happy about it?

"You two are so going to win," Lanie said. "You have nothing to worry about."

I shoved my fist into the ball of churning fire burning in my belly. She was so wrong. I had *everything* to worry about.

CHAPTER EIGHT

"Hey Mom," Angel said, strolling in as I slapped some mashed potatoes and deli turkey on a plate with a French roll, and drizzled some gravy on it. "Ooh, that looks good."

"It's always good when someone else does it and you don't have to help," I said with a smile.

She stopped in her tracks and gave me a guilty smile.

"Was it my night to make something?"

I was trying to teach her some skills, or at least get her in the habit of thinking about skills. Every third night was her turn to come up with a dinner plan and make it happen. I was happy to help, but it was ultimately on her. Or in tonight's case, on me. So I didn't wait. She'd *claimed* she was studying with her friend today while we were shopping, so I cooked, prepped, and was about to sit down with a plate of open-faced turkey and mashed potatoes.

"Yes, so I guess you're having cereal," I said, walking to the table.

"Seriously?"

I threw a dishrag at her. "Get a plate, dork."

She did, and we sat down to eat in peaceful coexistence. Except that it wasn't. Not for me. Angel scrolled through her phone as she munched in happy oblivion, whereas I sat there studying her for signs of sex. No hickeys. No afterglow. No whisker rash on her face—since she was evidently kissing a *man*.

"So—homework on a Saturday," I said. "Wow. Go you."

Angel looked up at me with a raised eyebrow. "Shopping. Go *you*."

I laughed. "Yeah, that was kind of an adventure. Sorry you couldn't be there."

Then again the eye-sex with Bash might have been significantly *more* awkward if my daughter was there.

"Did you find something for the—whatever he called it?"

Oh, I had better than words. Visual aids had come in the mail in the form of those laminated cards like Alan had. I reached behind me and grabbed one, holding it next to my head like I was one of those showcase girls holding things on game shows.

"The Honey King and Queen extravaganza?" I said dramatically. "Because what's sweeter than a crown made out of honeycomb? What's more amazing than a scepter carved from pure beeswax?"

The sneer on her face was priceless. "Seriously?"

"No," I said, chuckling. "God, I hope not, anyway. But yes, I found a dress."

"Hang on," she said, leaning forward and pressing things on her phone. "Say that again, I want to record it for posterity."

"I found a dress," I said slowly.

Two presses and my voice was playing back to me. "*I found a dress—a dre-dre-dress. I-I-I found a dress.*"

"Cute, now please kill that before I do," I said.

"*Dre-dre-dress.*"

"So, what does it look like?" Angel said, snickering.

I pulled out *my* phone and scrolled to a picture Lanie had sent me. One she took of me primp-posing when I first emerged from the dressing room. Before I saw Bash and lost all my feminine power.

"Holy sh—crap," she said, grabbing my phone.

"Nice save."

"Mom," she said, her eyes bugging. "That's you."

"So Lanie tells me," I said.

"That's like a—serious babe dress."

A serious babe dress! Would that make me a serious babe?

No.

Calm down.

"And that's a problem?" I said.

"Well, I thought you were just gonna get some—I don't know, some soccer-mom-looking dress," she said.

"You don't play soccer," I said.

"You know what I mean," she said. "Something that covers everything."

I looked at her profile. She was such my mini-me. In looks, anyway. Inside, she couldn't be more different.

"So this is too out there, you think?" I said.

"No!" she said, jerking her gaze my way. "This is so cool! Oh my God, Mom, I never knew you could look like that."

"Seems to be a common thread, today," I said, taking the phone back. "Why?"

I shook my head. "Good, I'm glad you like it."

"Has Uncle Bash seen it?" I closed my eyes remembering very well the moment he saw it. The eyes that went with the suit and the open shirt. I'd probably not forget that anytime soon. Or ever.

"Yes," I said.

"Did he like it?" she asked. "I mean he's a guy. He'd have to be dead not to like that."

I drew in a long breath. "He seemed to."

"So what's wrong, then?"

I made a face, and she rolled her eyes. "Oh man, here we go. You're wigging out about this dress, aren't you?"

"No, it's beautiful," I said. "It's just—"

Angel reached over and took my phone from me, pulling up the picture. "It's just amazing," she said, turning it to show me. "You don't ever treat yourself like that." She made a big production of pointing at it. "Go enjoy yourself being a little bit girly and crazy. You can be uptight Allie Greene the next day."

I would act insulted shortly. But first I had to take two seconds to just stare at this girl that could be an infuriating little brat one minute and then this budding mature young woman the next. The moment would pass, and I was sure it was already on the backslide, but I had to take a little snapshot while I could.

I scoffed. "I am not uptight."

"Um—" Angel opened her mouth to say something, and then picked up her fork and looked down at her food all wide-eyed and snarky. "Yeah, okay."

"I'm not!" I laughed.

"Aaron says his mom's a little wound up, too," she said.

Oh, Aaron. Here we were.

"You said she was in charge of the Sharp Group promoting the Lucky Charm?" I asked and Angel nodded. "I think I've seen her in the diner. She talks a lot."

She shrugged and kept eating, focusing back on her phone. We'd had about ten seconds of funny comfortable bonding, it was time to lose her again.

"So, tell me about this kid, Aaron."

She gave me a quick look before dropping her gaze back to her phone.

"This kid, Aaron," she echoed. Sarcastically.

"Isn't that his name?"

"Yes, but he's not a ten-year-old," she said, widening her eyes, not looking up.

A laugh bubbled up. "So I've heard," I said. "Rumor has it he's eighteen."

She frowned. "He's not eighteen. Yet. He won't be for another two months."

Yet. I nodded. "Two whole months, huh?"

Angel looked at me with a hint of a glare behind those dark eyes, and I watched all our good juju we'd had going on before start to trickle down some invisible drain.

"I'll be sixteen before that. He's not even two years older than me."

I took a slow breath as I moved mashed potatoes around my plate. I could tread lightly or I could be my dad—which worked so well for me. I could tell her what I heard about him hitting on older women and hurt her feelings, and I really didn't want to crush her self-esteem with that, either.

"Do you need reminding that you aren't allowed to date till then?" I asked.

She gave me the dead-eye look. "Seriously?"

"I don't remember it being a suggestion," I said. "It's the rule. And besides that, at your age, babe, two years difference is a pretty big deal, maturity wise."

Angel stared down into her plate and stabbed a piece of meat.

"Uh-huh," she said. "Because my dad was two years older than you, and all that went south and pear-shaped. So because of your bad choices, I can't hang out with a nice guy?"

The dad card, *and* the teenage pregnancy card, all in one. Nice. She was stepping up.

"Watch it, Angel," I said, not letting her push my buttons. "You'll mouth yourself right out of that phone you're so stuck to."

"Sorry," she muttered, still scrolling.

"This isn't a new rule, you've always known it."

"So I'm supposed to tell him we have to wait a month?" she said, looking at me like I just suggested she don a veil and a head wrap.

I set down my fork and gave her my have-you-lost-your-mind mom look.

"Baby girl, you wouldn't have to tell your boy-man anything if you hadn't started something you weren't allowed to do."

She huffed and a myriad of emotions played over her face as she shook her head and shoved her food around.

"It's not like we're *dating* anyway," she said. "We're just—hanging out. Talking and stuff. He's really easy to talk to."

And stuff.

"Then why are you arguing?" I asked.

"Because maybe I'd *like* to go to a movie," she said. "Maybe go wander around the Lucky Charm, ride the Ferris wheel and get some unhealthy food."

"You're welcome to go to a movie," I responded. "And cheesecake on a stick and rides are there any time you want them."

"With *Aaron*," she said, slamming her fork down. At my raised eyebrow, she picked it back up and set it down slowly, never breaking eye contact so I'd be sure to know her true feelings.

"In a month, we can have this conversation," I said, taking a bite of potatoes.

"He may not still be interested in a month," she exclaimed.

"Then why the heck do you want him?" I said. "If he's not interested in you a month from now, then he wasn't worth having."

Oh sweet God, even as the words were flying out of my mouth, I heard every old person I'd ever known. That logic was sound enough in theory, but I'd been young once, and you want them because you want them. There's no reasoning to it. Hell, most adults I knew had problems with that, how was a kid supposed to wrap their mind around it?

"Mom."

"Angel."

She blew out a breath in disgust and looked at me with all the toxicity a girl her age can muster. I'd be willing to bet I wasn't so cool now, serious babe dress or not.

"I'm not hungry anymore," she said. "I have homework."

"Again?" I said. "This is a banner Saturday for you."

"What can I say, I'm dedicated," she said, her eyes burning holes through me.

Fun.

"By all means," I said. "Go be brilliant."

Angel stalked off, banging the food off her plate with her fork so violently I was waiting for the sound of smashing stoneware. I sat there at the table alone, sighing as I speared another bite of gravy-laden turkey.

"That went well."

* * *

"Where are you going?" Lange asked as I left my office, keys in hand. Yes, it was still my office, so far. I felt like he was throwing me a bone with that, but I wasn't about to bring it *up for discussion.*

Everything was always up for discussion. That was his spindly, sleazy little way of taking over, by throwing me little breaths of air that sounded like I had a say when I really didn't. Not if he wanted to be an asshole about it. And from what I could tell, Lange frequently did. He changed the table order and sectioned them off. He took out the old jukebox, which didn't work anymore but still added ambiance. He had one end painted blue, which was kind of okay, but was talking about replacing a few of the tables with the standing variety.

Standing tables. In a diner. We weren't a nightclub. People came to eat lunch and dinner, and maybe dessert. As a general rule, most people like to sit down for that.

Now he was perusing the schedule, and had already fired my morning waitress when she showed up ten minutes late.

"I thought you normally stayed till after the dinner rush," he added.

"I do when I can," I said. "But I have excellent people here. I trust them." I held up my keys. "And today I have something I need to do."

"Well, I think it's time we discuss the new name," he said, nodding as though this was already done.

"New name," I echoed. "What new name?"

"I sent you an e-mail with some choices to consider," he said. "I'd be happy to let you choose."

"No," I said simply.

Lange blinked, looking a bit taken aback. "No, you won't choose?"

"Just no," I said. "That's not on the table."

"Allie," he said in his trademark condescending tone. "I told you it was up for discussion."

"It's not," I said.

"It's dumb and unappealing."

"It's personal," I said. "The Blue Banana Grille stays."

"Listen to the choices," he said, pulling a tiny notebook from his pocket. "I told you—"

"The Eatery," he said, flipping a page. "The Grille. Charmed Foods. The Charming Skillet. The Lucky Skillet. The Charmed Chef. The Honey Pot. Miss Sharp suggested that one."

My eyes popped open. "Miss Sharp?"

"We've been working on compiling a list for you," he said. "And I put customer cards out on the tables for people to make suggestions. Sometimes the best gem—"

"You did *what*?"

I dropped my keys where I stood and strode out into the diner, snatching up the little cards from the empty tables and trying to figure out a subtle way to get them from the occupied ones without having to answer questions.

"Allie," he said, clearly right on my heels.

"You don't get to do this on your own," I said under my breath. "You don't get to fire my waitresses. You don't get to make the schedules. I run this place. I don't care if you own *ninety* percent. You don't go polling *my* customers for a new name. We're called the Blue Banana Grille."

"I was thinking about that other stuff as well," he said. "I might take over the books and such. Free you up to manage the floor. Or look elsewhere, in case you decide to sell your percentage."

My mouth formed words but there was no sound. Sell my percentage. He wanted me to—

"I don't think so," I managed.

"Well, it's up for discussion," he said with a nod.

I headed back for my keys, plucked them from the floor, and passed him without so much as a glance.

"I have to go," I said. "Try not to put up a new sign while I'm gone."

CHAPTER NINE

I pulled into the trailer park at exactly 4:55 p.m., waving at Miss Gerry, Carmen's mom, as she swept the steps of the office trailer. She owned the place now. That was wild. Miss Gerry had gone from selling handmade hemp necklaces out of their trailer when we were little, to working at the Feed Store, the drugstore, the Walmart in Denning, a paper route for a time, and I think she'd done a stint bartending at Rojo's. Throughout all that was various other private little industries I'd hear about her trying out, mostly through my father, who thought her to be a supreme flake and yet he bought every single thing she ever tried to sell him.

I didn't know what to think when I heard that good old Larry was selling her the park after the land sold to Sully. I was a little worried that I'd have to move my father out of there, that she'd forget to pay the note or the maintenance on the rentals, and something would shut down or blow up while she was making candles out of pine cones.

I'd been pleasantly surprised. Miss Gerry had stepped up and formed a clean-up committee, had landscaping done with some pretty trees to fancy up what was just a bunch of trailers on concrete, had new lamppost lighting put in, upgraded the playground, and started a monthly potluck picnic by that playground for those who wanted to participate. It was pretty cool. People who barely talked to each other were now hanging out and eating good food, watching their kids play. And she was there for everything. It was like she'd wandered for decades just to find what she was supposed to do, and it was right there all along, right where she lived.

I was happy for her. I wish my dad had had that much luck. I wish I did.

Pulling up to his trailer at a couple minutes till five, I turned off the ignition and absorbed the quiet. I had to wait till exactly the top of the hour, or he'd get all bent up in a tizzy over the change, but that was fine. I happily took the three remaining minutes to breathe and calm my nerves.

Sell Lange my portion of the diner? *My* diner? I couldn't believe the audacity. Or I could, but it was almost too over the top to be imagined.

And then there was Bash coming over tonight. Then Mr. Mercer from the drugstore came up to the counter to say he needed to talk to me privately about something. Whatever the hell that meant. On top of that, I knew I couldn't put off coming to see Dad any longer. I had to face him, without being able to say a word about what he did.

My phone dinged with a text from a number I didn't recognize, telling me whoever it was, was about to call me.

"Okay," I said, glancing at the clock. Four-fifty-nine. "Get on with it."

The same number filled my screen seconds later and I answered with all the intention of saying I needed to go. I opened my door and turned to sit sideways.

"Hey Allie," said an older man's voice. Mr. Mercer. Who evidently got my number off an old prescription order. Wasn't that crafty of him.

"Hi, Mr. Mercer," I said. "What's up?"

"Well, like I said, I need to talk to you about something," he said. "It might be nothing, but it might not be nothing."

I sighed and checked the clock. Five o'clock straight up. "Um, I hear you, but can it wait? I'm about to go visit my dad, and—"

"Sure, but it's about Angel," he said.

The words already on my tongue dissolved. "Angel," I echoed. "Is she—" A million scenarios played through my head, and none of them resembling *I just wanted to track you down twice today to tell you that your daughter is the best thing since sliced bread.* "Did she do something wrong? Oh my God, she didn't steal from you, did she?"

I wanted to throw up. She'd never done anything like that, but every day was a new day and a new age, and a new opportunity to give me gray hairs.

"No, no," Mr. Mercer said. "Nothing like that."

I let go of a breath. "Oh, good," I said, chuckling nervously. The clock read two minutes after five. Crap, I was going to have to field drama for that. "So then, what's the issue?"

"Well, I hesitate to put my toe in other people's business," he said. "You know, people's private lives are their own."

Yeah, and a few months back, you announced to a field full of people that your cousin was a transvestite, so your sense of private is a little skewed.

"I understand, Mr. Mercer," I said. "But I'm afraid I don't know what you're getting at unless you tell me."

"Well, Allie," he began. "Angel was in the store yesterday afternoon with a young man."

"A young man," I echoed. "Let me guess, blond hair?"

"Yes, so you know him then?" he asked.

I shook my head, not that he could see it. "No, but I've heard about him."

"And—you know he may be a little older than our Angel?" he asked.

She was *our Angel* now. Okay. As in this boy is an outsider, and something really bad was about to be revealed. My stomach found everything I'd put in it today and went on standby.

"I might have heard that, too," I said.

There was a pause, and I swear if I could have reached through that phone, I would have yanked him through it.

"They bought condoms, Allie."

For the oddest, longest moment I had an entire conversation with him in my head that included a good laugh when he realized it wasn't Angel and this boy, but some other random kids…or that it wasn't really condoms they bought, but a package of sour gummy worms. They were innocent.

My baby was still innocent. My diner was still mine. My best friend was—

"They—" I attempted. "She—that can't be right. You had to be mistaken."

"I talked to her," he said.

My belly contracted. "You talked to her? She—she didn't even try to hide it?"

"Oh no, she acted like she was alone, but I saw them come in together," he said. "And they met back up outside the door."

I was sweating and in need of more air. Maybe I was having a heart attack. I looked around for something to fan myself with, but there was nothing. If I started my car back up for AC, my dad would hear and know something was up. If I got out and stood outside talking on the phone in the brisk air, he would know that, too, and come outside in his underwear and ask me just what the hell I was doing on his little patch of grass. Because there were days he didn't know me.

But right now that didn't matter. Because his stupid, idiotic, moron of a granddaughter was probably banging another moron.

"Oh my God," I whispered.

"I'm sorry to be the bearer of bad news," Mr. Mercer said. "But I thought you'd want to know."

"Yes—absolutely," I said absently. "Thanks for calling."

Thanks for putting the rotten cherry on a really shit-filled day.

I hung up and sat there, listening to my breathing. She'd already done this. Last night, when we had our fun little meeting of the minds—they'd already bought the condoms. Had they already done the deed? *We're just talking and stuff.*

I wanted to throw up. I also wanted to nail Aaron's dick to a tree. And pull Angel's hair out one hair at a time.

And more than anything, I wanted to talk to her dad.

That thought kicked me in the gut more than anything in a very long time, and knocked the wind right out of me. I sucked in a breath and clamped a hand over my mouth. Because it wasn't her actual dad I wanted to talk to, but the pretend one I used to wish for. The perfect one that would hold me right now and say all the right things and help me figure out the way to deal with our kid. And then head off to break the boy's fingers.

In other words, Bash. I wanted to talk to Bash. But I couldn't do that, because we were weird right now, and because he really would go break fingers. It pissed me off through and through. I missed my friend. I needed him.

I needed him for her, for the crap with the diner, for what was about to be crap with my dad. For this freaky-ass thing going on with a guy lately that I couldn't tell him about, even as a joke, because he was the freaky-ass.

I put the phone away. It was Sunday. Angel would theoretically be home when I got there, getting ready to go drive with Bash unless she was off doing homework again—and *fuck-a-duck.*

If *homework* was a cute little code word for sex, I was going to mess up that girl's world.

I swiped under my eyes and pushed open the door, pulling my hair down from the messy bun and fluffing it out. I felt so hot, it almost made me more nauseous, but Dad tended to place me better like that, so...

"Okay," I whispered, breathing slowly and shaking out my hands. Time to shelve the diner and the Angel issues for the moment and go face this one.

He opened the door before I even knocked, which told me he'd been watching out the window, and the set of his mouth told me I was eleven minutes late getting there.

"Hey, Dad," I said, hugging his neck.

He smelled of Ivory soap and cigarettes, the latter I'm sure he thought he was hiding successfully from me and from his home health nurse. He tended to forget we had noses. He hugged me back, so at least he didn't forget I was me. Not today.

"What were you doing out there?" he said, his tone irritable as he paced in front of the door.

"I was on the phone," I said.

He turned and fixed a look on me. "Don't blow smoke up my ass," he said. "Since when are there phones in cars?"

Ah. *That's* where we were.

"So what are you eating tonight?" I asked. "Has Bev been here yet?"

"Not yet," he said. "She's supposed to bring me extra puddings tonight. "Awesome," I said.

"You were late," he said.

"I know, Dad, I'm sorry," I said. "I'll do better next time.

He grunted and walked back to his recliner, next to which was a rickety old metal TV tray with a lidded cup, the remote, and a book. Add some Cheetos to that mix, I thought, and he'd never have to leave his chair.

The room was bright, every light on. He liked it that way, claimed it helped keep him from nodding off. Sleep wasn't usually his friend. The dreams he'd always been plagued with made slumber a miserable place for my dad. He could take medicine to knock him into the next planet, past dream level, but he hated how that made him feel. So the lights stayed on, the television stayed on, the AC stayed on—basically if it kept him cold and kept his eyes open, it was on.

A war movie was playing on the TV, which usually spurred him into a bad mood and quick tempers, but today I didn't care. I was kind of in a mood, myself.

I settled on the couch and pulled a worn throw pillow into my lap. "Whatcha watching?"

"Does it matter?" he asked. "War is life. It all has the same message. Get your shit together."

"Okay," I said softly. "Words to live by." I ran my fingers along a stray thread on the pillow. "Dad, do you remember how you and Mom named the diner?"

"Of course," he said. "And so do you. I've told you a million times."

"So go for a million and one," I said. I needed the nostalgia. I needed him to hear it, too.

There was a long pause.

"When I asked your mother to marry me," he said. "We weren't even dating. I just knew. She didn't, but I did. She laughed and said *Sure thing, Greene. When bananas turn blue.*"

His face softened with introspection. "So, I bought a banana, painted it blue and brought it to her." A smile pulled at his lips. "She said, 'Well, a deal's a deal. But how about a date first?'" Dad stopped and rubbed at his jaw. "We were never apart again. We'd joke that that blue banana was our good-luck charm. So when we bought the building for the diner, she painted one and put it in the window. I couldn't imagine a better name after that."

My eyes burned with tears. Not just at the story—he was right, I'd heard it a million times in my lifetime—but it was the longest dialogue he'd had in almost a year. There for about thirty seconds, it was like having my dad back, talking to me. Really talking to me, not just grunting at me in short little fragments.

"I can't imagine a better one, either," I said, shutting my eyes. I would rather run through town naked and on fire than have this conversation. "I'm fighting to keep it, but I don't know if I can."

He frowned at the TV, and I knew he'd gotten lost again.

"So, Dad, do you remember a guy named Landon Lange? Tall. Useless look about him."

"Carries a purse like a woman," he added.

I laughed. "Yes!"

He shifted in his chair and reached for his cup, and I took it that the subject was finished. Except that it couldn't be. Why the hell couldn't it be? I gritted my teeth together and willed my brain to let it go. I'd already determined that it would only rile him up, or he wouldn't remember it at all, that it served no purpose.

But there was an angry seven-year-old girl inside me, losing her purple-flowered room all over again and wanting retribution.

And the Blue Banana Grille was about to become The Honey Pot.

"He came to see me the other day," I said.

Dad grunted.

"Seems that you and he had a—transaction last year," I said, forcing the word over my tongue. "Do you remember that?"

Another grunt. "Bottom drawer." He twisted in his chair to look behind him.

"What do you need, Dad?" I asked, pushing back at the impatience shoving its way up my throat. "Bottom drawer of what?"

"I want some peanut butter crackers," he said.

"Bev'll be bringing supper soon," I said. "You don't want to spoil your appetite."

"I'm a grown-ass man," he said, twisting back to growl at me. "I can have crackers before dinner if I want to."

I held up my hands. Every day was different, and so were the boundaries. I knew that from before I hired Bev to bring him his meals and make sure he took his meds correctly. Soon, I'd have to concede to full time care or move him, and that was a battle I wasn't looking forward to.

"Fine," I said. "I'll get you the crackers."

I got up and went to what was always the snack cabinet below the counter, but it was empty. Bev must have moved some things around for easier access. I opened the pantry cabinet, which was at eye level, and there were what looked like fifty boxes of whole grain peanut butter crackers. I pulled a package out and brought it to him.

He took it and tore it open, giving me a double take as if questioning why I still stood there.

"Bottom drawer," he said again around a mouthful of peanut butter.

"What bottom drawer," I asked. "I don't know what you're talking about."

"My bedroom."

I shook my head and grabbed a nearby blanket to throw over his legs, and then wandered into his bedroom.

"What, is there food in here, too?" I said, cringing as I entered. The bed was unmade and the sheets looked like they hadn't been washed since I washed them. Two months ago. Two unfinished glasses of something kind of brownish sat on his nightstand with cracker wrappers scattered around them. Dirty clothes were wadded up in a pile on the floor, and there was a definite stench going on.

"Has Bev been cleaning in here?" I called out, wrinkling my nose.

"No," he replied.

"I'll talk to her," I said. "She's paid to handle light cleaning and laundry and it stinks in here."

"I don't let her in there," he said.

"What?" I said with a sigh as I opened his top drawer. "Dad, you have to let her do her thing." Top drawer was a mash-up of everything from questionable socks to fingernail clippers. I closed it. "Or hey, maybe wash a load of clothes," I said under my breath.

Next two drawers were T-shirts and shorts and jeans. Bottom drawer was—

"Holy fuck."

"Watch your language," he said casually from the other room.

I backed up to the bed and sank onto it.

"Fuck, fuck, fuck," I whispered.

All I could do was breathe. And stare. And listen to my heart shoving blood through my head at warp speed. A million questions asked and answered themselves in my head as I sat there in shock. I got back up and walked slowly into the living room, stopping to stand between him and the TV.

"Can you move?" he said, not looking up.

"Can you tell me why there's—" I took a slow breath and let it out. "Dad, how much money is in that drawer?"

He looked up like I'd asked him about the weather.

"A hundred thousand dollars."

* * *

I had to walk away. Well, as far as the kitchen, anyway. I made myself a peanut butter and jelly sandwich and stood in there eating it at the counter in shock.

What did he do? Why did he have that kind of money, did he win it? Would he even remember the answer to that? And why was it in a grocery bag in a dresser drawer in his bedroom instead of at a *bank*?

Why didn't he just pay Lange before the Blue Banana entered the equation?

He was asleep when I finally pulled myself together enough to go back, so I sat down and flipped through channels unseeing.

"Your granddaughter bought condoms with her boyfriend yesterday," I said softly. He snored louder. "Yeah. My thoughts exactly."

A few minutes later, he woke with a start, gripping the arms of the chair like he was on a carnival ride.

"Dad?"

He jerked to the right, staring at me with wild eyes. "When did you get here?"

"I've been here for a little bit," I said. "You fell asleep, so I thought I'd watch some—"

"Did you take the money?" he asked.

My mouth was still open, but words failed me. I couldn't tell if he was angry, paranoid, still in a dream state, or honestly asking me a question. It crossed my mind that he might not remember telling me, and I could pretend not to know, but that hurt my brain just to conjure that up. I was juggling too much already.

"No," I said. "It's still there."

"Well it's yours," he said. "You need to take it. I don't want it here."

I blinked. "Mi—Mine? What are you—"

The knock on the door made me jump. "Good God."

"That's Bev," he said.

"I know," I said, both palms against my temples. I felt like if I let go, everything might fall out. But he was halfway lucid, and I had to grab the moment. "Dad, where did that money come from?"

"From the trees," he said.

Well, so much for lucid. I sighed.

"Trees."

"Bailey's trees," he said irritably, like when I was little and bothering him.

"Bailey," I said, shaking my head as I walked toward the door. Mr. Bailey was an eccentric older man that basically owned most of Charmed and lived like a recluse in a house tucked away in the woods across the pond. My dad and Lanie's aunt had grown up with him or something, and they'd kept some semblance of a friendship as adults. I think. My dad only still spoke of him in dreams. "Of course. Big house Bailey?"

"Don't let her in yet!" he hissed, and I stopped cold. "Get some plastic grocery bags to double it up—triple it up—so it doesn't show. I'll stall her."

I gaped at him. "Dad—"

"Do it!" he demanded. "Put it in your car."

"My—" I had to laugh. This was insane, like we were pulling off some kind of heist. Except that the money was mine and it came from trees and landed in his dresser drawer. "I'm not putting it in my car."

He grabbed me by the shoulders. "Allie," he said. "Get it out of here, away from me. Now."

In that one split second of looking up into his eyes, my dad was in there. Goose bumps covered my body.

"Okay," I whispered.

Another knock at the door made us both jump, and I sucked in a breath as I went to the kitchen and pulled four plastic grocery bags from the drawer I knew he stockpiled them. On a whim, I tore a large black garbage bag off the roll under the sink.

"Mr. Greene?" Bev's voice sounded from the other side of the door. "Are you okay? It's Bev, can I come in?"

"Just a second," he called back, shooing me into the bedroom and shutting the door behind me.

"Jesus," I muttered, the insanity of the situation mixed with the rank odor of dirty clothes and sweat and funk overwhelming my senses.

I dropped to my knees and opened the drawer again, half expecting it to be gone like something I made up in my head. Nope. Still there. I reached out and picked up a bundle of hundreds wrapped in rubber bands. Some were like that. Some were twenties tied together with twine. Whatever the version, it was more cash than I'd ever seen in my lifetime and was likely to see again.

Take it away from me. Now.

My eyes filled with tears. Something buried deep under the dementia, something *him*, was still in there. And just tried to do the right thing. I think.

"What the hell am I doing?" I said under my breath as I heard Bev talking in the next room. I stuffed the tattered plastic bag into another, and then that into another, tying it all off at the top and setting it on the bed.

"Does it look like a bag of money?" I muttered.

Glancing around, I grabbed the garbage bag and fluffed it open, threw all his dirty clothes in it, and topped it with the bag of money. Tied that off. That worked. I opened the door and smiled at Bev as my dad turned around in surprise.

"What were you doing in there?" he asked.

I sighed.

"Cleaning up your mess," I said. I held up the bag. "I'm bringing his clothes home to wash. It's disgusting in there."

"I'd be happy to wash them," Bev said, reaching for the bag and retracting her hand when I yanked the bag behind me. "He—didn't want me to go in there."

"I know, he told me," I said, trying harder not to look like I was committing a crime. "But I'm overruling him." I chuckled. "I'm going to put this in my Jeep, and then I'll come strip the bed. If you'll take care of that from there, I call it good."

"Will do."

Fifteen minutes and half a melt-down later, the bag sitting like a slumped passenger on my right, I pulled into my driveway. Next to Bash's truck.

"Fuck," I sniffed. He was early, and sitting in the porch swing by the front door. Clearly the day wasn't done with me yet. "Shit, damn, hell, and every other word." I swiped under my eyes and took a deep breath. It was getting dusky dark. He wouldn't notice.

I grabbed my loot. God help me. And then—God help me.

Damn if he didn't look sexy sitting on that swing, one leg cocked lazily over the other at the ankles and his left arm riding over the top of the swing. Like he was waiting for me and had all the time in the world. Except that he wasn't waiting for me. He was there for Angel.

"Hey," I said.

"Hey."

"How long have you been here?"

He stood up slowly and I quietly mourned the loss of that visual.

"Not long," he said. "Maybe fifteen."

"Sorry, I got held up at my dad's," I said. I could feel the money like heat burning up through the top of the bags. I had to find a place for it. Where did one hide a hundred grand?

Bash gestured toward the bag. "Looks like you have his body in there."

"Almost," I joked, feeling the sweat break out along my spine. "All his dirty clothes he's been hoarding."

I wasn't good at this. I never had to be. Anything juicy going on in my life, I told Bash. Not telling him was like going against nature, but telling him about this money meant telling him about Lange. And Lange was now his partner of a sort. A partner he needed.

"Need help?" Bash asked.

"Nah, I got it," I said, walking past him to unlock my door.

Was it my imagination that I could feel him behind me?

"Angel didn't say anything about being late," I said, *that* subject now joining the party in my head and making my blood go a little warmer. *If she was with that boy...* I clenched my teeth together. "Did she text you?"

"No," Bash said, following me in. "Maybe she's at a friend's house or something."

"Or something," I said under my breath. "Let me go put this in the laundry room, I'll be right back."

I was shaking by the time I got the bag open. I didn't know from what. Anger, anxiety, nervousness over Bash—all of the above. My life felt like a giant melting pot of really pissed-off worms, all going in different directions. I pulled out the grocery bag of money and stood there holding it.

Take it away from me.

Okay. Done. Now what the fuck was I supposed to do with it? I yanked my phone from my pocket and typed out a text to Angel.

Bash is here. Why aren't you? Get home.

"Hey Allie?"

Bash's voice was coming down the hall, and the panic hit me like a freight train.

"Shit," I muttered, hitting send. Probably the same kind of panic criminals felt when they robbed banks or held up stagecoaches or broke into jewelry stores and museums. Because yeah—I was on that same level, holding a grocery bag of rubber-banded cash that my father may or may not have stolen.

Nevertheless, I did what any like-minded criminal's helper would do. I tossed the bag in the dryer with the towels I'd already fluffed twice and shut the dryer door.

"Yes?" I said, bursting through the door and nearly slamming into him. Finding my face just under his. "Sorry," I breathed, backing up.

His step forward seemed unintentional, like his body just reacting to mine. In a dimly lit hallway with nothing behind me but wall. His expression mirrored that, like he was fighting himself.

"I—was going to ask you if you wanted to just start working on the essay," Bash said. Too close. His gaze falling to my mouth.

All the magnets in the universe traveled through space in that four-second span, to land in the inches between us and pull me toward him.

"Um—essay," I managed. I could feel the warmth from his body radiating off him, and everything in me itched to feel more. To slide my hands under his shirt and feel just how hot his skin really was.

"Want to?" he whispered.

"Yes."

I wasn't talking about any essay anymore, and I didn't know if he was, but the moment I caved to the pull he backed off, leaving a cold vacuum where his body had been.

My head spun like I had a hangover, and as I watched him stroll back up the hallway with both hands raking his hair back, I suspected he'd gotten just as drunk.

Shit.

Weren't we a pair.

I, at least, had nightly dreams churning me up as an excuse. What was his?

"Okay," I said, grabbing a spiral notebook from the kitchen counter and fanning myself with it before turning my grocery list over to a new page. I glanced at him for a reaction check, and he was studying that spiral as if it was the most fascinating thing ever. "So. What are we doing?" His eyes flew up to mine. "The essay," I clarified super quickly. "What are we supposed to write about?"

He pulled out a chair at my table for me and I sat down while he went around to the opposite side. Good plan. He rubbed at his eyes with his thumb and forefinger and then sat down with trouble in his eyes.

"I think we're supposed to talk about what we'd do for Charmed," he said. "How we'd join together to do great things."

My mouth went dry at the thought of joining together to do great things. They would indeed be great things, if my dreams were any indication, but we couldn't write about that. We couldn't even look at each other about that. The memory of his eyes going so dark as he looked at me in that dress shot my heart rate sky-high.

Essay.

"Hang on," I said, my voice going gravelly. I cleared my throat as I pushed my chair back. "I need to text Carmen. Want some water or something?"

"I'm fine," he said. "Look, if you're too busy to do this, I don't need to just sit here."

He got up, and I turned to fix him with a look.

"What's your problem?"

"I don't have a problem," he said, pulling his keys from his pocket. "Tell Angel we can do this another night, when she can see fit to be here and not waste my time."

"Hey!"

"What?"

His jaw muscles were working furiously, and it was clear he wanted to be anywhere but there. What happened to the previous ten seconds?

"Why are you being a dick?" I asked.

He laughed. It was an angry laugh, but at least his eyes lit up a little. I missed that spunky side.

"*I'm* being a dick?" he asked. "What about you?"

"Me?"

He held his arms out and tossed his keys on the table as if to say *finally!*

"Yes, you," he said. "Where the hell are you?"

"Where—what?" I asked shaking my head in confusion. "I'm right here."

"You know what I'm talking about," he said. "Where's my best friend? Where's the woman I can talk to about anything? That I never have to be someone else around or watch what I say? What the hell is going on lately?"

My eyes went hot with embarrassed tears. Was I wrong? Had I misinterpreted that he'd been fighting the same attraction? I held up my chin in defiance, unwilling to be weepy.

"You know what? I could ask you the same questions," I said. "You've been like Jekyll and Hyde, hot and cold, laughing with me and then the silent treatment." I took a breath and gripped the back of the chair in front of me for grounding. "I have so much shit going on right now, and I can't talk to you—"

"Why not?" he demanded.

"Because it's different now," I blurted.

His eyes narrowed. "What's different now?"

"Everything, apparently," I said, flailing my hands. *Don't lose your shit. Keep this on the rails.* "Ever since—that."

"Since what?" he asked, but the look that passed over his face told me he knew exactly what "that" was.

I shook my head. "Don't be a girl. You know damn good and well what I'm talking about."

He put a *don't be ridiculous* expression on. "Because you kissed me? Come on. That was nothing."

I blinked through the smile I felt was tacked on. *Nothing.* Nice. Okay. I turned and walked to the kitchen cabinet and pulled out a glass, needing something to do.

"Well that *nothing* has made you weird," I said. "And probably made me weird, too, in response. Because we kissed *each other*, and maybe both of us know that's—not—what we do."

That made sense, right?

Turning around and finding him a foot from me made sense too, as my heart tried to slam its way out of my chest.

"You kissed *me*," he said.

I tilted my head. "Yes," I conceded. "But I wasn't there by myself, mugging with a dishtowel. You kissed me back."

Amusement danced with something else in his eyes. Something resistant. Something all too familiar lately that made his jaw twitch.

"If I kissed you, you'd know it."

"Oh my God," I muttered with an eye roll. "Save the macho for someone else."

He blew out a breath in frustration as he turned to walk away and then just made a circle back to me. "I'm not being macho," he said. "I haven't kissed you. Not like—"

"Whatever," I said, shaking my head and really just wanting him to leave. I didn't want to hear any more about how it was all me. "You know what? Never mind. I should have never brought it up. This is why everything is so different now. If you can't even own up to it—"

"Shut up."

"What—"

Hands held my head, hips pinned me against the sink, and his mouth landed on mine.

CHAPTER TEN

I felt every nerve ending in my body erupt in a million different directions as his lips hit mine with a hunger I never saw coming. Or I did. Every night.

It was soft, hard, tasting, searching. Oh God, it was Bash and I couldn't get enough. Fingers wound in my hair as his body pressed harder. I felt my fingers claw at his shirt, my mouth move on his lips—it was a full-on sensation party as every touch was heightened. And when he tilted his head to take more and go deeper, everything in my being melted against him.

It was so good and—so bad. So many reasons not to be doing this, and yet it was like the floodgates to my dreams had been opened and I'd been kissing this man for months. Except—okay, the little voices yelling in the back of my head saying *Wait! Wait!* were annoying, but I didn't care. I couldn't care. He tasted too good to care. My hands moved up his chest to his neck, to his head, to pull him in impossibly deeper, to kiss him harder, and the growl of desire that rumbled through him—

The sound of the front door opening was like a firecracker going off.

"Mom, I'm home."

A bomb exploding between us couldn't have had more force. We both sucked in air as he pushed away, hands in the air like he was being arrested, turning in circles.

"Fuck," he said under his breath, grabbing a dishtowel and hurling it across the room. "What the hell am I—"

"Hello?" Angel said as the towel landed at her feet. She looked down at it and then back up at both of us with a befuddled look. "Is there a problem?"

Bash was as far from me as he could possibly get in that room. Just about climbing out the back door window. I hadn't moved. I was still just as pinned to that countertop as if his body was holding me there, with my hands covering half my face.

What—what had we just done? What had I just done? How could we ever find normal again after—I mean, we'd done it once before and survived it, but we were really young and really drunk. Allowances were made.

"Where've you been?" Bash asked.

Angel. Focus on Angel.

"And with who?" I added, dropping my hands to cross my arms over my chest. Partially to look intimidating and partially to hold my racing heart inside.

I prayed that my lips didn't look as used as they felt. I could still feel him there.

"Jesus," she said. "Interrogation much?"

"Buying condoms much?" I retorted.

"What?" Bash quipped, pushing off his corner of the room like he was rocket propelled.

"Mom!" Angel yelled, looking at Bash, mortified.

I might have felt bad for her. If I weren't so angry and keyed up and wanting someone's blood today, I just might have. But I didn't. I felt a little bad that Bash heard it that way, but that's what I'd been trying to tell him before we fell into each other's mouths and got lost. Our communication line was off kilter. We were friends and then we were avoiding each other and then not talking at all and then… my skin went flushed as I relived that last *and then* on speed mode.

"If Uncle Bash knowing embarrasses you," I began. "Then think about that every time you decide to do something stupid."

"I didn't buy any—"

"Waiting outside the door while your boyfriend buys them counts, Angel," I said.

Her face went from self-righteous to *oh shit* to some other words I didn't need her to verbalize to know they were there.

"I'm going to my room," she said, her lips going white as she pressed them together. "I don't need to stand here and listen to this."

"The hell you don't," Bash said. "You're fifteen—"

"And you aren't my dad!" she yelled up into his face.

All the air left the room. All the sound. All the reason. Angel knew those words were eleven kinds of wrong the second she uttered them, I saw it on her face.

It was Bash's face that I would never forget. The hurt, the betrayal, the jerk backwards like she'd slapped him across the face. I saw a million walls go up in his eyes, and it broke me into as many pieces. No, she wasn't his, but he'd always treated her as if she was. She was the closest thing he had.

And Angel had just shattered that.

Over condoms.

He gave her a long look and then walked past her, plucked his keys off the table, and was out the door. I opened my mouth to call after him but nothing came out. Forcing my feet forward, I moved numbly.

Angel whirled around with tears in her eyes, as if she was unsure whether to be contrite or pissed off. I was pretty clear on the choice.

"Get—out—of my sight," I seethed. "Leave your phone on the table."

Big tears tracked down her face, but I didn't care.

"Mom."

"Now."

I made it out of my door as Bash slammed his shut.

"Bash!"

The engine roared to life, and I jogged to the open window. The one he wasn't using to look back at me.

"Bash, wait," I pleaded. "She didn't mean that."

"Did you?" he asked, meeting my eyes for the first time.

"What?"

"I know I'm not her dad," he said, pulling the seat belt over his body. "And *she's* supposed to say shit like that. She's a teenager. But you not telling me she's buying *condoms* with that little prick?" he said, his lip curling. "That *message* was much louder."

Shit.

"There's no *message*, Bash," I said. "It's exactly what I told you."

"That you can't tell me things anymore because we kissed?" he asked, putting his truck in gear. "That's bullshit, and that's your choice. That I've been a dick?" He held up both hands before he rested them on the steering wheel. "Then this is me being a dick."

The truck surged forward and I backed away, crossing my arms over my body and trying not to still taste him.

* * *

I was a zombie the next morning. One incredibly decadent, erotic-filled Bash dream, full of deep kisses that didn't end with my mouth and the aroma of him all up in my senses, making it all so much more real, finished me off and left me wide awake and panting. There was no sleep for the rest of the night. Instead, my brain was filled with bags of money, endless aisles of condoms, and images of Bash wrapped around me, his eyes boring into me. The taste of him, the feel of him, the what-the-fuck-happens-now of him.

As I stationed myself at the coffeepot—because it was the duty requiring the least amount of thought process—I stared unseeing at Carmen's wallet on the counter.

"So, you want me to ask Sully to set up a meeting with Mr. Bailey?" she asked, cocking an eyebrow.

"Can you?" I asked, keeping my voice low even though the counter wasn't full. For once, I was thrilled that it was a slow morning.

"He's gonna want to know why," Carmen whispered back.

I bit my lower lip. "I can't say right now," I said under my breath. "I just need to talk to him. About my dad. Tell him that."

Jesus, it was like trying to arrange a meeting with a mob boss.

Carmen gave a tiny shrug. "Okay."

"And then you'll have to take me there," I said.

Her eyes grew wide. "Hold up."

"I don't remember how to find it."

"I've been there once," she said. "In the dark. By boat. After having sex with Sully at the dock. I wasn't exactly firing on all cylinders."

"Well, the last time I was there, I was like eleven," I said. "Pretty sure you have a better shot."

"Allie—" Carmen began.

"It's important," I said.

There was a look in her eyes. Something saying that her reason was important, too. That she'd find fifty different reasons not to go back there if she had to. But I had a hundred grand sitting in a bag in my dryer that needed to trump that.

"Fine," she said under her breath, pulling out her cell phone. "I'll text Sully."

"Thank you," I said, my eye catching on blondness walking through the door. Said blondness caught on to me as well.

"Hi!" said Vonda Sharp, drawing out the word from the door to the counter. "I've been wanting to meet you!"

Oh? "Am I famous?" I asked.

"You may as well be," Vonda said, flashing sparkly teeth while the Sharp spawn hung back. "You and this diner are just indispensable," she said. She held out a hand with no rings or bracelets or adornments of any kind. "Vonda Sharp."

"Allie Greene," I said.

"Yes I know," she said. "You're one of my Queen candidates. Tickled to death to meet you."

She had a way. A way of making you feel good without really knowing why you felt that way. It put me on edge. Indispensable and all.

"I'm trying to get to all my candidates and talk in person," she said. "You do know there's an initial meet-up tonight, right?"

I had a schedule under a magnet on my fridge, but I hadn't paid attention. I certainly didn't know it was starting already.

"Of course!" I lied.

"And the first practice is day after tomorrow."

"Awesome." I plastered on a smile.

"I just know this will be a smashing success," she said. "Oh—" She turned sideways. "Have you met my son?"

He went from tragically bored to beaming in less than a second. Those Sharp genes were something else. I had to hand it to my daughter—she had good taste. This boy was beautiful.

"I'm Aaron Sharp," he said, holding out his hand.

"I know," I said, taking his with as much strength as I could muster. "I'm Angel's mom. You know, the girl you might be having sex with? You do know she's only fifteen, right?"

Aaron's smile faltered as he pulled his hand away, and the subsequent glow between them lessened.

"I'm sorry?" Vonda said. Her smile stayed on, but her eyes went somewhere else.

"Oh my God," Carmen snickered, turning to check out the room, probably for saviors.

"Oh, my daughter and your son have been hanging out *talking and stuff*," I said. "Have you met Angel?" Vonda didn't shake her head, or move, or even blink. "No? Well, she's fifteen, and they bought condoms together day before yesterday."

I didn't know this woman. I didn't know her habits, proclivities, or triggers, but she was a mother of a teenager. The facial body language of *what the fuck did my kid do* was universal even in its subtlest forms, and I wasn't seeing it on her at all.

Vonda turned to look at her son politely, questioning without words.

"Just in case," he said.

She nodded and faced me again. "They are thinking about safety. I find that responsible."

"You find that—what?" I asked, my voice cracking at the end. "No. It's not."

Vonda laid a cool hand on my arm, which was probably hot enough to burn her.

"I try to let Aaron make his own way, his own decisions about his life," she said. "I feel he is more mature for it."

"I'll bet he is," I said. "A little too mature for Angel. She's *fifteen*, in case you missed that. Inexperienced." I frowned at him. "And in school. How old are you?"

"Oh, I'm in a work program," Aaron said. "I go to school in the morning and work in the afternoons."

"He works as my intern," Vonda said proudly.

Proudly. I'd just informed her that her son was planning sex with a minor much more minor than he, and she was proud he was practicing safe sex in his off hours and following her around all day calling it a work program.

"Oh! Excuse me!" Vonda said, tapping my arm again as she did a double take on someone across the room. "I have to go say hello to Katrina Bowman real quick. See you tonight!"

"Nice to meet you, Allie," Aaron said, winking with a head toss as he followed his mother.

Breathe.

"Did he just call me *Allie*?" I said.

"And winked," Carmen said. "Did she just praise them for being responsible?"

I looked down at my hands. "I'm shaking. I don't shake."

"You did not tell me that Angel bought condoms," she said.

"Aaron bought condoms," I corrected. "Angel waited for him outside because she thought no one would pick up on that."

"She told you?"

"Oh hell no," I said. "Mr. Mercer called me with that fun little news."

"Oh God," Carmen breathed. "What did you do?"

I inhaled deeply and let it back out. What did I do? I made out with Bash.

"I called her on it," I said. "She got nasty and mouthy, Bash told her off, she told him he wasn't her father, and he left and I haven't heard from him."

Carmen stared openmouthed. "Holy hell."

"Something like that," I said.

"I can't believe she said that," she said.

"I can't believe she did *any* of that," I countered. "And now she has to come here after school and glare at me because I can't trust her to go home." I rubbed my eyes. "Want a teenager? She's highly discounted right now."

A familiar truck caught my attention outside the window, and I did a double take on the image of Bash leaning against it, talking to Lange.

Talking to Lange. What was Lange going to do to screw *him* over? I could go get that money out of my dryer right now and hand it to him with interest and tell him to get the hell out of Charmed. To leave me and everyone I know alone.

I could, but I needed to be sure where it came from. If it was legit.

I held my breath as Lange pushed the door open, waiting for Bash to follow him, but he didn't. He got in his truck and drove away, leaving my stomach in a state of flailing disappointment.

"So, what was Bash there for?" Carmen asked, as if she'd read my thoughts.

Whoosh. Heat rushed to my face as the topic landed on top of my heart. Or my libido.

"He—they—he's teaching her to drive," I said, picking up a menu and fanning myself with it. "And we had an essay thing to work on for the stupid contest."

"Uh-huh," Carmen said, leaning on her forearms. "Neither of those things will turn you as red as you just went."

"I—don't—" I dropped the menu and grabbed a clean wash cloth to wipe down the counter.

"Allie Greene."

I widened my eyes. "Carmen Frost."

She gave me a knowing grin, and I was hit once again with what having girlfriends in school must have been like. Hell, having girlfriends *now* was still a little foreign.

"What's going on?" she asked.

"Nothing," I said.

"Which really means?"

I closed my eyes, realizing I did need to say it out loud before my head exploded.

"We kind of kissed. Again."

She lunged forward and my eyes popped open.

"Kind of?" she whispered loudly, looking giddy.

"God, this is why I don't talk," I said, pulling a stool from under the bar and sinking onto it. Normally a no-no but I needed it.

"How do you *kind of* kiss?" she asked, chuckling. "Are we talking sweet, unexpected, or hard core? And who initiated it?"

My fingers went to my lips automatically at the memory of it. "Definitely unexpected. Him. And if Angel hadn't come home, I—don't know."

"The not-my-dad thing happened after *that*?" Carmen asked.

"Afraid so."

"Shit," she said. "Are you okay?"

I sighed. "Yeah."

"So what are we going to see Bailey about?" she asked, making me blink to find the my-dad-the-money-hoarder subject.

"I can't tell you yet," I said.

She laughed. "Hell, it was worth a shot my friend. You were on a roll."

CHAPTER ELEVEN

"Okay, everyone!" Vonda sang into the room later that evening, smiling at us all like we were her blessed offspring. Kia, the ex-carnie and Bash's ex-squeeze, was sitting up on a stool to her left, looking annoyed with her. "I hope you're enjoying the complimentary chips and salsa—and margaritas," she added with a wink and a giggle. "But it's time to get down to the nuts and bolts."

"She says complimentary like she did something special," Miss Mavis whispered, leaning over. "It's a Mexican restaurant. They always give you chips and salsa."

Miss Mavis being one of the contestants was hilarious. She didn't actually have a business, per se. She rode a giant tricycle all through Charmed and sold snack food from it. Sometimes. Mostly, she was just nosy.

What was even funnier, was her pairing with Mr. Townsend from the barbershop, since he tended to run the other way every time she came around.

"True," I said. "And I doubt she's comping the drinks," I said.

We were in the party room at Rojo's, the only Mexican food choice in Charmed. All the candidates for the contest were there. Except for Bash.

"Are we missing a king, Allie?" Vonda asked, winking at me. Again.

Okay, between her and her horny little boy, they had some serious eye twitching issues, and I had about had it. I came to the ridiculous meeting out of obligation, after leaving Angel at home under threat of never driving any car ever again if she let anything breathing into the house, while I still had a bag of money sitting inside my dryer. Not that I feared its discovery. Angel would die naked before stepping a foot in there to do laundry.

I had things to do. Things other than worrying about contests or who would do more for the town, or what we had to wear, or where my damn king was and why he wasn't there suffering through this crap with me.

"I don't know where Bash is," I said. "He must have gotten tied up."

Don't. Go. There.

"Uh oh," Alan said on the other side of the room. "Trouble in paradise?"

I sneered at him. "There's no trouble. There's no paradise. We aren't a couple."

"We aren't a couple either," Mrs. Boudreaux said, thumbing toward Mr. Masoneaux next to her. "But we do hook up now and then."

My jaw dropped an inch. My fingers inched toward my phone, instinct wanting to text Bash that those two were "hooking up" with a scared face emoji. But I couldn't.

"We don't—hook up, either," I said. "I'm just saying he must have gotten busy at the apiary."

"He texted that he would be a few minutes late," Kia said. "But he'll be here."

He texted Kia.

I might need one of those margaritas.

"Well, we'll catch your king up later," Vonda said.

I averted my eyes before she could wink again.

"He's—not my king," I said.

"I'd let him be mine," Katrina Bowman said, laughing. She nudged her husband. "You could join us."

I'll bet.

"So," Vonda said, clapping her hands together to get the class back in order. "First I want to introduce Kia Jadonovitz."

Jadonovitz? That was the first time I'd ever heard a last name. I'd started to think she was like Cher or Madonna.

"If you haven't met her yet, Kia was with the Lucky Hart carnival, and stayed behind to work on the Lucky Charm," Vonda said. "She's going to be heading up the contest activities and other promotional duties." She pointed at Kia. "Including getting with the local florist for décor and flower arrangements?"

Kia nodded and looked as thrilled as if Vonda had put her on cow-milking duty. I didn't blame her. From what I'd heard, I was pretty sure she and I had similar social skills. As in none.

"Graham's Florist, yes," she said. "Already met with them."

"Hey, Kia," Alan Bowman said flirtatiously. While sitting next to his wife.

Kia never even blinked. "So, first on the agenda is your essays," she said.

"Crap," I muttered.

"Everyone bring theirs?" she asked, panning the room.

"Bring?" I said under my breath. I glanced at Miss Mavis, who pulled a folded piece of paper from her bra.

"Haven't typed it up yet, but I scribbled it out in the line at Brewsters," she whispered.

I sighed. "Awesome."

"As you know," Vonda said, standing back up. "The townspeople will be voting. It will lie on whoever is attendance that night to cast a vote, so start working it in town. You have the rest of this week. Talk it up, get people out there. Get them wanting to come out and hear you read your essay—"

"What?" I asked.

"Did you have a question?" Vonda asked, raising her hand while Kia stepped back and just watched her take over again.

"No," I said, loading up a chip with salsa. "I have a reaction. No one said we had to read anything to the crowd."

"It's in the bylaws I e-mailed to you," Vonda said, tilting her head. The people sitting closest to her beamed up at her. "And your partner can do the reading if you aren't comfortable."

"Well, I missed that e-mail," I said. "And I'm pretty sure Bash did too—"

"What did I miss?" said a voice behind me as he pulled out a chair.

The chip all but fell out of my mouth as he sat down just inches away, those blue eyes landing on me for half a second. The smell, the warmth, the Bashness of him washed over me, whisking me back to being pinned against my kitchen counter and wrapped up in everything Bash while he kissed me like the world was coming to an end, and I reached for my keys in a desperate attempt at grounding. Good god, I was pathetic.

"Yay, Allie's king is here!" Vonda said, giggling. "So glad you could be here, Bash."

"He's not my king," I repeated softly, crossing my arms over my chest.

Kia smiled at him from across the room. To be fair, it wasn't a lover-ish smile. More like a buddy, like they had secrets and inside jokes. Like he and *I* used to have. Fuck balls, Kia was the new *me*.

"I was telling how the voting will work," Vonda said. "About reading the essays and working the crowd this week."

"Not a problem," Bash said.

"We didn't write ours," I said behind my hand.

His blue eyes rested on mine, stealing my breath. "I did."

"Oh."

Bash's gaze fell to my lips, making me lick them involuntarily, which made his pupils dilate as I looked at them.

Turn around.

I forced myself to turn back to where Vonda was droning on about the upcoming activity this week, all the while being hyper aware of the freakishly hot man at my back and imagining what his lips would feel like trailing down the back of my neck. How hot it would be if his hands slid up around me and palmed my breasts. How much we could get away with while Vonda went on and on, and would anyone notice if one of his hands got busy under my jeans?

"I don't think we should read them here," Bash said from behind me, making me jump so violently several people turned around.

I clapped a hand over my mouth just in case I might have yelped, and to cover some of the glowing that happens when all the blood that previously left your head for your privates, comes rushing back like a tsunami.

"You okay?" he asked.

"I'm good," I said, patting my face.

We needed to talk. To clear the air. To make things somewhat normal again. I was pretty sure we'd never have the original normal back, but we needed something in between that and dancing around each other's lips or avoiding each other completely.

"You were saying?" Vonda asked sweetly.

"If we read them here," Bash began. "It gives everyone else the chance to go change theirs."

"Are you saying we're all cheaters?" Katrina Bowman cooed at him, leaning on her section of table so that another inch or so of boob was revealed.

"I'm saying that we're all human," he said. "What's to stop me from listening to yours and thinking 'hmm, I need to use that line. I'm gonna make it even better.' And then Mrs. Boudreaux hears mine and says 'I didn't think about that point, I'll add it.' And before you know it, we all have the same speech."

"I agree," Kia said.

"Valid perspective," Vonda said, nodding. "Okay, we can go with that if you're all good with it. Essays will be a surprise element."

The next fifteen minutes were a boring combination of rules and Vonda's attempts at giving the stage to Kia and then yanking it back again. Then we were sprung. I took a deep breath as I scraped my chair back, hoping to have a real conversation, but when I turned he was already rising from his chair and in motion. Away from me.

Well, okay then.

Katrina Bowman stopped him at the end of the table, smiling, laughing; curling her red hair on a finger. To my knowledge, she hadn't seduced him into her nasty little web of extramarital boy toys, and it probably drove her crazy. Then again, he was smiling down at her and chuckling at whatever she was saying under her breath, as she touched his arm intimately. Maybe she had. She couldn't get Nick or Sully in the past because they were in love with Lanie and Carmen, but Bash was unattached. He normally had rules about married women, but maybe he'd made an exception. Maybe redheaded skank had been on the menu one night after he and Kia had split.

Kia, who had walked up and had a hand on his back that remained after he hugged her.

"Fuck me," I muttered, getting up and grabbing my keys.

"What was that?" Vonda asked, approaching me, a big perfect smile on her face.

That was ridiculous, stupid, infantile, beneath-me jealousy, that's what that was.

"Nothing," I said, pulling my mouth into a semblance of a smile. "Have a chat with Aaron, yet?"

She tilted her head questioningly. "About?"

Count to three.

"About what we talked about this morning," I said. "What he and my daughter purchased."

She gave me a placating look. "I get the feeling that you have an issue with that," she said. "Do you have problems with sex?"

"Prob—" I began. "What?"

"Hang-ups," she said. "Some people have these preconceived archaic notions about how sex should be approached, especially with young people. Like it's not to be enjoyed, but some big bad thing to be avoided until adulthood."

"*Motherhood* should be avoided until adulthood," I said.

"Hence the condoms," she whispered on a chuckle, touching my arm like all was going to be okay. Nothing was going to be okay. My life was twelve kinds of jacked up. I backed away from her touch and she clasped her hands, and my normal sense of snark mixed with partially impending doom came back.

"Intimacy before you're ready for it," I said.

"How about being used and dumped by a player before you even know what a player is," Bash said, suddenly at my side. "Because horny teenage boys have no idea what *intimacy* is."

Vonda raised her eyebrows just a fraction but her smile remained. "Are you calling my son a player?"

"I'm calling my daughter a fifteen-year-old," I said. "She's not ready to lose something precious to someone who'll be moving on to *enjoy* the next girl."

Vonda crossed her arms, the first sign I'd seen of her getting remotely uncomfortable with anything.

"Perhaps Aaron does need to move on," she said. "Rather than get caught up in your family's negativity. I'm surprised that you're so conservative on this stance, however," she added. "Considering."

"My family isn't negative," I said. "And what are you surprised about?"

"Well, with having a baby as a baby, yourself," she said. "And Bash essentially playing daddy while not playing hubby—it's a little nontraditional, you have to admit."

My blood flared to my skin's surface again, this time not in a good way, and the hand that came to rest on the back of my neck felt cool and calming. Except for that thing that made me want to curl into him. That wasn't cool. Or calming.

"It's a little not your business," I said. "I'll tell you that."

"Miss Sharp," Bash said, his thumb working on the side of my neck. "I don't play at anything. I'm whatever Angel needs as well as what Allie needs. They are the closest thing I have to family, and I don't need you to define that."

Vonda shrugged. "Fair enough."

"Angel may think she's ready for something adult," he said. "She may look at your son and go stupid, and I get that. But that's what the real adults in her life are for. For guidance."

"There's guidance, Bash," she said. "And there's dictatorial control."

"Dictatorial control," I said, raising my hand. "Otherwise known as parenting. It's not a democracy in my house. I have boundaries. I have rules."

"Which teaches her that she has limitations," Vonda said.

"It teaches her accountability," Bash said. "And we're done with this conversation." He pulled me against him, I guessed in a show of solidarity, and God help me, I was good with that. "Please just let your unlimited son know in one of your casual non-dictatorial chats that he needs to skip to the *moving on* part."

Vonda moved around us, reaffixing her smile as she approached some of the others. I watched their faces soften in contentment as she shook their hands, but my focus quickly turned to the slow trail Bash's hand took down my back.

And the slower way he stepped away from me.

"Thank you for standing with me on that," I said, turning to look up at him as he took another step back.

"Where else would I be?" he asked, meeting my eyes but then quickly looking away.

"Bash," I said softly. "We need to—

He shook his head, his expression troubled. "See you tomorrow."

"Bash."

My phone dinged with a text as he turned and walked away, nodding and smiling to people on his way out.

"Damn it," I muttered, pulling my phone from my pocket.

It was from Carmen.

Sully has to see Bailey tomorrow at noon, so we can ride along. See you tomorrow.

I sighed. Tomorrow was going to be a bitch of a day.

CHAPTER TWELVE

It was weird, riding through the old roads in the woods. You think you remember things a certain way as a kid. Smells, the way things look, the feel of a curve in the road. But it's all on a smaller scale. Time shrinks. Time fades. The last time I was out there, I was a kid with my dad. I had no need to pay attention to landmarks or directions. Now, as we twisted and turned and bounced along in Sully's pickup truck, I was hopelessly lost.

"I have some business with Bailey," Sully was saying, one hand lazily draped over the steering wheel. Carmen sat between us, one hand on Sully's leg. "But he doesn't draw things out. We'll be done in five minutes."

"Does he know I'm coming?" I asked.

"He does," Sully said. "But I didn't know what reason to tell him. Anybody want to share the big secret?"

"No secret," I said. "Just need to talk to him about my dad. They were friends—I think," I said, realizing just how little I knew about that situation. "When they were young. My dad used to talk about Albert Bailey and Ruby Barrett and hanging out in these woods."

"Yeah, I heard about that, too," Carmen said, an odd look on her face. "Have you ever met him?"

"He used to wave at me from the door sometimes," I said. "My dad would come by to—I don't know—drop something off, pick something up, I never really paid attention. I'd wait in the car."

"Well, I'd be sure to not get too close if I were you," Carmen said, glancing sideways at Sully.

"Yeah, avoid shaking his hand," Sully said.

"Avoid shaking his hand?" Carmen asked. "That's the same thing you told me, instead of *hey babe, do not touch the man under any circumstances.*"

He gave her a smirk. "Come on."

"Come on, my ass," Carmen said.

"What are you two babbling about?" I asked. "Why can't you touch his hands? Does he have a disease?"

She looked at me, a sense of uncertainty about her. Just as she opened her mouth, Sully spoke up.

"You can," he said, a look passing between them when she turned to him. "Just—some people claim they get a sense of something odd when he touches them," he said.

"Some people claim?" Carmen said.

"Odd?" I asked, even as a weird déjà vu settled over me. Like I'd heard all this before. I shook the thought away. "Look, I've lived with odd all my life. My dad thinks he has premonitions in his dreams and now he—"

I stopped myself.

"Now he what?" Carmen asked as we rounded a bend and a small-looking house came into view. A house surrounded and nestled by large welcoming trees.

"Nothing," I said. "I'm just saying that not much surprises me. Odd or not."

"Okay," Sully said, putting the truck in park and opening the door. "He's kind of weird about doing things one thing at a time, so give us a minute and then I'll call you over."

Sully got out and strode purposefully up the porch, tapping his work boots on the wood as he waited for the eccentric old man to come to the door. We watched in silence as a few moments passed and the front door opened, leading Sully to back up a step as he greeted him from a slight distance.

"Mm-hmm," Carmen said softly. "Some people claim."

We sat there watching the two men talk, until Sully nodded and picked up a small cabinet sitting on the porch, bringing it back with him to the truck.

"Your turn," he mouthed through the window.

"Coming?" I asked Carmen. On the one hand, I'd planned on doing this solo. I hadn't wanted to involve anyone else in my business. On the other hand, the slight memories I had coupled with Bonnie and Clyde here managing to sufficiently creep me out, kind of made me want a sidekick.

"Nah, I'm good," she said.

I raised an eyebrow. "Seriously?"

"Yeah, once was enough," she said.

I got out and shut the door. "Nothing spooky here."

"Need company?" Sully asked, strapping down the cabinet in the bed of his truck.

I frowned. "No, I'm good. Jesus, what's wrong with you people?" I added under my breath as I made my way up to the porch.

I'd grown up there in Charmed, so of course I'd heard the stories about weird old Mr. Bailey. How he stayed to himself out here in the woods like a hermit but always looked impeccable. Never had a family. Maybe that made him a little quirky, but surely he didn't eat puppies and small children.

Mr. Bailey came back to the door in the very second I approached it.

"Miss Greene," he said pleasantly.

Taken aback, I smiled. "You know who I am."

"Of course," he said. "You're the spitting image of your father," he said, tilting his head in speculation. "With just the hint of your mother's wary gaze."

My jaw dropped and my mouth went bone dry.

"Come in," he said, holding open the door. "I've been expecting that you'd want to visit."

Stay far away. Don't touch his hands.

Good Lord, so many rules.

"Really?" I asked, looking behind me, watching Carmen and Sully disappear as he shut the door. "Why did you expect that?"

He ambled past me as I backed up to give him room, and my eyes left him to take in all that I could see. For the first time, I saw the 'big house'. A high ceiling sported thick wooden beams and rich colors. The furniture was clearly dated but very high quality, and tapestries and mosaic wall hangings filled the walls. A fire roared in a giant stone fireplace along one wall, and when Mr. Bailey sat in his chair on what appeared to be an ancient Persian rug, he almost glowed from it.

Everything felt like more. Nothing on the outside would ever give an inkling that this is what awaited the senses within.

"Well, I suspect that it might have something to do with the package I had delivered to Oliver Greene," he said.

"A *package*," I said. "Okay, we'll call it that." I perched on a tufted stool. "Who delivers a package like that? And why?"

"To the point," he said. "I like that. Oliver wasn't like that so much."

"Mr. Bailey," I said. "My ride is waiting on me. Can you please tell me why my father had one hundred thousand dollars in a grocery bag in his dresser drawer, and says it came from you?"

He sighed deeply and packed a pipe, motioning me to sit closer.

"I'm good," I said.

"Do you want to hear the story?" he said.

I bit the inside of my bottom lip. "There's a *story*? Do I need to go tell Sully to—"

"Sully's fine," Bailey said. "He'll wait."

I glanced toward the door, kind of wishing I was out there with them. Reluctantly, I rose, and moved to sit on an ottoman closer to him. Within reaching distance. Hopefully, that choice wouldn't bite me in the ass.

"The money is Oliver's," he said finally, after lighting his pipe and puffing till he was satisfied. "It's what is left."

"Left?" I said. "Left from what?"

"From what we found," he said.

I sighed and rubbed at my eyes. "Mr. Bailey, with all due respect, can you just tell me and stop making me pull it out of you?"

"Certainly dear," he said, laying a hand over mine.

It was a good two to three seconds before it dawned on me that I wasn't supposed to touch him, and another couple before it registered in his eyes that it didn't do anything.

"Ah," he said, patting my hand and withdrawing his. "I should have known."

"Should have known what?"

"You're like your father," he said. "But stronger. The one who broke him seeks to break you."

I blinked in surprise. "How did you know that?"

Bailey shrugged and a small smile pulled at his lips. "Lucky guess." He sat back in his chair. "Oliver, myself, and Ruby Barrett—we were friends as children. We found each other, you could say."

"Because you're different," I said.

He shrugged as if he were talking about wearing blue instead of green. "To a degree. Ruby was always the intuitive one, your father had his dreams, and I—well, I was never really anything special, but I was a bit older and tended to lead."

"That's not what I hear," I said.

"Really?" he said, chuckling. "What do you hear?"

I crossed my arms. "That you're some force of nature and not to touch you."

His chuckle spread to his chest, pulling a hearty laugh from such a small and frail looking man.

"I love your honesty," he said. "Oh, that the people I pay to be honest with me would do it as well. So anyway, we ended up in these woods quite often, exploring; making up grand adventures for ourselves." His eyes narrowed as he studied me. "I'm going to tell you something that only two other people know, and one has passed."

"As long as you don't have to kill me afterwards, I'm okay with that," I said.

It didn't escape my notice that he didn't say he wouldn't.

"I assume you know about the caves down by the water?" he asked.

"I do."

"The three of us found a box buried in one of them one day," he said, smiling a faraway smile. "In it was an incredibly old dry-rotting leather bag. Oh, we fancied it some pirate's bag—not thinking that a pirate ship wouldn't be sailing on a pond," he added with a smirk. "But instead, it held money."

I knew I had to look like a kid getting a bedtime story, but my eyes got big.

"You literally found this money?" I asked.

"Up there on the mantel," he pointed. "You'll see a small shadow box with an old piece of leather."

I got up and went to where he pointed. The glass was yellowed, but I could see the strap. On it was a number three written in something dark.

"That was from the strap," Bailey said. "The only thing written anywhere. We called it the power of three and split it evenly among us."

"Oh my God, how old were you?" I asked.

He laughed. "Old enough to know we should have told our parents," he said. "Young enough to think making treasure holes in the trees and forming a secret pact to never tell anyone was better."

Money in the trees.

"That hundred grand was my father's take as a *kid*?" I asked.

Bailey took a puff of his pipe. "One hundred grand is what is *left* of his take," he said. "As we grew up, we all had our own demons to fight, but Oliver's was probably the hardest."

"Gambling," I said.

"Horrible thing to fight when you know you have secret money stashed away," he said.

"So he—we didn't have to lose the house," I said, really more to myself. "The car. Why—why didn't he just use that money?"

"I don't know," Bailey said. "But years ago, when it hit one hundred grand, he brought it to me. Asked me to keep it for you and your daughter, because he didn't trust himself."

"Oh my God," I breathed, leaning over on my knees, my face in my hands. "And now you sent it back?"

"My old friend can't do any damage with it now," he said softly.

My eyes filled with tears.

I could.

A hundred grand—could solve all my problems. Or at least a big non-Bash-related chunk.

Bailey scooted forward in his chair and laid down his pipe.

"So," I began, sitting up. "You never stopped to wonder where such a windfall might have come from? I mean, it could have been drug money, blood money, ransom..."

"It could have been anything," he said. "Where it came from became less important than where it went. It became an inheritance for Ruby's niece. A diner on Main named The Blue Banana. The trailer park you grew up in. Half this town."

"You're saying—"

"I'm saying it's getting late, Miss Greene," he said. "We should probably say goodnight."

"Goodnight?" I said. "Okay." Way weird, considering it was barely past noon, but whatever. "I can get out of your hair."

"Very nice to finally meet Oliver's daughter," he said, looking at me sincerely and chasing that look with a surprised one. As if he wasn't accustomed to feeling sincere.

"What made you tell me this story?" I asked. "If you don't mind me asking."

Bailey rolled his head a little and ran his hands up and down the arms of his chair.

"I can't honestly say," he said. "Maybe I just don't want to be the last of it." He gave a short little wink. "Maybe you have a little gift of your own, making me want to share. Take care, Miss Greene. Sweet dreams."

I rose to my feet and stretched my stiff legs, bidding him goodbye as I walked outside and closed the door behind me. Into the dusky night air. Wait—*night* air?

It was dark.

Goodnight.

I'd gone inside his house at twelve fifteen. How the hell was it dark? And where was Sully's truck? Where did he and Carmen go? What the—

At that thought, lights cut across the darkness and bounced along the road. Sully.

"Oh, thank God," I whispered, running toward the lights, and then stopping and waving my hands in the air as he slowed to a stop. I pulled open the passenger door to see Sully at the wheel. "Where's Carmen?"

"She's at home, she wanted to clean up after supper," he said.

"She—she what?" I asked. "When—how did she get home?"

"I took her home when you texted her that you'd be a while."

"When I texted her?" I asked, confused. "I didn't text her. Why is it dark?"

Sully looked at me funny as I climbed in. "It tends to do that when the day is over."

"Over," I echoed. "It's only like one o'cl—"

My gaze landed on his dashboard clock, and without blinking or looking away, I dug my phone from my pocket and hit the home button. The screen came to life, featuring the big bold numbers of my clock.

It read the same thing: 7:02 p.m.

CHAPTER THIRTEEN

"What's going on?" I whispered.

"About to ask you the same thing," Sully said, turning the truck around to head back the way he came. "You look freaked out."

I looked at him. "It was noon when we got here."

"Roughly, yes."

"You talked to Bailey on the porch," I said. "Got a cabinet."

"I did," Sully said, nodding. "Going to refinish it for him."

"Then I went in," I said, going through the steps. "You and Carmen waited out here."

"Yes." At my probable crazy stare, he added. "Until you texted her you'd be a while. We went home until you texted to come pick you up. I'm on my way to poker night with the guys, and told her I'd grab you on the way."

"I didn't text anybody," I said, clicking over to my text messages. "I was only in there for like twenty minutes."

Sully scoffed. "Allie, you were in there for a good hour before we left. There's an apple tree over there that I considered scaling for lunch."

I shook my head as I pulled up Carmen's name, and my jaw dropped. Sure enough. There they were.

2:06 p.m.

Me: Looks like this will be a while. Sorry! I should hv followed in the Jeep!

Carmen: No biggie! Do what you have to do & text me later. One of us will come bk.

6:45 p.m.

Me: All done!

Carmen: Sully's on his way.

"How did I do this?" I asked. "Where—where was I?"

There was quiet for a moment as we bounced softly over the uneven roads.

"All I can tell you," Sully said, "is that anything is possible with Albert Bailey. Did you shake his hand?"

"No, but he touched mine," I said. "Nothing happened, so that's—"

"*Anything* is possible with Bailey," Sully repeated, looking at me.

"Jesus," I muttered, raking my hair back. "Oh, crap. Angel's probably—and shit! We have contest practice tonight!"

"I'll get you home in just a few minutes," he said.

"Good God," I said, covering my face. "What the hell happened to me?"

I mumbled a thanks as I jumped out of his truck in my driveway and jogged to my front door.

"Angel?" I called out.

"Present."

Curled up on the couch with her laptop and an earbud in one ear, Angel looked up from a movie.

"Sorry I'm so late," I said, rushing past. "Did you eat?"

"Had some cereal," she said. "It was fine," she said when I stopped. "I had a big lunch, I wanted something light."

"Do you have homework?"

"Nope."

"No tests? Projects to do?" I asked, yanking off my T-shirt and kicking off sneakers.

"Nope."

I headed into my room, my closet, and stared. I wanted—*needed* something more than a T-shirt. We had to wear the shoes we'd be wearing on the day...it had been one of the rules Vonda had laid out. One I'd actually heard in the midst of my Bash fantasy. I grabbed the heels I already knew would be perfect with the new dress, and held them up to the shirts hanging there.

"Come on, somebody wave," I said.

"Going out?" Angel said from behind me, flopping onto my bed.

"No, there's a practice for the King and Queen thing," I said. "I'm missing the first thirty minutes, but I at least need to show up."

There was a small pause.

"The red flowy one," she said finally.

I frowned. "What red flowy one?"

"On the left," she said. "You keep skipping over it."

"On the—oh. Damn, I forgot about this shirt." I pulled it out and held it up. Dark red and sexy. Perfect show of a little cleavage without being overly boobed. Tight in the waist and then flared and flowy little pieces over the ass. I pulled it over my head and tugged it into place. "Yes?"

"Definitely," Angel said, propping up on her elbow. "Put on the shoes."

I strapped them on as fast as I could, pranced around a bit to make sure I wouldn't break an ankle, and held out my arms. "Am I good?"

"Good to go," she said, drawn back into her phone.

Well, it was fun while it lasted.

"Okay, I should only be about an hour, I'm guessing," I said, to which she gave me a thumbs up. "Angel."

She looked up. "No boys in the house, no anyone in the house, I don't leave. Keep the doors locked till I'm thirty. I know, Mom."

"And Bash?" I asked pointedly.

She frowned and looked down at her phone. "You shouldn't have told him."

"I didn't," I said, sighing that we were going to rehash this for the fiftieth time. "He happened to be standing there when you came home."

"And you couldn't wait—"

"Angel Greene," I said. "I don't have to explain myself to you. I'm the mother. You're the child. You're setting yourself up to make giant mistakes, and it's my job to steer you off that course. *You* made a bad choice, and then followed that up with treating someone who loves you very badly."

"I know, I know, I know," she said, getting up. "Don't worry. Your mistake is going to her cell now."

I whirled around. "*What* did you just say to me?" When she didn't answer, I stormed down the hall and nearly wobbled off course on a hard turn. "Angel!"

She was flopping onto her bed when I reached her, looking up at me with complete disgust. I knew the feeling.

"Don't you ignore me," I said. "Why did you just say that?"

"What, you're mad at *me* for being your big bad screw-up?" she said.

I stared at her and sagged against the wall. "Are you kidding me?"

"Do you not hear yourself?"

"Angel," I said, trying to draw strength from somewhere I hadn't tapped yet. "You are fif—okay you are almost sixteen," I amended. "And you feel grown. Your body feels grown. Guys are giving you attention, and they should, you're gorgeous. But baby, sex is about more than being physically capable. And once you give that away, it's gone."

"Like you did," she retorted.

I inhaled deeply and let it go. "Yes. Like I did. Even older than you, because a charming guy turned my head. Made me think I'd feel beautiful if I did that. But you know what? I didn't. Because I wasn't ready. A guy who really cared about me would have known that, and waited."

Angel shook her head and looked at her phone. "Grown-ups are so full of themselves with this stuff."

"Full of myself?" I cried, stepping forward. "I'm a thirty-three year old mother of a kid in high school. Other women my age have toddlers, Angel. That's not being *full of myself*, that's walking the damn walk."

"And I wouldn't be here if you hadn't *walked the damn walk*," she said. "Your grand mistake."

A little piece of my heart broke off and shattered into a million pieces. I nodded and swallowed past the crow in my throat.

"I deserve that," I said, pressing a hand to my belly as I sat on her bed. "Because if you've been feeling that way, that's on me and I'm sorry." I drew in a shaky breath. "Baby, from the moment you came into this world, I was yours completely. I've never been more in love and I have never thought of you as a mistake. But the way you got here?" I shook my head. "I wouldn't wish that teenage small-town, small-minded, high school drama on anyone. Least of all, you."

"Seriously, Mom, you go on and on about not making your mistakes, not doing what you did, not having sex, not getting pregnant—"

"Because I don't want you to be me!" I cried. I didn't mean to yell it, but the frustration of the day was demanding to be let out.

"I'm not you!" she yelled back, tears in her eyes. "I do the homework, I follow the rules, I don't do drugs, or drink, or have sex. I'm the most boring teenager to walk the earth, so if you don't mind, stop harping on me for your sins and wait until I actually do something, okay?"

"Well, to me, buying condoms is *something*," I said, swiping under my eyes as I got up. "But you're right, maybe I've been a little too proactive. So consider all that banked for this one, and we're all caught up."

"Can we say you still have more, and give me a bonus chip or something?" she asked, wiping at her eyes.

I raised an eyebrow. "A bonus chip?"

"Aaron invited me to dinner."

"No."

"With his mother," she added quickly. "She invited me."

"His *mother* would let you have sex in her living room while she knitted baby blankets," I said. "Free will and all that. No."

She scrunched up her face. "Ew."

"You have no idea."

"Then can he come over here one night for dinner with us?" she asked, eyes pleading. "To meet you?"

The *no* was right there tap dancing on my tongue, but I bit it down. I had to grow with this, too. Ugh.

"We'll see."

Best I could do.

I so much didn't want to leave. I felt like that boy—that *guy*—would be in my house before I even made it down the street. But I had an obligation, and she had a promise. I could trust her or lose my mind not trusting her. I really didn't appreciate those toddler years enough at twenty-one.

* * *

I nearly fell getting out of the Jeep, forgetting the heels I had on. I chose to believe that wasn't an omen.

The practice stage was set up on the pavilion, with speakers and wires and a block-styled set of bleacher steps probably twelve to fifteen feet high that made my progress falter halfway there. We were going to be expected to traverse that? In stripper heels?

"Allie!"

It was Vonda, hurrying toward me. Fabulous.

"Hey, sorry I'm late," I said. "I got stuck and—time got away from me."

Nothing had ever been so aptly described.

"Just head over there," she said, whizzing past me. "Bash will fill you in."

Bash, who was chatting it up with Kia by a table. My mouth went dry as I continued to walk toward their laughing, at ease selves. He never looked at me like that anymore. Like he was comfortable with me. With himself. He never had those friggin dancing blue eyes that were up to no good. Not with me. He looked at me like—

His head turned when my heels hit the wood, and I felt the flutter from my belly down to everything south of the border.

He looked at me like *that.*

And walked away from Kia as if she were a tabletop statue.

Wow.

I saw her eyebrows raise and an amused smirk touch her face, and for the first time I felt like—like *something.* Like she wasn't a threat, like no one was a threat, like I was actually the pretty girl for once in my life.

"Hey," Bash said as he met me, looking all kinds of tasty in a dark blue button-down shirt, tucked in to dark jeans. "I didn't know if you got held up, or—"

"Something like that," I said.

He nodded, and his eyes panned me. "You look really nice."

I winced. This wasn't us. *You look really nice?* I blew out a breath and made to move around him. I was too emotionally and physically wound up to play games with him tonight.

"Thanks."

"Hey," he said, putting a hand on my arm as I passed.

"Bash, I'm really tired," I said. "I have a lot on my mind, it's been an exhausting day, and I need to go ask Kia what I missed. I'm not in the mood to dance around you."

"Dance—what?" he said, looking ticked off.

Good. We got more accomplished that way. Well, except for the last time. In my kitchen. Yeah.

"You know what I'm saying," I said.

He held out his hands. "I'm standing all the way over here, what am I doing that you can't talk to me?"

I blinked a couple of times. "You told me I look nice."

One eyebrow raised in question. "And that's—wrong?"

I sighed and rubbed at my temple in advance of the headache I felt was coming.

"The old Bash would have told me I looked hot and then asked me if I wanted to get lucky."

A grin pulled at his lips, and my stomach shimmied at the sight of it.

"Do you realize what that would sound like now?" he asked, glancing downward. "I kind of have to pick my words."

I crossed my arms over my chest and looked away as I fought a smile, too.

"I hate that," I said. "That's not us."

"I know," he said. "So let's make it us." He made a gesture with his hands. "Talk to me. Tell me what's going on. Anything more with Angel? She's not getting married now, is she?"

"Not today," I said, still weary from the earlier conversation. "Tomorrow's a new day."

"Okay guys," Vonda called out. "Break's over. We have to stage the essay reading—pretend, of course," she added over her shoulder with a wink to Bash. Gah. "Then plan in the quick change—everybody find themselves a good spot, and then we'll practice the grand finale with the steps."

"I'm sorry," I said, raising my hand. "Quick change?"

"From your business casual clothes to your formal," Vonda said. She tilted her head endearingly. Well, it would be endearingly if she wasn't celebrating her son's manhood. "It's all in your e-mail. The formal attire is for the grand finale and the dance afterward."

"The formal attire is the dress you bought the other day," Katrina Bowman said, strutting by.

I smiled sweetly. "Yes, I'm quite sure I got that, thank you," I said. "But a quick change?" I pointed around us. "We're outside. That's a pavilion with—bleachers on it. Where is this change supposed to happen?"

"Behind the dividers we'll have up," Vonda said, as if that were perfectly clear. "Your assistant can help you."

"My—" I stopped myself and took a breath. "It's in the e-mail, isn't it?" I asked Bash quietly. He nodded. "And there's a dance. Got it."

"Are we ready?" Vonda asked. "Oh and take your hair down," she added, pointing to my head. "So much prettier with that outfit. Great shoes, by the way."

"Some might even say hot," Bash said as he passed.

I smirked. "Cute."

* * *

An hour in, my feet hated me, Angel had called once and texted twice to ask when I was coming home because she had something important to talk about, and Bash had disappeared with a phone call. In summary: a fucking fabulous night.

Now we were to the climb-the-stupid-mountain portion of the evening, and the only person who understood my insanity with heights was nowhere to be found.

My throat closed as I looked up. *Only ten feet.* Not fifteen or twelve. Only ten feet, Kia had said (when Vonda allowed her to), with no railing. No purpose. If it were steps from a building I'd think nothing of it, but this was climbing what was essentially a glorified ladder on steroids to stand atop a reasonless block, looming above the stage. No sides.

I felt hot. Katrina went up first and I watched her navigate over the top like it was nothing. I was going to choke. I was going to make a giant fool of myself.

Miss Mavis headed up next, maneuvering the rungs just fine in her Keds. Christ, I was doomed to die on a ladder. If the height didn't give me cardiac arrest, my shoes were destined to take me down.

Breathe.

My hands shook, so I pressed them against my ribs. Hard. One over the other, making sure to slightly pinch the back of one hand. Anything to keep me present and breathing.

The guys were lined up like show ponies on either side, hands outstretched to greet their queens. *Fuck.* All but Bash. My eyes darted frantically for him, in desperate need of that contact to ground me, but he was nowhere.

"Okay, Allie," Kia's voice said over the speaker. "Head on up when you see her disappear over the top."

Bash was still out of sight. Gone. I had to do this on my own.

The floor felt like liquid as I looked up. Like I was standing on a water bed. I gripped the railing, but the attack was coming on fast, the blackness touching the corners of my vision. I lifted my hair off my neck, fanning myself with it.

"Shit," I whispered, mortified at what was about to happen in front of everyone. What was I thinking? I couldn't do this. This stupid weakness of mine was sabotaging me again.

"Allie?" said one of the other women behind me. I couldn't tell who. Everyone sounded alike inside a well.

"I'm—" I began. "I—"

"I've got you."

Solid man was suddenly at my back, a hand against my stomach pulling me tightly against him. I gulped in air like he'd just delivered it, and let my weight rest against his body.

"Just breathe, Al, you can do this," Bash said, his breath warm against my ear. "It's just perspective, remember?"

"Perspective," I echoed, breathing deep and closing my eyes, letting the oxygen reenter my blood.

"One step at a time," he whispered. "I'm right here. When you reach the top, I'll be right where you can see me."

"Swear?"

"Swear to God."

Leaving the solid warmth of Bash's body was the hardest thing ever. I grabbed the railing with trembling hands and started up on shaky legs I didn't feel, praying my shoes didn't stage a coup.

"Please," I whispered with each step.

Focus. Perspective.

"It's just steps," I said softly. "It's solid."

There were handles that went over the top, much like I imagined the last ladder should have had. Then I was topping it, and suddenly up went down.

"No," I cried, a choked sound down in my throat.

"Focus, Allie," I heard Bash say behind me, and the sound propelled me one more step. Then one more. And—

"Holy shit," I said, standing at the top like a deer in the headlights.

"Okay, come down," Kia was saying. Vonda was a few feet further, nodding.

Walk down. Don't fall. You can do this.

Then there he was. Running to his spot up front so that I could see him. Holding out his hand and waiting for me. Looking up with those eyes that said *I've got you.*

I was halfway down before I knew I was moving, and my hand was in his a second later. His expression beamed with relief and pride and things I felt too emotional to attempt to name. So I did the next best thing. I flung my arms around his neck.

He caught me, laughing; his arms coming up around me in a tight embrace.

"You did it," he said against my ear.

"I did!" I chuckled.

"I'm proud of you, Al," he said, putting me down slowly and keeping his hands in place. His eyes were dancing. Like they used to, except there was more.

"Um, are we missing something?" Vonda asked, coming forward.

My hands were still on his chest, and I reached up to touch his cheek.

"No, but *we* were."

CHAPTER FOURTEEN

I sat on the edge of the pavilion, drinking a water and absorbing the peace of the light chatting and laughter in the background with the crickets chirping nearby. Home wasn't that peaceful. I'd either have snarky and rude Angel back (I held no delusions that the girl who helped dress me two hours earlier would still be hanging around), or I would end up in my kitchen reliving that kiss, or in my laundry room staring inside my dryer and hyperventilating.

I chose crickets for the moment. Because whatever was eating at Angel tonight could wait a minute. I'd had enough of that. Kiss-obsessing was ridiculous at my age, and plus it felt like we'd gained some of our old ground back tonight. And hyperventilating wasn't just about the money, but now the holy fuckedness of how I'd lost an entire afternoon talking to Mr. Bailey, when I distinctly remembered every word. Sully told me to let it go, but—

He didn't understand. He didn't get growing up with something kind of off-color in your house. Something you deny so much that you start to believe your own protests.

My dad was a gambler, and that was bad enough. It was embarrassing enough to lose everything and the whole school know that you're poor enough to be on the charity list for holiday food drives. I couldn't handle the extra talk like Lanie Barrett had to deal with. Her Aunt Ruby was always rumored about with her eccentric ways and hints at premonitions. I could never have shouldered my dad's wacked-out dream life making the circuit along with everything else. Not like that. And now—I mean, I knew they were friends, but to find out that they were evidently a *special* little trio—and they found enough money back then to still be making a difference today.

Lanie inherited eight hundred thousand dollars that no one knew the origin of. So my dad had at least that much at one time. I had to shut that thought out. My fingers curled into fists at the swirls of things that swam through my head if I didn't. The things we'd lost. The things we had to fight for, because he "never had enough" to cover his debts. And now the diner...

I closed my eyes. "Crickets, damn it."

"What was that?"

My eyes popped open to see Bash strolling up, shirt untucked, hair looking as if he'd rifled through it a few too many times. A lazy smile on his face.

Basically, even in the dark after the main lights were shut off, he looked good enough to eat and come back for dessert, and my entire body reacted accordingly.

"Sorry, I was trying to drive out all the outside noise from my head and let the crickets have their way with me," I said.

He stopped about two feet away and tucked his hands into his jeans pockets. He didn't speak for a while and neither did I. It was bizarrely okay, and us, and not us, and normal, and not normal and sexy as hell to do that.

He pointed to the spot next to me. "Can I sit down?"

"Sure."

Bash's height allowed him a simple shift to slide up next to me. His leg was a whole three inches from mine. I calculated it immediately. He knocked his ankle against mine playfully and I did it back.

"Didn't you have poker tonight?" I asked. "I saw Sully earlier."

"Also had this," he said. "Told them to find someone else. You look—" He stopped and gestured up and down at me as I sat next to him. "I don't see you like this very often."

"Nice save."

"Caught that, did you?"

I chuckled. "Yeah, this doesn't really work well with grease fryers and mayonnaise stains. Not to mention I'd be ready to take one of these shoes off and stab someone with it by noon."

Bash laughed. "I can imagine. I'm glad I don't have to wear them."

"Yeah, they wouldn't really go."

He pretended to look down at himself. "You don't think they'd up my ranking?"

"I think you're doing just fine," I said.

He looked at me sideways. "Fine? Is that the new *nice*? You know, the old Allie would tell me I was smokin'."

I nearly choked on a laugh. "I'm pretty sure I've never used that word. Ever. In my life."

"Or something close."

"Okay, how about—" So many words came to mind. *Fuckable* was first, delicate flower that I am. "Delicious."

Stepping. Way. Out. There.

The look on his face, even in the dark, said he was having the very same reaction.

"Delicious?"

"I'm trying new things," I said. "In light of our—" I gestured in a circle with my hands. "Our new normal."

He gave me a long look. "I like it."

I chuckled and leaned sideways to bump shoulders. We sat quietly for a moment, and it was nice. Not formal and crappy kind of nice, but really and truly awesome.

"So, tell me what's been going on," he said finally.

"Tell me what's going on with you and Lange."

He gave me a funny look. "You first."

I gave him the rundown from the time Lange made his big announcement, to finding the money in my dad's drawer, to the conversation at Bailey's house earlier. Minus the time warp. When I was done, he pushed off the stage and walked off a few steps, staring into space.

"I'm going to talk to Lange tomorrow," I said. "Tell him I have the money to pay him off and ask him to tear up the deed paperwork."

"He's out of town till day after tomorrow," Bash said. "And I doubt he'll care."

"What?" I said. "Why?"

He turned back and covered the few feet between us, crossing his arms.

"Because he has money. He doesn't need it," he said. "He's more about collecting businesses and putting his name on them than in anything financial."

I frowned. "He wants to change our name and I told him hell no, I didn't care how much his percentage was. Did he do the same to you?"

"He's trying. He doesn't have any ownership, but he wants controlling power of some of the products. He's held up deliveries because I won't agree," Bash said. "That's why there was no delivery this week."

I shook my head in disbelief. "I wondered." Actually, I assumed he was avoiding me, but I'd go with his version.

"He's even messing with the hives now," he said.

"When does he have time for that?" I asked. "He never leaves the damn diner."

"Not physically," Bash said. "He's communicating with my customers about their rentals." He ran a hand over his face. "Cherrydale Flower Farm and Kaison Orchards suffered serious setbacks when Dean screwed me over last summer. I couldn't get them all the bees they needed, and I've kissed some major ass to keep them working with me. Now Lange is emailing them about paying higher rental fees for fewer hives? Shit, he's gonna put me out of business."

"Are they local?" I asked. "Can he go schmooze with them? Because he would."

Bash took a deep breath and let it go. "Kaison's a half day's drive. It's on the other side of Austin. But Cherrydale is just an hour away."

"We could kill him," I suggested.

"Poison his coffee?"

"Get some killer bees and put them in his man purse," I said.

Bash laughed. "Oh, if I only had the time."

I nudged him. "How's the new shop? I suck as a friend, I keep forgetting to ask you that."

"You do suck, but I'll let you slide," he said, the hint of a grin pulling at his lips. "It's okay. Doing better than I hoped. I think having a location out here was a good step."

"Glad to hear it."

He looked at me for a moment.

"I miss you, Allie," he said finally.

Didn't see that switch-up coming. My belly did a tumble on the words, and it was everything I could do not to jump off that pavilion and wrap myself around him.

"I miss you, too."

"I'm sorry I've been acting like a jerk lately," he said, raking his fingers through his hair. "I haven't known what to do with—things."

I narrowed my eyes. I was pretty sure I knew what those *things* were, but I wasn't about to assume it.

"And this conversation just proves that we have to figure out how to handle distraction better, or—"

"Or don't let ourselves go there," I said.

His eyes were shiny in the dark.

"That's getting harder," he said softly.

I nodded. "I know," I whispered, the words barely making sound.

"I lied," he said.

I frowned. "About?"

"It being nothing."

I shouldn't have had any earthly idea what that meant. As it was, I knew *exactly* what he was talking about, and the breath I had to stop and take was proof of that.

"You're my best friend," he said.

I nodded in lieu of words, even though he probably couldn't see it. I couldn't trust words right then.

"You're the one I can't wait to tell things, the one that knows everything—the good and the crap—and doesn't care," he said, moving forward and stopping short like there was a wall there.

"You're that for me, too," I said.

"And yeah, maybe back in the day, there was that thirty second drunken blink of a moment—"

"*Was* it a whole thirty seconds?" I asked.

"Come on, you gotta give me at least that," he said, laughing. "I did my best for being barely coherent."

We laughed and then the quiet returned. An easier quiet, but troubling at the same time. There was always something else hovering now. Something I couldn't quite decide on the good or badness of.

"The thing was, I knew even then what was more important," he said. "I'd lay in my bunk in San Diego thinking, *God, I want to do that again*, and then, *Fuck, I hope I didn't mess us up* in the very next breath."

I chuckled. "I know what you mean."

"I don't have family, Al," he said. "Y'all are it. I can't afford to fuck that up."

Ah. So we *were* on the same really back-assward, twisted, unfair, and jacked up page. That was good. So why did it not feel good?

"I know," I said. "Me either. I mess up every relationship I have."

"I don't do relationships," Bash said. "I don't even do overnights. No one sleeps in my bed but me."

"True," I said, keeping it light for sanity's sake. "You *are* a man whore."

"Guilty," he said, raising his hand. "And that usually works for me. No feelings. No complications."

"Usually?"

He exhaled slowly and lowered his hand. "Usually." He moved closer and went to lay his hands on my knees but then rested them on either side of me instead as if he and his hands were battling. "And then you kissed me."

He was close enough that I could feel the heat off his body. I could smell the uniquely delicious simple aroma of soap and man that was always Bash.

I could pull him into my arms if I wanted to. Oh God, I wanted to. My heart was racing and the only thing I could think of was *focus.*

Focus. Perspective. He'd just echoed every thought I'd had for months. We were talking again. Agreeing that we were fighting the same battle. We couldn't afford to lose the very rare and precious thing we had. The thing we were so lucky to find all those years ago. We needed to not be this close!

"This argument again?" I said, attempting light.

"You kissed me," he repeated. "And then I kissed you back. And for God knows how many months afterward—"

"Three."

"I have not been able to think about anything else."

Oh, fuck, light was jumping in the pond and swimming away. What the hell were we talking about a few minutes ago? I had no idea. I wanted to touch him so badly. *Don't touch him. Focus.* But he had me in this little arm cage of his, and...God help me.

"Yeah," I managed. "Me too."

"It's turned me into a lunatic."

"Yes it has."

He grinned, and I wanted to pull that grin closer. Get to know it up close and—

"And that little—"

"Nothing?"

He laughed and dropped his head, and it took all my power not to reach out.

"That nothing was everything," he said. "That one little kiss turned us inside out. What the hell would more do?"

He lifted his head on the question, and his face was so close I forgot the question entirely.

"Then," I breathed, staring at his mouth. "My kitchen happened."

"That it did," he whispered, leaning in, resting his head against mine. Touching. "And I've been totally fucked ever since."

I was totally fucked right now. Super magnets were tugging my mouth toward his, and I had no say in the matter. Not that I would have argued. I wanted to kiss Bash again more than breathing, more than friendship, more than any of those logical thoughts I'd had earlier.

"You're my best friend," he said slowly, drawing the words out and diverting his mouth from its direct path to around by my ear. Sweet Jesus, that wasn't any better, and my hands lost their battle. They moved up his chest to his face, his hair, pulling him closer as he brushed his lips against my ear. His breath quickened at my touch, making me heady. "We need to be able to talk."

"Mm-hmm."

Hands slid around to my ass and up my back, slowly squeezing me against him as his lips trailed down the side of my neck.

"Fuck, this is such a bad idea," he said against my skin, setting me on fire.

"Worst," I breathed. "In the history of bad ideas."

Focus?

One hand came up in my hair to cradle my head and give him better access to my neck. Hot breath rippled over my skin as his lips kissed the sensitive spot under my ear.

Focus left to hang out with light. Sensation took over and, oh God, he knew just how to touch me. My fingers fisted in his hair as I arched against him automatically.

It was like a switch flipped for both of us. That switch that signals the train about to go flying off the rails. He pulled his head back just enough to be face to face, where we were both breathing raggedly.

"This is why I can't be trusted when I get near you," he said. "All common sense takes off and—" He pressed a soft kiss to my lips and I closed my eyes, willing to stay like that for days.

"It feels really good," I whispered against his lips.

"It feels so fucking good," he said against mine.

I kissed him once, twice...

"We—we'll never survive a dance," I breathed.

He claimed my mouth, enveloping me with a head to toe rush.

It started softer, more intimate that time around. We just kissed in the dark. Slow. Sexy. Deep. It was hot and erotic and all sensation, but there was that something *more* again. Something foreign that hit my heart with every kiss.

I felt every inch that he touched, his hands moving slowly on my body. Finding skin under my shirt and teasing close to the sensitive places. Moving deliberately slow down my legs and back again, as if imagining the feel of me under the denim.

I knew the feeling. I wanted skin. His kisses and caresses had me trembling with need, and I craved more than my hands could feel through the heat of his shirt. I finally left his mouth, unable to restrain any longer. I trailed my kisses down over his jaw, down his neck. His breathing was as erratic as mine, his skin hot as fire against my mouth as I let my hands slide down his chest to his waist, letting my fingers travel up under his shirt, skimming along his abs to stop at the waistband of his jeans.

A rumble of desire ran through his chest, and his fingertips dug in to my upper thighs, just inches from ground zero, while his thumbs continued to stroke in a dangerous tease. Bash finally backed up an inch or two, looking down at his hands as if they were acting on their own.

"Bash," I mouthed as my breath felt like it went away.

He dragged his hands up along my ribcage, letting the backs of his fingers trail achingly slow up between my breasts to my neck, breathing in deep through his nose as I slid my fingertips just under the waistband along his abdomen. By the time his gaze met mine, and he cupped my face with his hands, we were both wild-eyed with need.

"You need to go home, Al," he said, his voice thick. "Before what we're trying to avoid happens right here on this stage."

Holy mother of shit storms, that shouldn't have been hot, but everything inside me lit up at those words. Just the imagery of primal, naked, wild and uninhibited sex with Bash under the stars was enough to take my breath away.

He ran his thumb over my bottom lip. "Before it feels too good to stop."

It was already there in my book, but he was right. We'd just said all the right things, and understood all the same boundaries, just to fall back into each other mouths again two seconds later. Plus some. Every time we did this, there was a plus some.

"Yeah," I said, closing my eyes as he stepped back from me and I slid down to my feet, dizzy and unsteady with no blood in my head.

I instantly missed him. The cool air had nothing on the awkward chill I felt without Bash wrapped around me. He walked me to my Jeep, and because I lost my spine somewhere back when he was groping me, before I got in, I turned and walked into his chest, wrapping my arms around him. I just wanted—I just needed to feel him one more time. To hug him, feel the solid warmth that I'd know was him in my sleep. He wound his arms around me and held on for longer than we probably should have, pressed a kiss to my head that he probably shouldn't have, and finally made sure I was in my Jeep and safe just like he always had. All without saying a word.

That embrace could have been any other day, month, or year in our lives, but it wasn't. It was the one after the make out after the kiss after the nothing that meant everything. None of which should have happened, because while yay, great, we were open about it now, we still hadn't mastered how to make the things work. Things we needed each other for, as part of that can't-afford-to-lose business that kept getting pushed aside for magic tonsil hockey.

And it was going to happen again, of that I was certain. Because it was a horrible idea, and that seemed to be in our wheelhouse.

I was still trembling when I walked through my front door, and I shook my hands out.

"Angel, I'm home," I called out, trying to get my body back under control and stop reliving the feel of his hands roaming my skin and getting lost in his mouth.

"Kitchen table," she said, her voice sounding odd.

Alarms went off in my head, and I almost ran around the corner as my heart sped up. Something was wrong. Something was—

Angel sat there like a mafia princess, her hair spilling around her shoulders as a backdrop for my torn and ragged grocery bag full of money laid open on the table.

My breath caught in my throat.

"Hi, Mom," she said. "Nice evening?"

I stared at the money, still shocked every time I looked at it. Really shocked to see it sitting in front of her like a sacrificial offering. My eyes finally met hers.

"You did laundry?"

CHAPTER FIFTEEN

"Really?" Angel said. She picked up one of the bundles of hundreds and waved it at me. "*Laundry* is the shock value here?"

"That's—"

"That's a shit ton of money," she said.

"Watch your language."

"I'm sorry," she said. "But I don't know how to talk when I find a hundred thousand dollars in our dryer."

Look calm.

"You counted it?"

"I've had some time," she said. "You were busy."

I pulled out a chair and lowered into it, scrambling frantically for a spin. I was caught. I was busted. But I couldn't tell her the truth. I couldn't tell her that her Pop had a secret stash of cash his whole life, cash he'd found in a cave on the island of misfit toys with his magical friends. I couldn't tell her it was mine, either. Or that the diner was in trouble. I rested my face in my hands and prayed for a believable answer.

"It's not my money," I said. "I'm holding it."

"In the dryer?"

"Let go of the dryer thing, Angel. It was a last minute—"

"Is it illegal?" she asked.

"No!" I cried. I didn't think so. Mostly. Probably not. "It's—Pop's." Okay, now what? "He won it on a big bet. A while back. And—I'm holding it for him because you know, he's not really all there anymore, and so..."

She was looking at me like I was a loon.

She wasn't far off.

"And it's not in the bank?" she asked. "It was where—his underwear drawer?"

I clamped my lips together before I blurted out just how close she was.

"I didn't know about it, okay?" I said, deciding to go for a little truth. All the best lies have a foundation of truth. "I was surprised, too, and he asked me to take it and keep it safe."

"Safe from—what?" she asked.

"He's a gambler," I said.

"He's housebound," she retorted. "He had to be keeping it someplace better than the dryer."

"Angel," I said, rubbing my face. "It's been a really long day, followed by a whiplash of a night, so can we just agree that I stashed it someplace I figured you'd never go, and now we can put it somewhere better and go to bed?"

She shook her head and got up from the table.

"You—you are nine kinds of crazy," she said.

"And don't mention this to anyone." My eyes went wide. "Angel, you *cannot* tell anyone we have this kind of money in the house, do you hear me?"

She gave me a look. "I'm aware, Mom."

"Not Aaron. Not anybody."

"I didn't!" she said. "And I won't. I was too terrified we were hooked up with the mob or something to tell anyone."

"Oh God," I said on a sigh, laying my head on my arms. "If only it were that simple."

"You're delirious," she said. "Did you ever eat?"

"No," I said into the table.

"Do you want some fruit or something?" she said, sounding genuinely worried for my mental state. "Um, a sandwich?"

"A sandwich would be nice," I said. "Fine. Good. Delicious." I started to laugh a little maniacally. "Hey, can you be my assistant on Saturday and help me change my clothes in the middle of the park?" I asked.

"My mom has gone insane," she whispered on the way to the fridge.

"Is that a yes?"

"Sure. Why not?"

* * *

"Kerri, Carmen Frost is coming by," I called out on the way to my office after making my post breakfast rush rounds. "Send her back, please." Saturdays were always crazier for breakfast. Everyone and their mother, aunt, cousin, and secret baby snuck out on Saturdays for someone else to cook for them. Not that one could ever be blamed for wanting that someone else to be Nick. He could make toast exciting.

I always did my best to make it around the floor, helping the waitresses pick up and clean, filling drinks, ringing up orders, even helping Nick in the kitchen if he was swamped. With the easy stuff, anyway. I never wanted to short anyone on the exciting toast.

Some owners—one I knew in particular—preferred to stay in the back and make worksheets and lists. Sometimes I had to do that, too, but I felt more in tune with my customers and just more *alive* while I was out there.

Or I did before Lanie and Nick had a giant poster made for the bar and the door with my picture and VOTE FOR OUR VERY OWN ALLIE GREENE FOR HONEY QUEEN!

"Ugh," I said, passing it. Lange would have taken it down immediately if he'd been here, and for once I would have actually agreed with him.

"You have my vote tonight, Allie," said Mr. Wilson as I picked up his napkin for him.

"Thank you," I said, squeezing his shoulder and swallowing past the tennis ball-sized lump in my throat.

The noise from the diner floor dulled to a low chatter as I circled into the back and pulled my door partially closed. I sank into my office chair and clicked my computer to life.

"An assistant," I muttered. "What the hell do I need an assistant for?"

I'd been meaning to look for the e-mail for the past two days and hadn't had a chance (or forgot), so tonight being the night, and Angel being by my side, I thought I'd better get this Girl Friday thing figured out.

I scrolled frantically through my e-mail, looking for the idiotic message from Vonda. Or Kia. Or whoever sent me the crazy message rambling about quick change dividers in the park and assistants and did they think this was the Miss America Pageant or something? Seriously, this was about being a matriarch of honey. In Charmed. Bash made sense. His business actually was honey. He should be king. I wondered if he'd get to hold a staff and go shirtless.

There was a knock on my office door, and I waved whoever it was in, grateful for the reason to shut my mind up. With Lange out, it was so much more freeing. Like it was just my diner again. Good Lord that seemed like a long time ago.

"Hey you," Carmen said, making me turn and smile. "You rang?"

"Oh, thank you," I said. "I have a favor to ask, and thought giving you a free meal might sweeten my odds."

"Uh oh," she said, tossing her keys on my desk and landing on a stool. "What are you bribing me into?" She glanced over her shoulder. "Where's MP?"

"Man Purse is out of town till tomorrow," I said, clicking on a message that might be the one. "And it's about the contest tonight."

"I'm not taking your place," she said casually. "No matter how tasty Bash looks in a suit. And I don't know how to twirl fire batons."

"No fire batons," I said. "They nixed the talent competition, thank God. But no, I'm not asking you to take my place. I'm supposed to have an assistant, and Angel said she'll do it, but—" I paused. "She's not the most reliable person. Can you possibly be on standby?"

Her eyebrows lifted in amusement. "You need an assistant for this thing?"

"Evidently," I said. "I'm looking for the e-mail that's supposed to tell me why. The only thing I know for certain is that I have to do a quick change behind some flimsy divider in the park before the grand finale, and I might need some help there."

"Getting naked in the park?"

"Basically."

"I bet Bash would be glad to lend a hand," she said, crossing her legs. *And we would never make it to the bleachers.*

"Please?"

"Of course, silly," she said. "I'm just messing with you. I'll even come hang out if Angel does come through. Sounds like an adventure."

"Sounds like the Twilight Zone," I said, rubbing my eyes.

"Ironic that you say that," she said. "Sully said you had an—odd experience at Bailey's place?"

I dropped my hands and looked at her. "Carmen."

She was shaking her head. "Unexplainable?"

"To any sane person," I said.

"What's with the posters?"

Carmen and I both jumped at the sudden presence of Landon Lange in the doorway.

"Shit," I muttered. "Knock, maybe?"

"To my own office?"

"Uh, to *my* office," I said. "I share out of the kindness of my heart. And Nick brought those posters to rally customers for the contest tonight."

"Isn't that conflict of interest?" he said.

"It's a contest for business owners," I said. "It brings attention to the diner."

"I don't know if it's the kind of attention we want," Lange said.

"It's a small-town contest, representing a small-town diner, in a small town," Carmen said. "It's pretty much tailor made for what you should want."

Lange looked at her without blinking and then walked to the corner I'd put together for him with a table and chair so he'd stay away from my desk. He pulled a small laptop out of his man purse and sat down.

"Why are you here?" I asked. "I thought you were out of town."

"I was," he said, tapping on the keyboard. "Came back a day early."

"I have something I need to talk to you about later," I said. I didn't want to waste any more time, but I couldn't venture into the money with Carmen there.

"Send me a calendar notice," Lange said. "I had some mock-ups of new sign ideas made. I'm e-mailing them to you."

My jaw tensed. "I told you no."

"I told *you* it needed to change," he said. "I'm being nice in giving you an opinion on choices, but I don't have to. I'm happy to do it all myself."

"Lange—"

He closed the computer in disgust. "That's another thing. It's Landon, which I'm perfectly fine with, or Mr. Lange, but we are not in the military or a locker room. I realize you grew up just short of barn level, living in a trailer park and all, but please don't refer to me like that."

Speech failed me.

"What the hell did you just say?" Carmen said, coming to her feet faster than I could even process the words.

"Mom?"

Carmen and I both spun around.

"Angel!" I said. "What are you doing here?"

"I was just—walking around town, and thought I'd come talk to you for a minute," she said, one eyebrow raised at Lange. "See if you're ready for tonight."

"You were just walking fifteen blocks?" I asked. "You don't walk *three* blocks."

"Well maybe I wanted some exercise," she said, crossing her arms.

"Or maybe you're grounded and you're looking for any way to get out of the house, even stooping so low as to come see me."

"Wow, thank you for thinking so highly of me," she said.

"Thank you for thinking I'm a pushover," I said.

"I'll thank the both of you to please stop bickering," Lange said, not looking up.

Angel pulled a smirk. "Who's the gripey guy with the purse?" she whispered loudly.

"Excuse me, it's a messenger bag," he said. "And the gripey guy owns this place, so…"

She looked taken aback, and I wanted to go lunge onto on Lange's laptop and slam his fingers in it.

"No, you don't," she said. "My family owns this place. My pop, actually."

"No," Lange said, his tone disinterested. "He doesn't anymore. I own more of a percentage. He's a minority owner."

"What?" Angel said.

"Angel," I said. "This is business, honey. I'll explain it to you later."

"It's basic math, Allie," Lange said. "I own fifty-one percent. Your father owns forty-nine, and so do you by proxy."

Angel shook her head slowly. I felt like that's what I looked like when I found out.

"No," she said. "That's not right. Why—"

"Oliver defaulted on some money owed," Lange continued droning on as he stood and walked past her to the door, as if he were talking to an adult and not my teenage daughter.

"Stop," I said, getting to my feet. "Lange—*Landon.*"

Carmen looked at me with a troubled expression as she attempted to corral Angel.

"Come on," she said. "Let's go out here. Let them talk business for a minute."

"And now I own a diner," he continued, turning back to her, and unfortunately causing her to dig in her heels. "You've learned about business in school, right? It's the American way. See how that works?"

He disappeared through the doorway. If ever in my life there was a time to feel blinding rage-filled murderous thoughts, it was then. I didn't even feel that much hate toward her father when he left me alone and pregnant.

Angel blinked and jerked her head at me. "Pop owed—no!"

"Angel."

"No, Mom, he *has* money! You know he has money!" she said, running after him. "Hey!" she yelled.

Oh, fuck.

"Angel, quit," I cried after her, glancing at Carmen and trying to keep her from overhearing. The staff from overhearing. The friggin *town* from overhearing. The balls were getting difficult to juggle and this was about to go very bad. "This stays at home!"

"Mister!" she yelled from behind the counter. I ran up behind her just as Lange turned around. Along with about twenty other people. "You don't have to do this, we can pay you. My Pop has—"

"Stop." I said through my teeth.

She whirled around. "Mom, this is important," she said, tears in her eyes. Damn it, she actually cared about this place. "You just let him take our diner? That money Pop won, give it to this dude!"

I closed my eyes as I envisioned every ear in the restaurant going on super radar mode, and every mouth priming for afterward.

"I will talk to him *privately*," I said in a clipped tone under my breath. "Please stop making a spectacle."

Her jaw set and that cliff sensation hit me again. *No.*

"We have Pop's money," she blurted, walking toward Lange. "Cash. It's yours. Put it toward whatever he owes you and—"

"Angel Elizabeth Greene," I said, raising my voice. "Go. Home. Now."

The look she gave me ripped me apart. Like she didn't know me at all. Sometimes I had that same look lately when I was getting ready in the mirror.

"Seriously?" she said, two tears falling down her face. "You're just—"

"You don't know all the facts, Angel, and you're making it worse, so please stop talking," I said, seething with anger. With embarrassment. With about as much self-loathing that could still fit in with everything else.

"No, please," Lange said on a laugh, holding up a hand. "Don't stop on my account. This is entertaining."

Angel's eyes turned to slits of pure disgust before she turned them on me. "This guy?" she whispered in a broken voice. "You're giving it all away to *this* guy?" Her chest heaved with a frustrated sob. "You tell me to have integrity and not sell myself out, but you just sold our *family* out."

Slap.

"Mr. Anderson!" Lange said, chuckling, bringing everyone's attention to where Bash stood, wiping his feet on the doormat, mine and Angel's included. My stomach came up in my throat, and I thanked every entity there was that I'd told him last night. "I was just coming to see you. Why don't we go out to your new shop, it's a little melodramatic in here. Allie's offspring needs a leash."

"Excuse me?" I said, my feet propelling me forward.

I saw Bash's eyes glaze over and I felt like I couldn't get there fast enough.

"No thanks," he said quietly. "Allie's *offspring* might not have the best approach," he said through his teeth, glancing at Angel with a hard glare. "But her point is spot on. Are you going to talk to Allie *privately* like she asked?"

"Ah," Lange said, oblivious to the raging lion he'd just provoked. "That's right. You're her guard dog. Maybe I was wrong about you being a professional, Bash," he said. "Maybe you need a leash, too."

The move was so fast, I never saw it. Bash had Lange by the stupid sweater vest and was up in his face.

"You need to remember that you are a guest in this house," Bash seethed. "That applies to this town, this establishment, and mine."

Lange's expression changed to fear before the sarcasm replaced it. "This guest pays the bills—"

I was between them, chest to chest with Bash before his other hand could come up and do real damage.

"He's not worth it, Bash," I said softly. "He's a weasel." I spread my fingers across his chest and pushed gently. He was as tight and hard as a boulder. "Hey." I reached up to touch his face and that broke the intensity. His eyes dropped to take me in, the glaze lifting as he saw me. "Hey," I repeated in a whisper. "He's not worth it."

Bash inhaled slowly through his nose and let go of Lange, who straightened his vest and looked at us both like we were beneath him.

I was boiling and I felt every set of eyes in the room. I didn't want all this crap publicized, our dirty laundry out there for everyone to speculate on. I'd had enough of that in my life. I needed a trap door. A large vacuum cleaner. Something to beam me up after I helped Bash shove Lange through the plate glass window.

"Please leave," I said quietly, turning to Lange with as much dignity as I could. "I can pay you what you're owed. Please just take it and leave us alone. All of us." I walked back to the counter, moving around it so that I had something to hold on to.

"No need," Lange said pleasantly. "I'm not interested."

CHAPTER SIXTEEN

"What does that mean?" Angel asked, looking around in embarrassment as if she just that moment realized there were other people in the room.

"It means no," I said in a monotone, shooting as much hatred as I could at Lange.

Lange shrugged. "Money's easy," he said. "I can get that anytime. Ownership is much more challenging." He smiled at me and ignored Angel. "Think I'll stick around. Sticky buns on the house, everyone!" he called out. "If you haven't tried them, I recommend it. I have a great chef, here."

He walked outside to answer a call, and Angel turned on her heel and glared at me before bolting out from behind the counter and out the front door the opposite way.

I turned my back to the room, staring at the coffeepot like it might save me. I was so angry, I was shaking, but I wasn't even sure at who. At Angel for putting us under a spotlight? At Lange for being so smug? Or at myself for being such a dupe.

I heard Kerri and the others start to ask for orders and drinks to get things headed to normal again, and I was grateful, but I'd been in Charmed long enough to know that nothing was going to be normal for some time. In fact, I wasn't even sure that sales would survive it. No one wanted to go eat somewhere full of drama, and if they thought that my family was in trouble in addition to the Blue Banana, that was even more fodder.

I already heard the whispers. *That guy's the owner now? What was that about money? Yeah, I heard the old man gambled their home away. That's why—*

Strong hands landed on my shoulders, squaring my back solidly against the body they were attached to. Blocking me from the world. Protecting me.

Protecting *me.*

Hot tears burned my eyes as I sucked in a breath. I was always the one looking out for someone, taking care of them, putting up the shield. Angel, my dad... There was only one person who consistently looked after *me.*

"Thank you," Bash said into my hair. "For talking me down."

"Hey, it was my turn," I said, hating the shake in my voice.

"Just breathe," he whispered. "Get your game face together. You've got this."

I snorted and swiped under my eyes, grabbing a napkin off a stack.

"You gonna tell me it's about perspective next?"

I felt a small chuckle roll through him. "I might."

I shut my eyes tightly as my fists clenched on the countertop. "Do you know how hard I worked to *not* give people a reason to talk about me?"

"I know," he said.

I took a deep breath and blew it out very slowly. He was right. I had to pull it together. I had to be the face of my business, even when someone threw a pie in it. I rolled my head back, met with solid chest, and he squeezed my shoulders.

"Okay," I said. "I've got this."

"You've got this."

I turned around, taking a chance on looking up into those eyes, knowing how dangerous it could be at that proximity.

"Keep holding your head up," he said softly. "Look people in the eye like you are right now. You have nothing to hide from."

"Do you think I sold out my family?" I asked on a whisper.

"I think you've done everything under the sun to *protect* your family," he said. "Including your dad's honor. Don't worry about Angel. She just has a mouth."

"You know he's gonna be ruthless with you now, too," I said.

Bash didn't blink, the same serious affection burning in his eyes.

"Bring it on."

When he left—or to be exact, when he poured himself a to-go cup of coffee, grabbed a cinnamon roll, stared down exactly nine customers at the bar who were not being subtle in their whispered conversations, hit up Nick in the kitchen to keep an eye on things and let his fingers brush mine in passing—Carmen finally spoke.

She'd been hovering in the hallway entrance since Angel's big show, soaking it all up in her introspective way, no doubt.

"You okay?"

I nodded. "I'm fine."

"That fuckhead is lucky Angel came in when she did," she said. "I was about to show him what we learn growing up in a *barn*. Seriously?"

I chuckled in spite of nothing being funny. "I know you were."

"You and Bash," she said, skipping ahead to the lighter subject, almost making me laugh as I wondered when that became the lighter subject. "When did that happen?"

I gave her an innocent look. "Nothing has happened."

"So, you and Bash," she repeated. "When did that happen?"

I rolled my eyes. "It's—complicated."

"Aren't they all," she said drolly.

I sat on the stool for the second time this week, and once again thought of the stern look my dad would give me for that. He wasn't a big believer in showing weakness. Neither was I, and right now I was having a hell of a time. Especially knowing that Angel had left angry and disappointed and wasn't answering phone calls. Not just mine. I saw Bash try her a couple of times, too.

"You know, Bash isn't your only friend," Carmen said, making me meet her eyes as she leaned against the bar. "There are other people you can trust, too. That you can talk to."

"I know," I said. "I kind of suck at that, but I know."

"Well, it appears that you're back to needing an assistant tonight, possibly," she said.

"Yeah," I said, my gut hurting that I didn't know where Angel went. "She will most likely refuse the job, now."

"What time do we need to be there?" she asked.

I crossed the space between us and hugged her.

"Thank you," I said. "For agreeing to probably the dumbest job ever assisting the most ridiculous position ever."

"Well, when you put it like that, how can I turn that down?" she said. "I'll bring my party shoes." She grabbed my hand. "Allie, Angel will be okay. She'll be back and she'll be fine."

Hot, angry tears burned my eyes. The way she'd looked at me—

Don't show weakness.

"Yeah," I breathed, blinking away.

Lange took his time coming back in, and when he did, my eyes followed him.

"Excuse me," I said to Carmen as I headed the same direction.

"Something I can help you with, Allie?" he said, his back turned to me.

I didn't stop at my desk. I followed him all the way to his little corner, and when he turned around his expression was surprised if not a little bit afraid.

"It doesn't take a big man to pick on a little girl," I said. "You can do and say what you want to Bash and I, we're pretty tough. But if you talk to or about my daughter like that again, I will rip your head off and shit down your throat. Are we clear?"

Lange's eyes widened. "Classy. Is that a threat?"

"I grew up in a trailer park, remember?" I said. "Try me."

* * *

I paced our little self-claimed space behind a wooden folding screen draped with blankets. Carmen brought a large fold-out table and a basket of sodas, waters, and snacks, along with three chairs. She came prepared.

I came a nervous wreck. I'd spent the entire afternoon on the phone, trying to find out where Angel was. I knew where she probably was, but I didn't have that number, and no one else was spilling. Vonda wasn't there yet, or I would have spilled plenty. Bash and his truck had hit the road looking for Angel, telling me not to worry. He'd be there before it started.

I could care less when it started.

"What am I doing here?" I said behind my hands, poking holes in the sod in my very spiky heels. Brilliant idea to put us back there.

We were supposed to wear what people would associate with our jobs. I'd never in my life worn heels and slacks and such a nice blouse to work, but my sneakers and jeans and T-shirt weren't quite the attire for this.

The formal dress hung on the screen. I couldn't wait to strip under the stars with the Lucky Charm teeming with people on the boardwalk behind us. That was going to be awesome.

"You're trying to win some money and get your picture on the town's travel brochure at the Chamber of Commerce," Carmen said, fiddling with my hair. She'd fixed it for me, fastening it over one shoulder with a black ribbon that went with both outfits and would show off the bare back and shoulders of the dress. Also, supposedly, the stage was being decorated with a variety of wildflowers from the florist, and that would complement me well. Like I knew anything about any of that shit.

"God," I muttered.

"Anything on Angel yet?" she asked.

"Out of my 240 calls? No," I said. "But I'm about to pull out the big guns."

At the police station putting out an APB on you. Now would be a good time to answer me.

I clicked send on the text and showed Carmen.

She snorted. "That ought to make her shit her pants."

"Or make me shit mine if she doesn't ans—" My phone dinged.

Jesus, Mom, I'm fine.

Relief, immediately followed by white hot anger flooded my veins.

I jabbed at the button and it started to ring.

"She'd better pick up," I muttered.

"Yes, Mother," she answered, her tone sarcastic.

"When I call you, you'd better answer," I seethed.

"I just did," she said.

"Not the other forty-five times, you didn't," I said. "So I suggest you find a job to pay for that phone, because come Monday I'm not anymore."

"Mom!"

Funny how the sarcasm left.

"No. You make a scene, storm out, leave me high and dry with no help tonight, and then play me by pulling a disappearing act?" I said. "If you're adult enough to do all that, you're adult enough to pay your own phone bill."

"Mom, seriously," she said.

"Do you know Bash isn't even here getting ready because he's been driving all over town looking for your pouting little ass. All because you were upset?" I continued to pace. Thank God I wasn't wearing the spiky shoes yet or I'd be aerating the grass. "You didn't like what you heard? Well, guess what, baby girl. Grow up. We don't always get things our way. I certainly didn't get my way when you informed half of Charmed about Pop's money and what he did. Right before a town vote where I could have actually won enough money to pay for two years of college."

There was silence on the other side.

"Wherever you are, little girl," I said. "You'd better be home when I get home."

I hung up and put the phone on Carmen's table with a loud *thunk* as Alan Bowman sauntered by.

"Hey, Greene Bean," he said. "I heard about all the teenage angst at your place today. Sorry to hear about all the drama."

I'll bet.

"Yeah, Alan," I said. "You and Katrina need to pop out one or two so you can truly appreciate the glory."

He barked out a laugh. "Well, no kid of mine would embarrass me like that in public, I know that. I'd control that kid like a puppet." He winked and walked on.

"Uh-huh," I said to his retreating back. "Because it's *just* like having a puppet. Total control." I sighed. "Douche."

She winced. "You make such a strong case for having kids."

"Oh, my God," I said, sinking into a chair. "I don't have enough lives for all the heart attacks."

"What?" said a familiar voice to my left. I turned to see Bash frowning at me. "What's wrong?"

I held up a hand as I stood. "Nothing," I said. "I just talked to Angel, she's fine." I closed my eyes. "Or she is until I get home and duct tape her to her bed."

"Where is she?" he asked.

"She didn't say, but I can guess," I said.

"Damn it, where's Vonda?" Bash said, enunciating her name like it had gone rotten.

"I haven't seen her."

"Are you two ready?" Carmen asked.

I blinked and reminded myself why we were here. And then let my eyes see past the red haze of my blood pressure.

Bash had on the suit without the jacket. Black slacks. Black shirt. Both looked as if celestial beings had come down to sew them perfectly around his body.

"So unfair," I breathed.

"What is?"

I licked my dry lips and almost had to do it again as his gaze dropped to watch. I cleared my throat.

"Um, your quick change isn't much of a change," I said.

"I don't think they'll sue me over it," he said, smiling, letting his eyes drift over my face. "You doing okay, Al?"

I gave him a fake perky smile. "Game face."

Bash chuckled. "Let's do this."

"Okay guys," Kia said, coming around back of all the dividers with a clipboard in her hand. "We're about to begin. You should have the schedules posted on your tables—"

"I'm here, everyone!" Vonda sang through a microphone, cutting off Kia as she jogged up from the Lucky Charm. She must have parked at the bakery. "So sorry I'm late!"

Kia didn't even have a microphone. I watched the look on her face as the clipboard dangled next to her side and her shoulders dropped. She handed the clipboard to Vonda as she ran up in all her glory, and turned and walked out of sight.

"I think we just lost Kia," Carmen said.

"And Miss Sparkly has no idea."

Bash met her at the end of the tables.

"Miss Sharp," he said.

"Oh," she said, looking a little flustered and harried. Possibly also wondering where her female parts melted to in his presence. "Hello Bash, don't you look nice."

Any other circumstances, I would have laughed out loud.

"Where's your son?" he asked.

"My—" Her expression changed from confusion to mild annoyance as it probably dawned on her what he was asking. She put a hand over her headset mic. "My son is out with a friend," she said. "And we don't have time for this tonight, guys. Let's focus." At the seriousness in Bash's expression, she sighed and added, "I believe he's out with a *guy* friend."

She moved on with a flourish, chattering into her mic as if we were going live to the world.

"We're getting an audience guys, so let's keep the backstage chatter down to a hum, please," she said.

"Backstage?" Bash said. "We're standing outside in the grass behind the pavilion."

We did our intros, at which time we got to see just how many people were interested enough to show up. It was a decent enough showing. Carmen kept sneaking around the pavilion to get updates, telling us the crowd was growing.

Fabulous.

When it was time to do the essays, we were last on the list. The backstage hum quieted as we all listened to where the others had gone with it. Being last could be a death march, if the crowd was bored and started tuning out, but if Bash could be Bash—it might be the final impression to undo the public debacle of the day.

Alan and Katrina took turns reading in a very cute back-and-forth exchange. Bash glanced at me sideways, and I shook my head. He chuckled, knowing fully well that wasn't going to happen. Mr. Masoneaux and Mrs. Boudreaux were pretty straight forward, and poor Miss Mavis and Mr. Townsend sounded as if they left theirs at home at first and then pulled it off with self-deprecating humor and drew a big applause.

I felt the warmth of Bash's hand on the back of my neck, sending happy shimmies everywhere else as I looked up at him. His eyes looked up to something.

"You trust me?" he asked, a smile pulling at one corner of his mouth.

"Oh shit."

The smile turned into a laugh as he dropped a kiss on my forehead and grabbed my hand. "Come on."

CHAPTER SEVENTEEN

As we walked hand-in-hand out of my little hidey-hole to the path where the other nominees were standing and listening, I couldn't help but sort of pretend that was normal. I liked holding his hand like we were a couple—in public. I liked watching Katrina's eyes widen when he let go of my hand to rest his low on my hip possessively as we walked the three steps up to the pavilion. Like we were more than friends. Familiar with each other. Almost—

No, we weren't that, but familiarity had definitely changed. He'd been all over my legs and ass just two days ago, so as far as I was concerned he could claim and possess whatever of mine that he wanted.

My thoughts stumbled over each other in shock at that realization. At knowing how far we'd ventured into very foreign territory in such a very short time.

Bash pulled me tightly against him as we took the stage and waved, and my heart sped up when I saw the crowd. It had doubled since the intros. Holy Jesus.

We did another quick introduction, this time of each other, completely off the cuff in a kind of *look at us, we can be cute, too* thing.

Then he signaled to Vonda. "Can you bring me a chair?" The look of alarm was all over her normally beaming face, but she grabbed the nearest folding chair and met him across the stage. "Thank you."

"Have a seat, Allie," he said, placing the chair behind me.

"What are you doing?" I whispered, trying not to move my lips.

His gaze slid over me. "Trust me."

He turned back to the crowd as I sat down and crossed my legs, unsure what I was really supposed to shoot for.

I watched him gear up for the crowd, and watched them automatically fall in love with him. It was like going back in time to high school, when all he had to do was walk down the hall and his charisma made everyone want to be near him. I always felt a mixed bag of reactions on that. Like I had some sort of special code that gave me back door access to Sebastian Anderson. The vulnerable side of him no one else saw. That could talk with me for hours and share his life over leftovers that were just going to be thrown out. That was precious. But on the flip side, they got him in public. They got to hang out with him, have lunch, go to parties. They got to touch him and live in the world with him. I got the real boy. They got the public one.

I always wished for both.

"I wanted Allie to get to sit for a second," Bash said into the microphone. "As you all know, she runs the best eating place in town." There was a pause for clapping and I smiled and wished he'd get the spotlight off me. "This lady has been on her feet all day, and now has to wear these—ice picks strapped to her feet—back there in the grass. Do you see her shoes?" I laughed and wiggled a foot as the crowd laughed. "Seriously, I don't know how you ladies do it. But she's doing it."

He paused and pulled the mic free from the base and looked at the ground for a moment.

What are you doing, Bash?

"We had to write an essay," he said. "About how we'd help this town. What we bring to the table. And why you should vote for us to represent the heart of Charmed." His head moved slowly from side to side like he was in deep thought. "I have the assignment," he said, pulling a folded piece of paper from his slacks pocket and holding it up to chuckling from the crowd. "But if you'll indulge me for a second, I think I'm just going to wing it."

He turned to meet my gaze.

Trust me.

"I could say that Allie and I grew up here among you, but so did the others," he said. "I could talk about the glory days in high school," he said with a grin, bringing smiles from below. "But so can Alan Bowman. I want to talk about Allie and I as a team."

My stomach flipped a hundred times a second as he said those words, looking at me.

"She's my best friend," he said. "She has been since we were teenagers and worked together at the Blue Banana." He paused for a breath and I held mine as his eyes bored into me. "I delivered her baby there, almost sixteen years ago." He glanced away from me at the crowd when some surprised murmurs rippled through and I let my breath go. "Yeah, not that many people know that. I'm also her daughter's godfather and honorary uncle, another not-well-known fact but something I take enormous pride in." His eyes landed back on me with something else in them. Something scary and new and terrifying and wonderful and something I couldn't put a name to but I wanted so badly it brought me to my feet.

"Allie sells my honey in her diner. I post her menu in my apiary. We've talked each other out and down from some pretty precarious places, because that's what friends are for. Not just when you fall, but when you soar."

It was like everyone else left. My vision swam with tears and all I could see was him. Talking about our life together like we—

"Allie and Angel are my family," he said. "It's not perfect, and if you've ever experienced a teenager, you know what I'm saying." I laughed through my tears and I heard the burst of laughter from the crowd but I couldn't look away from him. "But we are there for each other in good and bad the best way we can be because that's what *family* does."

Bash's voice caught, and he stopped to clear his throat. My feet started to move on their own as the tears fell freely from my eyes.

"What he's saying," I said, taking the microphone from his hand. My hands trembled, my voice shook with emotion, but what he'd started had to be completed. "Is that we are already a team. In all the important ways. We already serve this town in ways you love. We're not perfect, either. We have flaws." I stopped and laughed as I swiped at my eyes, and was amazed to hear them laughing with me. "We have problems, just like you do, but we stand together, so if you'll put us together as one with Charmed, you'll have the representation you can be proud of." I drew a tear-filled breath and smiled the best I could. "Thank you."

Bash pulled me into his arms, and everything drained from me as I buried myself in his chest and the applause roared from seemingly everywhere. I didn't care anymore. If they liked us, great. If they didn't, none of that mattered, because—because this man that was wrapped around me, that held me so tightly with his face in my hair had stood before our world and told it that we were us. He'd given me the gift of both sides.

Someone took the mic from my hand as I wrapped my arms around him, wishing I never had to let go. Nothing ever felt so good. So right. If only there weren't hundreds of people watching the goodness.

I pulled back and looked up into eyes probably as raw as mine felt.

"All right, that was amazing," said Vonda's voice over the speakers. A low rumble of thunder could be heard miles away. "Let's move on to the grand finale before it decides to rain on us," she said, giggling. "Everyone who hasn't changed yet, go get changed!"

We walked off, back through the pathway, back to our hole, where Carmen was crying. She picked up the paper schedule and smacked Bash with it.

"Damn you," she said.

He laughed, but he looked like he'd been punched between the eyes. He sank into one of the chairs and ran his hands through his hair.

"You okay?" I asked him, still dabbing at my eyes.

Carmen grabbed the dress in one hand and a blanket in the other, trying to figure out how we were going to do this.

"That just—went somewhere I never saw coming," he said. "That was—"

I knelt to my knees in front of him. "That was amazing."

The look he gave me melted me right into the ground and I was totally okay with that.

"Come on," Carmen said. "Bash can you help me hold up these blankets so she can get naked without everyone seeing?"

I think we both heard *get naked* and knew that was a bad plan. He pulled keys from his pocket and gestured with a nod over my shoulder.

"My shop is literally right there," he said.

I turned to follow his gaze to the building next to the bakery. He was right, it was almost throwing distance.

"It's locked up tonight, no one is there. You can change and be back in five minutes."

I pulled off the shoes. "Without these, I'll be back in three. Let's go."

We were off at a run, had the door open and I was in Bash's office and literally naked except for my panties within thirty seconds. I stepped into the dress and pulled it over my boobs, still unable to believe I actually bought a backless dress that I had to wear with no bra, for an event with Bash. Granted, nothing was going on then except some dreams, but—

And that's when I realized I hadn't been dreaming about him. Interesting. I guess my real life with him had become active enough not to need the supplements.

Carmen helped me fasten the clasp behind my neck, I was already wearing the jewelry that sparkled well with it, and she'd been dead on about the hair style. It was both pretty and sexy with the bare back, and—once again, the thought of standing so exposed like that with him now—it was making my blood rush to some serious places.

"Okay, am I good?" I asked. I knew my face was probably a wreck, now, but I didn't have time to worry about that. And this was mostly for distance viewing, anyway.

"You look stunning," she said. "My lord, you and Bash will make a hot couple."

My gaze flew to meet hers.

"Tonight," she added quickly. "You'll make a hot couple tonight." She glanced around. "Wow, he's got a lot of pictures around."

"Yeah, he had a bunch at the apiary, too," I said, glancing cursorily at the black and white photos in his office and also in the showroom up front. My eyes stopped on one that was framed by his computer: A close-up of Angel a couple of years ago, laughing at the camera, her hair blowing around her. Goose bumps covered my skin. He had that photo there like a parent would. "He likes old pictures of the town. We ready? I'll just leave this stuff here and come back for it afterward."

We ran past the stacks of honey jars and packages of things I didn't have time to check out, locked the door behind us and back up the hill. A little more challenging with the open concept, trying to keep things from bouncing out.

I could see Bash walking back to his table to get his jacket, so I pulled my shoes back on, pulled a powder compact from Carmen's everything basket to pull things slightly more together, and swiped some sparkly gloss on my lips.

"You're not cold?" Carmen asked. The air was thick and warmer than it had been, but the pending rain had it feeling damp and it was getting chilly.

"I'm okay," I said. "My nervous breakdown will keep me warm."

We were last on the list, and I was thoroughly giddy about that. I was behind Alan and Katrina in line, however, and I wasn't particularly fond of that. Especially when Alan turned around.

"Holy shit shows," he said, looking me over.

"Really?" I said.

Katrina turned around, her eyes going from me to her husband, and she whacked him on the back of the head.

"Really?" she echoed, as he turned back around.

I concentrated on the big evil mountain ahead. I blew out a breath. It was okay, I'd conquered it, I could do it again. Bash was here. If tonight proved anything, it was that there was nothing I couldn't manage with him by my—

When he walked around the corner, buttoned up and adjusting his cuffs like something from a James Bond movie, all other thoughts left my head. When he looked up and did a double take on me, I knew we were done for. I took a deep breath, and attempted normal, while my very exposed cleavage suddenly felt every molecule of air move as his eyes blazed a path.

"Wow," I breathed as he walked closer.

"Still delicious?" he asked, his gaze burning into me with a wicked playfulness.

"I—can't even be trusted with that word right now," I managed, running a finger down his lapel and watching his pupils take over the blue at both my touch and probably my chest.

I turned around to get in line, reveling in the sound of the strong exhale as he got my naked back.

"Fuck," he muttered.

Okay, there was a rush in that much power. I was lightheaded with it. I tilted the bare side of my neck to tease him a little.

"Problem?"

"Not as long as I keep this jacket on," he said. "God, you kill me in this dress."

I giggled. "Oh? As in?"

"As in I have a wood the size of China," he muttered.

I had to clap a hand over my mouth. "Really?" I whispered.

The finger that traced down my spine as his lips brushed my ear made me suck in a breath.

"Care to check?" he breathed.

Yes. Yes, I would.

"Probably shouldn't," I said with a grin over my shoulder to match his.

His lips were right there. Apparently many things were right there. Dear God, we weren't going to survive these clothes, much less this night.

The mountain was looming and his hands slid up my arms to my shoulders. We both blew out breaths as if to remember where we were and what we were doing.

"You know what I'm going to say, right?" he said as he pulled me back against him.

"I've got this?" I said weakly.

"You've got this."

"Okay."

It was my turn to look up the ladder.

"Just like last time," he said.

"Okay," I repeated.

I heard Katrina and Alan's names announced as she no doubt flounced down the stairs, and I knew I had to get up there. One foot stepped above the other as my heart pounded in my ears.

"Don't look up my dress," I said.

"Wouldn't dream of it."

"You're looking now, aren't you?"

I heard a chuckle. "Only as moral support."

"You're a prince," I said, hearing the shake. "Okay," I whispered to myself as I topped the surface. "You've got this. Just hold on. Keep walking."

I didn't stop. I kept moving blindly over the top on trembling legs, thinking of that suit waiting for me on the other side. All I had to do was lock eyes with Bash and I'd be fine. Just—

Light so blinding it could have come from heaven hit me with a *ffomph* sound. Our names were announced and I was supposed to come down, but I couldn't see anything.

I couldn't see anything. Or anyone.

"Allie, I'm down here," I heard.

Panic, deep-seated and fear-driven, washed over me as I flailed with a hand in front of my face, desperately trying to find Bash. Find the steps. Find the earth. I sucked in a gulp of air and forced myself to stay on my feet—to not react like I always did. Like everything in me wanted to. Flattening myself to the ground.

People are watching. You can't do that. Fuck. Shit. Please don't do this.

"Turn that damn light off!" Bash yelled, his voice getting closer as I felt his steps jogging up to me. "I've got you," he said then, grabbing my hand. "Stay on your feet, we're walking down together."

"I'm sorry," I said under my breath, holding onto him with a death grip.

"Nothing to be sorry about," he said. "They already love you. Just smile."

We made it to the bottom, all lined in various flowers I tromped in my heels, and all my newfound confidence and girly power vanished. All I wanted was to go home and put on my normal clothes and be me again. I could be strong and deal with weakness when I felt like myself. This had me all out of whack and embarrassed and put in a literal spotlight for the second time that day, and I'd had enough.

"Okay folks," Vonda was saying. "Time for you to vote and head over to the new banquet building. Go to charmed royalty dot com and click on your favorite King and Queen choice."

"It's like a reality show," Miss Mavis said, shuffling by. "We're famous."

Famous. I wanted to tell her I'd always been famous in this town and it wasn't what it was cracked up to be.

"You okay?" Bash asked, his hand on the back of my neck. "You look—off."

I laughed, feeling exhausted. "Off. Great."

"You know what I'm saying," he said, taking my hand and pulling me back out of the crowd, out of the flow of the herd. "You went a little gray up there. I'm worried about you."

I shook my head. "Just—some things never change," I said. "You can dress the girl up, but the same crap's still underneath."

"Same crap?" Bash said. "What, because you're afraid of heights?"

"This isn't fear of heights, Bash," I said. "That's *ooh, I don't want to look down*. What I experience is unforgiving, unreasonable, heart-stopping, anxiety-ridden, paralyzing terror to the point of blacking out."

"I know."

"I know you know," I said. "Until tonight, you're the only person I've ever let see that, and it's humiliating. I've—"

I couldn't talk about it anymore. I had to keep walking. Get back to my table and get my shit so I could move on to the next stop and get this damn night over with.

"You've what?" he asked, making me stop and turn around.

"I've managed to unveil every weakness I have in one day," I said. "In front of the whole town. My dad. My daughter. My fear." I took a deep breath. "You."

"Me?" He walked closer, hands in his slacks pockets, looking like something out of a magazine. "Are you saying I'm a weakness of yours?"

"I'm saying you broke me out there." I gave him a small smile. "My feelings for you were all over that stage."

His progress stopped, and his gaze dropped to some point on the ground as his expression went troubled.

"Yeah," he said softly. "I guess mine were, too."

When he looked up, the unspoken question was so loud, so intense, it made me pull in a quick breath and grab a support pole nearby.

What are those feelings?

Did my eyes say that, too?

Because I couldn't answer that. I couldn't honestly say I'd ever been in love, or had strong feelings for anyone, or at least anything I could identify as that. I didn't see a lot of romantic love growing up, I only saw reasons *not* to get my heart involved. So, what was this thing I had going on lately with my best friend? I had no idea.

"Come on, y'all," Carmen said, speed-walking past us as we stared at each other. "Let's get over there before the rain hits. Vonda said we can get our tables tomorrow, and I've already put the basket in my car, so..." She turned around when we didn't answer. "Am I—interrupting—"

"No," I said.

"No," Bash said simultaneously. "We're good," he added, putting his carefree smile back on. "Let's go dance."

"I'm not dancing," I said, falling into step beside him.

His fingertips skimmed my back. "You are *so* dancing."

CHAPTER EIGHTEEN

I could not believe the amount of people turning out for this thing. It was a dance. For nothing. No festival, no carnival, no honeycomb anythings. Just *hey, let's dance after we vote for the world's stupidest contest.*

That was evidently my town.

I probably wouldn't call it stupid if we actually won, and twenty grand slid our direction, but I didn't see that happening. Other than the big emotional tug Bash had mastered, all I'd done for us is show how many problems I have. I needed to let go of any notion that we had a chance.

"Holy glitter balls," Carmen said as we walked through the doors to the thump-thump of some high energy retro dance tune. "It's like—prom came back and exploded all over this room."

"I never went to prom," I said, looking around at the cheesy sparkle everywhere. And I do mean everywhere. Every corner, table, and ceiling space was draped, pinned, or stuck with something shiny. Most of which also shimmied, spun, or swayed when air hit it. "But if this is what I missed, I'm okay with it."

"I must have been drunk enough to forget all this," Bash said. "Good God."

"Weren't you prom king?" Carmen asked.

"No, that was—what's his name with the Camaro," Bash said. "Alan would remember. He keeps up with all that."

"Of course, you'd remember the car," she said.

"Hell yeah," he said. "That car was fine."

I listened to them with an increasing distance, as one who couldn't relate whatsoever. My senior year was spent waddling down judgmental hallways, planning for a baby. When they were worrying about what to wear for prom, I had to borrow my dad's car to go find secondhand maternity clothes. Once again, knowing now that he had a windfall of money at his fingertips that would have made life a million times easier, poked at me.

I had to let that go, too.

"Earth to Allie."

I blinked myself back to see Bash gazing down on me. We were alone, as Carmen had run off to greet her handsome guy.

"I'm sorry, what?" I said, pressing a hand against the butterflies in my stomach.

"Where'd you go?" he asked.

I shook my head. "Nowhere, really. Just—" I smirked. "I'm probably having a pity party for myself and someone needs to kick my ass."

Bash turned to face me head-on, resting both forearms on my shoulders, essentially pulling me in toward him but in a casual way. Not that anything felt casual with him anymore. Close was close. And a slow song came on. God help me.

"I'd be happy to kick your ass," he said softly, humor dancing in his eyes again. "But you have to dance with me first."

"I don't dance."

"Because?"

I tilted my head, getting a little of that previous thrill back when his eyes lowered to my exposed neck.

"I never learned."

He pulled me closer. "See, now I take that as a challenge."

I was all too aware that we were just standing next to a table, not on the dance floor, and that there were a million other people in the room, but the way he was looking at me...

His hands slid down my back ever so slowly, prompting mine to creep up his chest as I felt my breathing quicken.

"Feel that little sway?" he said, his face achingly close to mine as we moved the tiniest bit.

"Mmm," I said, feeling those damn magnets tugging us together.

People, Allie. There are people. Judgey people.

"We're dancing," Bash said. His lips brushed my forehead.

"You know, we don't do so well close up," I whispered, closing my eyes. The people were gone.

It was intoxicating. The smell of him. The feel of his hands on my bare skin. The sensation of the heavy slow music soaking into my bones. Him holding me tighter until we were moving as one. I slid my arms around him under his jacket, and he sighed into my hair.

"I think we're doing just fine," he whispered.

I chuckled, and lifted my face to look at him, knowing it would be a mistake. Knowing his mouth would be right there. Knowing we wouldn't be able to resist.

He was only centimeters away and his eyes went serious.

"God, you're beautiful," he breathed. "You take my damn breath away and you don't even know it."

I knew the feeling. All the air left my lungs, left the room, the planet, the universe. All there was in my head space was Bash. His voice, his body, his eyes, his smell, and his mouth that was right there saying things like that, and I wanted to kiss him so badly I could taste it.

"When did this happen?" he said, the words barely making sound, but I felt them.

"Everyone!" screeched Vonda's voice throughout the room, a sound so jarring that Bash and I both jumped.

My heart felt like it skipped about eight beats, and I had to grab a chair to steady myself as I let go of Bash. The four people sitting at the table next to where we were doing whatever the hell we were just doing all looked up at us with knowing grins.

Sweet Jesus.

They knew. I didn't know shit about anything, I barely remembered my name at that moment, but *they knew*. Bash and I exchanged looks that said we both looked like we'd been hit by a bus. We needed to get out of there. Go anywhere. *Be* anywhere but there, surrounded by fifty million eyes.

"We have the results!" Vonda exclaimed.

"So, we can go as soon as they call this thing, right?" I asked.

"Absolutely," he said.

"It was kind of a landslide," Vonda said in her singsongy voice. "Are you ready to hear who your new royalty will be?"

Good grief.

"Really?" I said, as everyone yelled their excitement. "Cheesy, much?"

"Your new Honey King and Honey Queen of Charmed and winners of several local business prize packages and a cash prize of ten thousand dollars each, is—Sebastian Anderson and Allie Greene of An—"

The names of our businesses were drowned out by the roar of crazy, and Bash turned to me with stunned exhilaration on his face.

"We did it!" All I could do was look at him wildly as all the clapping and hooting and hollering went on around us. I couldn't even speak. His hands cradled my face. "Baby, we did it!"

My hand was in his and we were walking up to wherever Vonda was before I realized I was moving, and the only coherent thought I had as I walked on numb legs was *he just called me baby.*

Silly little crowns went on our heads, and we laughed as flashes went off everywhere and people cheered. Lanie and Nick had shown up from out of nowhere, and it warmed my heart to see Nick whistling and doing a fist pump. Carmen was jumping up and down and Sully was laughing at her. Alan and Katrina were smiling *fakily* and basically sulking. Kia was there, standing off to one side, alone. Smiling and clapping, but looking ready to bolt. I felt a little envious.

I had never made it to a prom, and now there I was, amidst all the glitter and paper ribbons, voted prom queen.

Except better. Because it came with ten grand.

And Bash.

Did I just think that?

"Okay, we're going to let the King and Queen dance, and then you all can do whatever you want," Vonda said as another slow song began.

"I don't—" I began, but my words were cut off by being lifted off my feet into Bash's arms. I shrieked but the crowd loved it, applauding louder.

"I don't want to hear it," he said, depositing me on the dance floor but not letting go.

I laughed as I held onto my plastic crown and him. Definitely him. I never wanted to ever let go of him. And that was a rocketing sobering thought.

I let my hands slide to the back of his neck, as those eyes I adored so much drank me in, my fingers going into his soft hair. It was fair game for what his fingers were doing on the skin at the base of my spine. He was teasing along the line of my dress, and it was maddening.

"This is crazy," I said on a laugh. "What were they thinking?"

"I know, right?" Bash said. "Maybe they just think we're hot."

I laughed out loud. "Well, then they should be bowled over by these sexy crowns," I said. "I think half the glitter on mine just fell down my chest."

Which of course brought his gaze exactly there. "They are looking extra sparkly—"

"Stop," I said, laughing, pulling his head so close that the natural thing—what had *become* the natural thing—happened. He kissed me.

Just a brush of lips. Soft. Sweet. Another one, and my head started to spin. Our bodies swayed, our lips found each other. It was a potion like none other I'd ever experienced, and I felt myself getting drunk on it. On him. A flash went off nearby, and then I remembered.

My eyes popped open.

"We're in public," I said. Way more than public. We were dancing alone in front of the entire town.

"Do you care?" he asked, his gaze uncharacteristically serious.

I was so dizzy with the need to kiss him again, I could barely process the question, but I shook my head slightly and smiled up at him.

"No, but maybe we need to figure out what we're doing before the *Gazette* tells us—and Angel—what we're doing," I said softly.

Humor tugged at a corner of his mouth. "You might have a point."

"So…"

The floor started to fill with couples congratulating us and then wrapping themselves around each other, and I met Bash's eyes.

"Let's go."

* * *

The sky opened up thirty seconds after we were out the door. Bash's shop and vehicle was easily only maybe fifty yards away, but in full blowing downpour, it took forever. He gave me his suit jacket when we left the banquet hall, and even with that I was soaked through by the halfway point.

"Hang on!" I yelled over the din, pulling off my shoes. "I can't run in—"

My second shriek of the evening happened as he swept me off my feet and kept going.

It wasn't graceful. It wasn't the romantic-looking gesture you'd imagine, since one leg didn't make the swoop and so was dangling and flopping very ladylike as he ran. If my hoo-hah hadn't seen rain before, it did now.

We were laughing when we made it under Bash's awning and he set me on my feet, him leaning over on his knees to catch his breath.

"I need to start running again," he wheezed.

"Carrying a woman?" I added.

"I used to carry a heck of a lot more in the service," he said standing upright and sucking in air as he dug out his keys. "I'm getting weak."

"Some people might call that getting normal," I said, slinging the wet locks from my face and pulling the useless pretty hair ribbon free.

He slid me a sideways glance. "Like I said."

I texted Angel.

Please tell me you're home and not out in this.

He left the light off and locked the door behind us, not that anyone else might still be out there in this weather. But the indoor warm security lighting illuminated the room beautifully. Honey glowed from the stacked jars arranged randomly among the other products. Candles of all different fragrances sparkled in pretty wrappings. Boxes of household wax, raw beeswax, a cosmetic line of lip balm called WaxMackers, and a variety of other products filled the room. I knew Bash didn't physically make all these things, he contracted some of it out, but all of it came from his hives. His bees. His vision. His copyright.

"It's beautiful in here, Bash," I said. "You've really outdone yourself."

"It was a team effort," he said. "Everyone at the apiary had a part in this, and they still split their time to help work sales here." Even in the low light, I could see his frustration. He raked his wet hair back and ran that hand over his face. "Losing so much of my hive this summer—that wasn't part of the plan. I should have four new hires by now, working here solely."

"And then Lange."

He laughed bitterly. "Yeah. Lord only knows what that cost me. But it's my own fault."

"How's that?"

"I got cocky," he said. "Bee farming is a gamble, like any crop. You're at nature's mercy, and anything can go wrong. You have to keep a comfortable buffer in case that happens." He shrugged. "I had a long stretch of success, and instead of socking that away into my buffer, I thought hey, a shop at the Lucky Charm! Wouldn't that be awesome? I have the money, let's do it. Signed the papers, wham, bam—Dean."

"Ugh," I said. "That was a mess."

"That was a lesson," he said, chuckling. "I knew better, and I didn't listen to my gut. I won't make that mistake again."

"All these pictures," I said, turning in a circle as I tried to call Angel. It went to voicemail and I jabbed angrily at the end button. The honey-tinted light brought a warmth to the black and white photos, almost a sepia tone, and I blew out a calming breath and tried to let it soothe me. I wandered into his office where they continued. They were from all different times, in the apiary, around town, old and new, a couple from the diner, and—"Oh my God."

I walked forward to see it better. It was from before. Way before. A double-framed snapshot of me and Bash in the diner in our teens. The first one was pre-pregnancy, I remembered it. My dad was trying to take a picture of me at the counter, and Bash had run up and photo bombed it before that was a thing. We looked so young. I looked exactly like I remembered feeling. Absolutely ecstatic that Bash Anderson was goofing around with *me*.

The second one brought tears to my eyes, because I'd never seen it before, and because I remembered that moment, too. I was very pregnant, and I'd just endured a particularly harsh ridicule from Stacey Keener, a girl from our class who'd come to eat with her friends and left a penny on a napkin with the words *cheap whore* scrawled in lipstick. I'd gone into the kitchen to cry alone, and Bash had been in there sweeping. He stopped and held me, and for a second we'd just stayed that way, his hands over mine on my swollen belly.

"How—who—" I managed, swiping at my eyes.

"Your dad," he said, walking up to stand next to me. "I've had the first one forever," he said. "Always a favorite of mine. But he gave me the other one a little over a year ago."

I turned around. "Seriously?"

"Yeah," he said. "Said he took it through the service window. Y'all weren't really getting along then, so I guess he didn't say anything."

I stared at it in awe. "What, he walked around with a camera?"

Bash held out his hands. "I don't know," he said. "I didn't ask. I just—I love that picture. Not what it represented, because you were sad, but it was like the first photo of the three of us."

Emotion, hard, fast, and immense slammed into me like a rogue wave. I looked at his profile as he gazed on the photo, and his image swam in a sea of tears. This man. This *man*. Who'd made us his family without—

"What are we doing, Bash?" I asked, my words more of a whisper.

He looked at me and frowned as I whisked two tears away.

"Hey."

"No, I know I'm being a girl, here, but seriously." I crossed my arms, still wearing his jacket. "I don't know—" My voice caught and I closed my eyes to pull it together. "It's not just about me. It never is. It's why I'm so clueless and never know what I'm doing—"

"What are you talking about?" he asked, looking genuinely dumbfounded.

"I'm a package deal, Bash," I said, my voice quivering. "What I do affects her. If I just mess around, it has to stay under wraps, but if I go somewhere—more serious with it, well—I've got nothing for that because I've never done it."

"Neither have I," he said.

It was falling out of me in a rush. All of it. And I was about to lose him, this version of him, lose this amazing ride we were on, because we couldn't do it.

"I can't just mess around with you, Bash," I said, more tears filling my eyes. "You're—you're—" I pointed to the picture. "You're Uncle Bash. If it goes bad, I—" I shook my head, realizing for the first time that his eyes were shiny, too. "I can't afford to lose you."

"Is that what we're doing?" he asked, his voice rough. He swiped two fingers over his eyes. "Is this just messing around?" He snorted. "Because I gotta be honest with you, Al. I'm out of my element, here. I've never—" He stopped and walked away a step and then turned back. "I want you so badly I can barely think sometimes, but it's not about that. I know sex. I can deal with sex. This is—I can't *breathe* when you're close to me. The second I leave you I'm thinking about when I can see you next, because *nothing* feels as good as this." He pointed at the ground between us. "This. This crap right here where we might be saying to hell with it all, and it might be about to come crashing down and kill me, but right now you're standing two feet away in my jacket and I am possibly the happiest man ever."

CHAPTER NINETEEN

It was impossible, the words he was saying.

I was shaking. Either from emotion or from cold, I didn't know which. No one had ever talked to me that way before. It was like watching a movie where it was happening to someone else and hollering at the character to do something. *Say something!*

Thunder crashed, rattling the building as if to highlight that.

"Please say something," he said, closing his eyes like he just gave himself a migraine.

I licked my lips as everything other than my eyes had gone as dry as sand.

"I'm not just messing around," I said, my words hushed as if maybe saying them louder would make it scarier. Even so, they felt like they were yelled through a megaphone.

He breathed out a sigh that almost sounded like a chuckle, and looked at the floor.

"Five words?" he said. "I just dumped my soul out on the floor and you give me five words?"

I was laughing through my tears before he finished.

"I'm profound like that," I said behind my hands.

My feet moved on their own, closing the space between us until one of his hands laced fingers with mine and the other wiped the stray tears from my face. His words were bouncing around my head in a haze of happy-scary, and it was terrifying and liberating and I felt like I'd just that very second graduated to adulthood.

"What do you want to do?" he asked after a moment's pause.

"I want to hear your breath catch when I get close," I said, hearing the shake in my voice but it all going away when I felt his warmth. "I want to see your eyes go all dark and sexy when you touch me." His free hand moved along my jawline, almost taking my next words away. "I want to feel that growly sigh you make in your chest when we kiss."

I looked up into his face, into his eyes, and saw more there than I knew I'd ever see in ten lifetimes. It felt like my heart was squeezing.

"Anything else?" he said, his breath warm as he hovered over my lips.

"Just that if you don't kiss me soon, I'm gonna lose my sh—"

I thought he'd land with a hunger, but it was soft. A tease. He kissed my top lip, then my bottom one, pulling that one softly into his mouth and then drawing his tongue across it.

An audible sigh escaped my throat on that one, and I felt him grin against my mouth.

"Now who's making the little noises?"

"I liked that move," I said, running my hands up his chest. My brain was already humming for more, as if it instinctively knew the doors were open. It was all I could do to stay at the slower pace he was setting. "Nice way to shut me up. Do you have more?"

He chuckled and backed up to his desk, perching on the edge of it as he pulled me tightly against him. "I'll see what I can do."

The kiss was more intense that time, his hands going into my wet hair and tilting my head the way he needed it. He dove deeper, curling my toes with the thorough exploration of my mouth, the tease of his tongue along mine that accompanied the gentle push of his jacket from my body.

Bash's mouth was hot and wet as he moved down the side of my face, down below my ear, moving down my neck. My trembling fingers worked on his buttons. I needed skin if he was going south.

"Mmm, Bash," I mumbled as he tasted his way down and I arched myself against him.

"You like that," he whispered.

"God, yes."

I leaned my head all the way back to give him access to my throat and—oh fuck, there it was. That deep growl resonating through his body as his kisses turned hungry. He moved lower, lower still, sending shooting bursts of desire to all places south as he tasted me, palming my breasts to lift them to his mouth, kissing the inside of each one before running his thumbs over my hard nipples.

My whole body moved against him in response as I moaned.

"Fuck," he muttered, his eyes taking on a dark edge as he lifted me up to straddle him.

"Mmm," I moaned again as he put all the right parts pressing together. I unzipped his pants. "Oh, God, you feel—"

He held my hips. "Jesus, Allie, you're killing me. You're gonna have me done in thirty seconds again," he said, reaching behind my neck and unfastening me in one click, peeling the wet fabric down.

Oh, there was no being fucking still when his hot wet mouth closed on my nipple, his hands caressing. Making love to my breasts with his mouth.

"You—oh God, oh God, yes—fuck."

"Shit," Bash said, his voice strained, his breath hot on my skin as I ground against him. "Allie—"

Fingers moved my thong aside, and dove inside me, making me moan as he curled his fingers against that very sensitive space and worked my clit with his thumb.

"I can't stop," I gasped. I moved on his hand, against his mouth, and I was nearly done for. "Bash—please—"

In seconds, he was inside me, growling in exquisite agony as he filled me up, stretching me.

"God, baby," he groaned, shoving the words out as if they hurt. "Fuck, you feel so good."

I was on the brink of convulsing around him, but I had to hold back. Had to watch this. Had to watch his beautiful face. The muscles in his neck tensed as he dug his fingers into the soft flesh of my ass, helping me move on him. The storm outside was like background music with a light show, every clap of thunder rumbling around us. He was gorgeous to behold as we moved with each other, but it was his eyes that captivated me. He could have watched us fuck, he could have focused on my boobs in his face, but his eyes were on mine, linking us together as we climbed.

It was the hottest, most erotic experience I'd ever had.

He shifted his hips then, his whole upper body straining with exertion as he moved me like he needed, and I gripped his head as he hit different places and the freight train came rushing in. He was bottoming out inside me, moving me up and down like I weighed nothing as we slammed into each other.

My body arched. Everything tensed as breathing ceased to be important. All that mattered was the glorious wave that was about to crash. My toes curled and my head fell back as I shook uncontrollably.

"Look—at me," he forced out.

I looked down just as it hit, primal sounds coming from me I didn't recognize. I had no control, all I could do was cry out his name and ride it out as the body-wracking orgasm slammed through me.

His roar joined my cries as he let go, his climax crashing out of him with a ferocity I'd never seen before. Hearing him growl my name as he lost all control—it was mind-blowing. Earth-shattering. And as we came back down to the planet together, wrapped up in each other and fighting for air in our lungs, I prayed it wouldn't be heartbreaking.

Several moments went by before I dared to look at him again. Burying my face in his hair as he buried his in my chest seemed much safer. It was one thing to look in his eyes while I came. Facing each other now, after *that*, and after everything that was said—that was something else entirely.

Bash was the one to take the leap, in a way that only Sebastian Anderson could get away with. Looking up at me all adorable with his face lying on my boob. I yanked his head back down and smirked.

"You're impossible."

And brilliant. He managed to make this normal.

He looked back up at me, and I was hit in the gut with déjà vu. Not the good kind. We'd been here before.

"So, I finally get to do that again after—how many years?" Bash said. "And I still don't make it longer than thirty seconds. But I blame you."

"Me?" I said, trying to go along with his banter.

"I might have been thinking about you in that dress since I saw you in it before," he said. "The live version just put me over the—"

"Well, cool," I said, dismounting him and reattaching/adjusting clothing. "Always good to be a fantasy."

Bash fixed himself, looking at me oddly. "You okay?"

"Great," I said, looking around for the clothes I'd left behind earlier. "I'll just grab these and g—"

"Whoa, whoa, whoa," Bash said, on his feet and holding a hand in front of my stomach. "What's going on?"

"Nothing," I said, avoiding his eyes. "Just getting my stuff, and—oops, my crown," I said, holding it up.

"Allie," he said, physically stepping in front of me. "What just happened?"

I raised my eyebrows sarcastically. "Seriously? An orgasm like that, and you've already forgotten?"

"Stop." The seriousness in his voice sent my gaze up to meet his, and my stomach felt like it came with it. "What are you doing?"

"The same thing you're doing," I said. "Making small talk to kill the awkwardness like you do with the *messing around* people. It's how it was fifteen years ago, and—just how it is, I guess."

His eyes closed. "Shit."

"It's okay, Bash," I said. "I get it."

I walked out of his office, needing desperately to get the hell out of there so I could come apart in the rain and no one would know the difference. I looked out the window, praying it would lighten up just a tad.

"You clearly don't," he said. "Did the sex knock your short-term memory loose? Because I could swear we said—things."

I laughed, turning around. Good God, he still stood there all warm and delicious with his shirt open, looking this time like he really had fucked someone on a table. Me. "Things. Yeah, see how grown up we are? We can't even say what those *things* are. And after we get the hot-and-bothered stuff over with, we go right back to what's easy."

"Excuse me?" he said. "I may not be great at pillow talk, but *I'm* not the one bolting out the door right now."

The words hit home. Enough to make my next comeback hold back a second.

Then my phone rang with Angel's ringtone.

Bash turned around, shaking his head as he buttoned his shirt back.

"Are you home?" I answered, feeling every last nerve ending on perma-fray.

The first thing I heard was the thing no parent ever wants to hear from their child on a phone call, when you can't get to them.

"M—m—mom?"

Hysterical sobbing filled my ears first. Rain and wind, next.

Fear, like no height had ever teased me, clenched down on my chest like a vise.

"Angel—what's wrong?" I said, my voice cracking. Bash spun around and I hit the speaker button with suddenly trembling fingers. "Where are you?"

"I don't know," she sobbed, her voice almost drowned out by the wind. "Aaron—"

There was more crying, and my brain went on overdrive.

"Where's Aaron?" I asked.

My first thought was a car wreck. My God, they were in a ditch somewhere, bleeding. She was hurt. Aaron was dead or dying. When I looked at Bash, all those same thoughts came flying out of his eyes. My heart slammed against my ribs so hard it hurt.

"I think we passed—the—the—sign for Denning," she sobbed, sounding far away like she'd dropped the phone to look around. "Maybe Forrester?"

"You're in *Forrester*?" I yelled. A wooded area about thirty minutes away with lots of twisty dark roads. Lots of prime make-out opportunities for horny teenagers. Bash's hand came up on the back of my neck. "Where's Aaron, Angel? Are the two of you okay?"

"He left."

I blinked and stared at the phone, at Bash, back at the phone. "What?"

"What do you mean, he *left*?" Bash said.

"Uncle Bash!" she said, the sobs starting up fresh. "I'm so—so—sorry!"

"Angel," Bash said, closing his eyes. "What's going on? Are you hurt? Did you—"

"We had—a fight," she cried. "He left me h—h—here. And I'm so cold!"

Rage and shock filled my soul.

"Aaron left you in the woods, in the dark—in a *storm*—and drove away?" I asked, hardly able to form the words.

"Do you have enough battery to leave your phone on?" Bash said, suddenly moving.

"Um, it's—only at ten percent."

"Don't turn it off," he barked. "Leave it on till it goes out."

He opened the door and yanked me through it, barely stopping to even close it behind him. "Hold that phone and plug it in when we get in my truck."

I didn't argue. I ran. Rain whipped into my face, but I didn't feel it. I'd forgotten my shoes, but I ran barefoot after him, not even breathing until we got in his truck.

"We're in the truck, Angel, are you still there?" I asked, staring at the snarky smiling girl in the picture on my screen.

"I'm here," she cried. She sucked in a breath. "I'm sorry, Mom."

"We'll deal with that later, boo," I said. "Just look around you. Are there any signs, any—"

"It's just dark," she said, her whispered sob shaking. "It's just me and the dark."

I held the phone to my chest as everything inside me broke. She sounded six instead of almost sixteen. Terrified.

"Are you off the road?" Bash asked, kicking the truck into gear.

"Yeah," she squeaked. "I walked for a little bit, but I couldn't see anymore, so I got behind a bush to block the wind."

"Good." He hit a button on his phone and put it to his ear. Barely three seconds passed before he spoke again. "Hey," he said in a low voice. "I know. I'm sending you a cell number. I need the coordinates immediately. It's a child in trouble and her phone's almost dead."

Her phone's almost dead. It was almost a whiteout. All the headlights illuminated was a wall of churning water. I didn't know how Bash could even tell where the road was.

"We'll never find her in this," I breathed, my stomach clenching.

He hung up, hit a button, and handed me his phone, taking mine from me. I felt like a useless shelf holding items while he went from one task to the other.

"Type in her number and hit send while I cover some ground," he said quietly. "Allie?"

I looked at his profile, stern and hard in concentration.

"Trust me," he whispered.

I looked at him with all the courage I could dig up. "Always."

"Hey, baby girl, we're coming for you," he said into my phone.

"Okay," she hiccupped.

"Just stay as low and as dry as you can."

"I think dry is over with," she said.

"Remember what I've told you," he said. "Curl yourself up, so less of your body is exposed. Protect the core. Make yourself into a ball."

There were noises of shuffling. "Okay. My phone's at three percent y'all."

Damn it, it was dying fast.

"Okay," Bash said. "Just stay like that. We're coming." His phone dinged in my hand and he glanced over. "Copy and paste that into the GPS."

I was already on it. I hit the go button and watched it think. *God, please find it. Please—*

"Got it," I said, telling it to route us and holding the phone up to Bash. "It *is* Forrester Hills. That son of a bitch," I added under my breath. I could see Bash's jaw muscles working overtime. I didn't want to ask the question, but I knew I had to. I closed my eyes and gripped the phone tighter. "Angel, are you okay? Did he hurt you?"

"Just my pride, Mom," she said. Her voice was a little stronger now that she had a lifeline and knew we were on our way. "Aaron might have a black eye, though."

Bash looked like he might rip the wheel right out of the dash.

"That's my girl," he said.

The phone beeped and hung up.

It was dead.

CHAPTER TWENTY

"Fuck," I cried, feeling the burn hit me hard now that Angel wasn't on the line. "Fuck!"

"We got it, Al," Bash said, grabbing my arm. "I will find her. I swear it to you."

Fire burned hot in my gut.

"That entitled little prick," I spat. "He—I know they bought condoms together, she wasn't clueless in this, but—he brought her out in the woods and then—" I couldn't see straight, and it had nothing to do with the rain. "He *left* her there when she changed her mind?"

"That's what I'm getting out of it," Bash said, his tone dark.

"Who does that?" I said, covering my face with my hands.

"Someone about to die," he said.

"You can't kill him," I said, dropping my hands. "I can kill him, but you can't. You have training."

"That *bitch*," he said, shaking his head. "So smug, telling us she doesn't put restrictions on him."

I closed my eyes. "She's mine."

"You get both of them?" he said. "I don't think so."

"Honestly, we can't do anything, Bash," I said. "She'd be mortified."

"Honestly, I don't care," he said. "I love that little girl more than life itself. I'd go to hell and back for her. For both of you. But I don't think he kidnapped her and dragged her out there against her will."

"No."

He flexed his hands on the wheel. "I just want her safe in this truck and then she can be all the mortified she wants."

We rode in silence for a bit, both of us lost in wherever we were. I was having sex while my daughter was trying not to. *That's* where I was. That was a messed up thought. As far as me and Bash and where we'd left off back there—I didn't know. He'd had a point. Somewhere back before Angel called me, ripping my heart out, he'd called me out, but that was a hundred miles away right now.

"Bash," I said. "Back there—"

"Not right now," he said. He rested an elbow against his window and rubbed at his chin. "Let's just deal with her first."

I nodded. "That's what I was going to say."

He nodded too, and we went back to silence. Yeah, we were great.

We turned into Forrester Hills and wound around as fast as possible, in fact Bash almost misjudged where the ditch was once. It was a hairy mess.

"Left at that road," I said, pointing.

"It's barely a road," Bash said, leaning forward to see.

"The GPS calls it a road," I said.

"Okay, I'm turning."

"Twenty-five yards," I said, straining to see ahead. "It says—we're here."

We both looked around but there was nothing to see.

Bash stopped and reached behind the seat for a big Q-beam flashlight. "Stay in here," he said.

"The hell I will," I said, opening my door. "Angel!" I yelled into the wind, a blast of cold rain slapping my face.

It was dark and cold and intimidating, and it chilled me to the bone to know she'd been out here alone like this, the wind and rain slicing at her.

Bash came around his side with the flashlight, shining into the bushes. "Angel!" he yelled.

Where was she? Wouldn't she be right there, waiting?

"Angel!" I screamed louder, the needles of fear piercing my chest. *Don't panic. Don't lose it.* "Bash, where is she?"

He yelled as loud as he could, walking in a circle, shining the light into the bushes, the trees, and adrenaline surged through me, pushing past the sick fear. I ran to the side of the road, oblivious to the cold and the sting of the wind on so much exposed skin and the gravel on my bare feet. I screamed her name into the trees, over and over, but the wind took it almost as quickly as it left my mouth. Gasping for breath, I backed up to the truck and grasped for hope as my next cry of her name was full of tears.

He was there in an instant, the flashlight propped on his hood and his hands on my face.

"Hey," he yelled. "Breathe."

The rain blown into his face was highlighted by the light. He looked like some Viking hero. And he was. He would die out there looking for my baby. I knew that. He wouldn't leave until she was found.

"What if the coordinates were wrong?" I yelled.

He shook his head. "She's here somewhere. Keep—hang on."

He left me and ran around the truck and laid on the horn.

Brilliant.

"Angel!" I continued to scream as loud as I could.

"Mom!"

I spun around at her voice. It was tiny and far away and I still couldn't see her in the rain but I had to trust that she could see the lights.

"Angel?" I cried. "Bash! Over here!"

The light swung around, and bounced as he ran around the truck. Within moments, her shadow broke through the beam and the three of us collided in a giant embrace with his arms around both of us. I felt her body shake with cold and sobs as she clung to us, and I buried my face in her wet hair.

"I'm so sorry!" she cried. "Uncle Bash, I didn't mean it, I didn't—" Her words broke as she crumbled into him, and he wrapped her against him, shielding her from the wind.

"Baby girl, you can't get rid of me that easily," he said, his head against mine and leaning over hers. "You may be a pain in the ass, but you'll always be my girl." He squeezed us against him. "Come on, get in the truck. Let's go home."

I gasped at how pale she looked when the inside lights bathed the cab. Bash nodded toward the back seat.

"There's a blanket under the seat."

Of course there was.

I found it and got in the back seat with her, wrapping it around her as he turned the truck back onto the road. Angel curled up against me like she used to when she was little, tugging on every heartstring I had.

I focused on smoothing her wet hair back, and not thinking about what could have happened. On *how many* things could have happened.

"I'm so glad we found you," I said.

"You aren't mad at me?" she asked, her voice small.

"Oh, baby," I said, my eyes fluttering closed in exhausted relief. "Mad doesn't even begin to cover it. But right now, just let me be glad you're alive, okay?"

Angel nodded, and we rode in silence for a moment.

"Do you want to tell me about it?" I asked finally.

"No," she said, her word breaking.

That one utterance ripped me in half. I wrapped my arms tighter around her and rocked side to side. In anger. In despair. In commiseration. Bash ran a thumb and finger over his eyes up there in the driver's seat.

"Uncle Bash?" she said.

"Yeah, baby."

"Thank you."

I saw his eyes in the rearview mirror. They closed for a second, and then he sighed deeply before reaching back and squeezing her hand.

"I'm really sorry about what I said the other day," she said. "That was mean, and I—I shouldn't have said it. I've been wanting to tell you that."

He nodded.

"Are you?" he asked. "Sorry?"

"Yes!"

I felt tough love coming on, and I braced myself for it. She needed it. I, however, felt about as tough as a wet noodle.

"Because I didn't hear anything from you at the diner today about it—when you weren't supposed to be there—but now you're suddenly all distraught over it. Or you just need me now."

Angel's eyes squeezed shut and more tears flowed. He'd hit his mark.

"Sweetheart, I love you," he said. "I will always love you, no matter what you do. I'd lay down my life for you in a heartbeat, but I really don't like you very much right now."

Wow. Knife to the heart. Knife to mine, even.

"I'm sorry," she whispered.

"You've been acting like a brat, the way you talk to your mom—to me—the people that love you? We don't deserve that. We don't deserve what you did today, the stunt at the diner, disappearing in a pissy little huff just to show your mom that you could, and knowing damn good and well that we'd be worried."

"I know," she said, the sobs returning. "I was just mad."

"Welcome to our life," I said, pulling a wet lock of hair off her face.

"Tonight went twenty kinds of messed up for you, baby girl, and God, I want to make him pay for that," Bash said through a tight grimace I could hear in his voice. "You didn't deserve *that.* Even though you went and bought condoms like a stupid little girl, thinking you were all grown up, you still didn't deserve to be treated like this. No man, no boy, no *anything* should ever treat you this way, do you hear me?"

She nodded. "Yes, sir."

Sir! Damn, he must have scared her senseless.

"Okay," he said. "Get your act together. That's all I'm saying on the subject."

A few moments passed.

"I just—" She stopped and took a breath and let it out slow. "He acted differently with me than most guys do. He made me feel like I was something."

"You are a million somethings," I said. "You don't need a man to give you that."

"No, I mean, he made the big gestures, you know?" she said, sitting up. "The wow kind of moments that make memories."

I couldn't imagine what kind of romantic wow moments a fifteen year old could be blown away by, and I was a little afraid to ask.

"The big gestures?"

"You told me a long time ago that you missed getting the big moments," she said. "The big cheesy proposal. Asking Pop's blessing. Somebody making you feel special."

"You can't remember being grounded but you remember that?" I said.

"I'm just saying, I thought I met somebody special, because he would take the time to think about stuff like that," she said. "I thought I was making memories." Her chin trembled. "I've never seen anyone get so mad." She took a shaky breath and wiped at her face. "It's like he turned into someone completely different. He just yanked me out of his car like I was a rag doll."

My heart was pounding so hard in my ears, I thought my head would explode. I wanted to hurt this boy-man in so many ways, and all I could do was find something meaningful to say.

"Baby, when it's someone special, he won't ask you to break rules and do things you know aren't right," I said. "He'll never hurt you like that. He'll want what makes you happy."

"But what if I never get that, either?"

Fifteen. Seriously.

"I promise you, you have time," I said.

"You're thirty-three, how old do I have to be?" she said.

I caught Bash's look in the mirror and tried to laugh, but emotion caught it up in my throat when I remembered him bearing his soul to me in his shop. On stage giving his speech. Giving her driving lessons. Talking me through the bleacher steps, rescuing me from my roof, etcetera, etcetera. Not to mention what he was doing *right now* and had done for the past sixteen years.

"You know what? I think maybe I actually did," I said, unable to look away from him. "I want you to go by Bash's new shop when you get a chance. There's a picture in there I want you to see."

She nodded. "Okay. Mom, where are your shoes?"

I licked my lips and tore my eyes away from his.

"We left in a hurry," I said, gazing out the window at the rain that was beginning to lighten up. At the Welcome to Charmed sign and the oh-so-familiar streets I'd traversed my whole life. At the diner, closed and dark, and still called The Blue Banana Grille, thank God. I had been gone a whole afternoon and evening, so it was a valid concern. And past—

"You passed our road," I said.

"Have a stop to make first," he said.

Angel looked at me questioningly, but I didn't know. When he pulled into the parking lot next to the banquet hall, however, I felt the dread creep into my gut.

"Bash?"

"I'll just be a minute," he said.

It was just drizzling now—barely a hint of what we'd just endured showed, except for some pretty significant standing water in the low spots. An inside light glowed from the door as a couple came out, and then several more people started to follow, laughing and looking happy. That was us, what—three hours ago? It felt like three days.

"Bash, look."

Vonda was walking out, her arm looped through none other than—

"Aaron!" Angel gasped, lurching forward like she was poked with a fire iron. "What—what are we doing?"

"Saying hello," Bash said, shutting the door behind him.

It was like watching a meteor headed for an unfortunate planet. The kid had no idea.

"Mom," Angel said, scrambling to get out of the blanket.

"Angel, stay in this truck," I said. "He just finished telling you—

"He's gonna kill Aaron!" she said, looking at me wild-eyed.

"No he won't," I said, following Bash's movement. I crossed my fingers. "Too many witnesses."

She was out the door anyway.

"Damn it," I muttered, shoving open my door. "Will this night ever end?"

"Aaron!" Angel yelled, running around the truck.

Bash whirled on her, about to tell her off again, but she held up her chin.

"It happened to me, I deserve to be here," she said as I joined them.

"Do either of you know how to stay anywhere?" Bash said, exasperated.

"It's our King and Queen!" Vonda sang out with a smile and maybe a little happy juice as the other patrons went around her. "I wondered where you two went." Her eyebrows lifted as she looked at each of us. "Get caught in the storm I'm guessing? Allie, where are your shoes?"

Enough with the shoes.

"We had to go rescue my daughter up in Forrest Hills," I said.

Aaron disentangled himself from his mother and tried to keep walking, but Bash moved in front of him.

"You know where Forrest Hills is, don't you, Aaron?" Bash asked, getting close up in his face. He tousled his hair, making the boy duck and tighten his jaw in defense. "Yeah, your hair's still a little damp. How's your eye? I heard you got whopped."

"What are you talking about?" Vonda said, looking from Bash to me to her son.

"I'm talking about your boy here—you know, the sexually enlightened one with no need for rules?" Bash said. "He took our fifteen-year-old girl out to the woods in Forrest Hills tonight."

Our fifteen year old girl.

My heart both melted and panicked all at once.

"He—he what?" Vonda asked, looking confused and glancing around as people slowed to listen.

"And when Angel said *no*," Bash said, his eyes unblinking on Aaron. "He yanked her out of the car in the middle of the fucking woods, in the middle of the fucking storm, and *left* her there."

Aaron looked defiant. Vonda looked about ready to throw up. People gasped around us.

"That's a lie," Aaron said.

"Bullshit!" Angel said, surging forward, angry tears in her eyes, Bash catching her with one arm. "You asshole! I thought you were nice. I thought you were *something*."

"Yeah, well I thought you were more than a tease," he seethed at her.

I didn't even see Bash move. Before I could blink, he had Aaron's arm in a vise, a handful of hair in his fist, and had slammed him up against his truck. I sucked in a breath, and Angel let out a yelp. Vonda and some other females screamed, and Sully and Nick appeared out of nowhere to stand on either side of Bash like bodyguards.

"Boy, you may think you're a man," Bash growled into Aaron's ear. "But I'll bet you'd scream like a girl if I let Angel kick you in the nuts right now."

"Bash! Stop!" Vonda cried. "I'll sue you for slander! For injury to a child!"

"Lady, I'll personally make sure that Allie sues you for everything I can dream up, and make sure your lovely son gets a juvie record for sexual assault," said Carmen, as she and Lanie stood next to me and Angel. She handed her a card. "That says Attorney-At-Law, in case you missed it."

Vonda ignored the card and looked ready to self-implode. She whirled around to me.

"Make him stop!"

"Funny, I believe I said something similar to you the other day, didn't I?" I said. "But no. You didn't want to be a parent."

"That's right, you told me they bought condoms together," Vonda said, crossing her arms over her chest. "So then she planned on this, too, and led him on? Sounds to me like your daughter is nothing but a—"

"You finish that sentence, and you'll have to sue me for assault," I said, my voice low. "And I say bring it on. I'd love to see what the cops think about your son leaving a young girl out in the woods to die from hypothermia. *Telling no one.*" It was my turn to get up in her face. "Her phone was almost dead, Miss Sharp. She had three whole minutes of calling me before it died, and we were lucky to find her in that storm."

Vonda's face went ashen. "You all heard her threaten me, right?" she asked, raising her voice as she looked around me to make sure Bash hadn't killed him yet. "You heard him threaten my boy?"

Heads shook everywhere, as people who'd been frozen with curiosity suddenly started moving again, walking off. Many of them patted my shoulder, stopped to hug Angel, whispered things to each other about not hearing anything… It nearly brought me to my knees, as I watched them all go. They stood up for us. This town, the one that had been nothing but brutal to me my whole life, was standing up for us.

"Guess that answers that," I said.

Bash pulled Aaron off his truck and shoved him back at Vonda, who wrapped her arms around him like he was five and someone had said *boo.*

"You don't talk to Angel," Bash said, pointing a finger in his face. "You don't look at her. You don't bad mouth her to anyone else. If you see her, you go the other way. If you see *me*, you go the other way. Because if I hear differently—" I saw the glaze come over his face and the light go out of his eyes. "Let's just say you *never* want to see my face again."

He turned and walked away. "Let's go, ladies." He stopped to shake Nick's and Sully's hands. "Thanks for having my back, guys."

I hugged Lanie and Carmen with tears in my eyes, unable to form words for what their standing by us meant to me. My girlfriends. I actually had those now. I truly felt it.

"You're part of this place, Allie," Lanie said. "You're Charmed family. We've got you."

Angel tackled Bash in a monster hug, and he hugged her head with both arms.

"I love you," she said into his chest.

"Back atcha, baby girl," he whispered. He kissed the top of her head and walked around to the driver's side.

"There's your very first grand gesture, Angel," I said softly, as her eyes filled with new tears. "It doesn't get better than that."

We got in, and drove out of the parking lot in silence, each lost in our own thoughts.

"Wait a minute," Angel said after a couple of minutes. "Y'all actually *won?*"

CHAPTER TWENTY-ONE

I sent Angel inside with orders to take a hot shower, and told her I'd be in in a minute. Then I opened the front passenger door and got in. Neither of us spoke, we just sat in the dark breathing the same air.

I reached for his hand and he took mine, resting them on the console.

"Three hours ago, this wasn't how I thought this night would end," he said finally.

"Three hours ago, we were about to howl at the moon." I thought I saw a small smile in the dark, but I couldn't be sure. "Bash, you were right earlier," I said. He looked at me then. "I was bailing before you could." I snorted. "Story of my life."

"I wasn't going to bail," he said.

I closed my eyes tight and willed the tears not to come.

"You are the best—" Damn it, this *feeling* shit was going to kill me. I stopped to pull it together. "The best thing that ever happened to us. To me," I added.

"So, why do I hear a *but* in that sentence?"

"There's no *but*," I said. "Just a fact. You're too important to lose, Bash."

"Why do you think you're gonna lose me, Allie?" he asked.

"Because that's what we do," I said, the words rushing out with round 584 of new tears. "We don't stick. We don't keep people. We don't do relationships. We have no damn idea how, so we float on surfaces and keep things easy."

I was breathing faster and harder at the end of that. And it was about to get worse.

"You and I—we can't float," I said, emotion catching my words. "We're too important for that. You are. I—can't lose you, Bash. Angel can't lose you. It's always been she and I against the world, and I don't know how to do—this. I can't afford to screw this up."

"You're screwing it up right now," he said. "I would never not be there for either of you. You should know better than to even think that."

I rubbed my eyes, and wiped at my face.

"I don't know anything right now," I said. "I'm delirious."

"There's nothing to be delirious about," he said. "What *I* did tonight is nothing new. It's what I've always done. Taken care of my girls. What the *town* did tonight?" he said with a look. "That was epic."

"It was," I said.

"They made a statement," he said. "*Allie and Angel Greene are our people. We have their backs.* But you go on in. Go be Allie and Angel against the world some more, and shut everyone else out. It's what you do."

I stared at him in the dark. "Why do you have to be a jerk?"

He ran both hands over his face and then back through his damp hair.

"Because maybe I'm tired of having to knock that chip off your shoulder and convince you that you aren't alone," he said. "I don't know what else I can say or do to prove it. I spilled my guts to you tonight, the whole damn town just shunned Vonda Sharp for you, and yet here you are, still on the defensive."

"Because defensive is all I've ever known, Bash." I didn't know how to be any other way.

He looked at me in the dark. I couldn't see the expression in his eyes, but I felt it to my core.

"It's safe, Allie, I get that. Believe me," he said. "But does it keep you warm at night?"

He let go of my hand and rested his on the steering wheel. I instantly missed the connection.

"It's late," he said. "Go get some sleep."

I looked at his profile. "Why do I feel like once I step out of this truck, I'm losing something?"

He shook his head. "I told you, you'll never lose me. But you're the one defining the boundaries," he said. "That's on you."

Slowly, I got out of the truck, and waited before I shut the door. "Good night."

He turned his head.

"Night, Allie."

* * *

Today was a week.

A week from last Saturday, when everything turned on its ear. I hadn't seen Bash. Not once. Not even from a distance, or in passing. I almost caved to go get a donut at the bakery next to his shop, but I talked myself out of it.

I felt so empty without our conversations, without his laugh and his smile, and lately, without his touch. Carmen and Lanie were doing their best to keep me occupied with dinners and silly get-togethers. Lanie even gave Angel a makeover one night, and it was worth enduring the girliness of it just to watch Angel soak in the female bonding. She needed that. I did too, I just never realized it.

But I missed my friend. I missed my Bash. He said I'd never lose him, but I had. He'd be there in a second if we needed him, I knew that, but I lost what made us—us. I wanted more than just the emergency responder. I wanted him. I wanted all of him.

This was safer, though. It was smarter, right? No one had to step outside into the unknown and fall into holes and traps and heartbreak. Everyone would be happier, and no one got hurt.

Yeah, how's that working for you, smart girl?

It was working my imagination into a frenzy, that's what. Every night, I'd close my eyes and wish he was wrapped around me, his warmth at my back and his kisses on my neck. I missed him so much, that late at night when things got really quiet, I literally ached inside. I'd never tell a living soul that, but there it was. I begged the universe for dreams, but they were gone. Replaced by my dad, of all things.

Every night, at some point, my dad would be there. Sitting at a table, cooking eggs at our old stove, watching TV, loading things into an old truck (that we never had), but always saying the same thing.

"Say yes, Allie."

Say yes to what? It was driving me crazy.

The money? I already had. Once Bailey told me it was legit, I opened a separate savings account at the bank and deposited it, holding a little out for a blow-and-go fund. Because we were going to do that, I decided. Since Lange wouldn't let me use it to get the diner back free and clear, I was going to start taking my daughter places. Seeing some things, having fun with her, letting her see me do something besides just work all the time.

And possibly, maybe, once I didn't have a heart attack over the idea, buy her a used car. I could buy *me* a new car and give her mine, but I loved my Jeep too much to do that to it.

"Hi, Queen Greene," said Mr. Wilson from his seat, giggling at his rhyme for only the thirty-ninth time.

Yeah, that was going to be fun.

"I didn't see that big fat check of yours in the ledger file," Lange said as I walked back to my office to get some headache medicine from my desk.

"Really?" I said. "Imagine that."

"Pretty sure you won that for the *business*, last I checked," he said, leaning back in his chair.

"Pretty sure I told you to stay out of my files, too," I said, not giving him the satisfaction of a look his way. "But life's just unfair like that."

"Thought you were going to put your crown out on the counter somewhere," he said.

"I am."

And I would. When I got it back from Bash's shop, with my shoes, and my clothes, and my heart. None of those things were knocking on my door, and I hadn't drummed up the nerve to do any knocking, either.

Yes, *heart* had joined the list of what I'd left over there, and I wasn't too thrilled with that so far. At least I had the advantage of not looking at my desk every day and reliving it again and again. Then, who was I kidding? I was totally reliving it every spare second of the day.

"I'm running to the bank, we're short on small bills," I said. "I'll be back in a few."

I walked out, keys in hand, ready to open the register when I rounded the corner and a pair of sexy blue eyes nearly took me down.

He was sitting at the bar, waiting for me, arms resting on the counter casually, a small smile saying he was trying to pull that off. The eyes, though. There was nothing casual there. They looked like they just got slammed with the same wall I did.

I pulled in a breath, grabbed the counter, dropped the keys, and tried to speak through the mad flush of blood that all went to my head at the same time.

"Bash," I said, my voice cracking like a pubescent boy.

"Hey," he said. "How's it going?"

I raised my eyebrows. *How's it going?* "Uh, okay. You?"

He nodded, and I wanted to cry. To break something and yell and throw a fit and say *This is what I was talking about!* But it wasn't quite like that. There was a dark intensity there that stole my breath and made me dizzy.

"You look good," he said.

I looked like I'd just worked two rushes, and probably smelled like it too. He, however, looked—I couldn't even think it.

"Thanks."

He wouldn't blink, wouldn't look away, and it was hypnotizing. Made me feel like if I looked long enough, I could just get lost in there. Dear

God, if I hadn't had a restaurant full of people, I would have hopped that countertop and climbed him like a tree.

He cleared his throat and finally averted his eyes, and I took a breath like I'd been underwater for an hour.

"I brought your stuff," he said, unlooping a plastic grocery bag from a knob on the counter and holding it up.

My gaze fell to the bag, and I realized I hadn't wanted to get that stuff back. As long as he had it, I'd still have to see him again. Now—now there was no reason.

"Oh, yeah," I said, taking it from him. "I've been meaning to—"

Our fingers brushed, and heat swooshed through me as if someone lit my blood on fire. Good grief, we were dancing, holding hands, and bumping sex parts the other day, and now finger touching was the big moment.

"Well, I've had it in the truck," he said. "I've just been busy, and—you know."

"Mr. Anderson?"

Bash turned as a middle-aged lady blushed and laid a hand on his arm. No one was immune.

"Yes, ma'am?"

"I just wanted to tell you two how much you moved me last week," she said. "The way you are together. The way you talked about each other and—" She laid a hand on her heart. "The thing about always being a team. People can spot the real thing, you know? It reminded me so much of my late husband and me, and I just wanted to tell you thank you and congratulations."

"Thank you," I managed to push out over the lump in my throat.

"Very sweet of you," Bash said, patting her hand.

He turned back to me as she walked away, but he kept his eyes on the counter, resting both hands there. He looked exhausted, troubled, tormented when he finally met my gaze, like a man who hadn't slept, and all I wanted to do was go around the counter and wrap myself up in him.

We were a team. The real thing.

The real thing.

We weren't being shit, now. He opened his mouth to say something, when there was some hushed talking by the front window that caught both of our attention. When Sully appeared in the doorway, I wondered what the big deal was. When he held the door open for Albert Bailey—

"Holy shit."

Bailey didn't come out in public. Very, very seldom did he venture into town, he paid people to do that for him. He was always just rumored to be eccentric that way, a bit of a hermit, but after meeting him myself and what I experienced there... it seemed to be a much simpler, basic reason.

It's hard to interact in public without touching people.

He leaned heavily on his cane, and walked in slowly, nodding curt greetings at people and doing a double take on Mr. Wilson.

"Leroy," he said.

"Albert," Mr. Wilson responded.

And that was that. I was on the other side of the counter before I realized I'd even made the trip.

"Mr. Bailey," I said.

"Miss Greene," he said, his expression changing into a pleasant smile. "Good to see you again."

"You as well," I said. "I think."

He chuckled, and I glanced at Sully, who raised an eyebrow.

"That brutal honesty of yours," Bailey said. "Never lose that. Pardon the intrusion today, but I asked Sully to give me a ride into town to visit Oliver, and I wanted to meet your—partner."

"My partn—Lange?"

"Yes, please," he said. "Is he in?"

"Unfortunately," I said, turning to Kerri, who was behind the counter. "Kerri, can you ask Mr. Lange to come out here for a minute?"

She disappeared around the corner and Bailey looked over his glasses up at Bash.

"Mr. Anderson, I presume."

Bash smiled and held a hand out. "Mr. Bailey. Have we met?"

I took his hand gently down, and didn't let go quite yet. "You don't want to do that," I whispered.

Bailey chuckled again. "Not in person, but I've seen your name and face, and I'm a big fan of your honey. I get a case delivered every quarter."

"Yes you do, I've seen the order," Bash said. "Thank you very much."

"Well, I believe in supporting the local industry," Bailey said. His eyes narrowed keenly as he peered up at Bash. "And local royalty, I hear," he added, sliding his gaze to me.

"Oh Lord," I mumbled.

"Can I help you?" Lange said, walking around the counter.

"Landon Lange," Bailey said heartily. Too heartily.

Lange slowed his steps for a half-second, then kept approaching. "Yes?"

"I hear that you and I have a mutual friend in common," Bailey continued, holding out a hand to Lange. I had only a split second to process that before he took his hand. "Oliver Greene."

CHAPTER TWENTY-TWO

I didn't have to wonder if that was a mistake. Whatever it was, Landon's expression said it all. The look of surprise, and what-the-fuckness could have—to an unknowing outsider—been attributed to the mention of my father's name. It was pretty common knowledge now, since Angel's fun little show, that Lange and my father had some bad blood.

The *bleakness*, for lack of a better word, that came over him in the seconds following their union was almost scary.

Lange pulled his hand back and looked around as if he were a little lost.

"You know Oliver," he said, his demeanor quiet.

"We go back a very, very long time," Bailey said. "And you know Mr. Anderson, of course," he added, gesturing toward Bash.

"Of course," Lange echoed. He paused to blink a couple of times and then looked at me. "I'll be leaving," he said matter-of-factly, much like I'd just mentioned going to the bank. "The diner's yours."

"What?" I asked, looking from person to person.

"I don't want to deal with bees, either," he said, looking at Bash with calm, clear eyes.

"You—already put money into it," Bash said, looking wary.

"My gift," Lange said with a shrug. "Enjoy."

"And my customers?" Bash said, his tone baffled. "The Romans at Cherrydale Flower Farm? Kaison Orchards?"

Lange turned to head back to the office room. "Not interested," he said over his shoulder. "I'll void our contracts."

My mouth hung open in shock.

"What just happened?" Bash asked.

"No idea," Bailey said, winking at me. "Some people are just flaky like that. Sully, can you bring me by Oliver's now? Then that other stop."

"Will do," Sully said, his mouth fighting a smile as he glanced at me.

"Miss Greene," Bailey said.

"Yes?" I almost yelped as I jolted out of my stunned state.

"It was a pleasure," he said. "And a tip, if I may?"

He could do whatever the hell he wanted as long as he never did to me whatever he'd just done to Lange.

He leaned in a little closer. "Safe is overrated," he said. "Take a leap."

"Leap," I echoed. "Got it." Bailey smiled at both Bash and I and turned, leaning on his cane. "Thank you," I called to his retreating back.

"I'm sure I have no idea what for," he said, waving a finger. "Everyone have a good day."

I swiveled around to look at where Lange had disappeared, and then around the room. Everyone was eating and chatting as normal. I looked back at the windows. Still sunny. The big clock behind the counter had only moved about fifteen minutes. Good signs.

I met Bash's gaze questioningly. "You saw all that, right?"

"Seriously, what the hell *was* that?" he asked. *Whew.*

"I think that was—" I stopped. "A second chance." I held my hands to my hot cheeks. "Holy crap."

Lange came back out with his man purse, a plastic bag holding the few personal items he'd brought, and a Blue Banana Grille coffee mug. He held the mug up.

"You don't mind, do you?" he asked me.

"Not at all," I said.

He nodded at us both. "Nice to meet you," he said, and left.

"I'm—" I had nothing. My experience with Bailey had been different— had certainly not been like this.

"You're going to explain this to me, right?" Bash asked.

"After Sully or Carmen explain it to me, sure," I said. I took a deep breath as I suddenly realized how close we were and how easily I could now do what I'd really wanted to do since I'd come around that corner. Since we'd gotten lost in each other for a moment. Since he'd been about to say something. Something important, maybe. "Another time. I need to—go dig my keys off the floor back there and get to the bank for some change, and—wow. I guess I need to make this place mine again."

Bash nodded and ran a hand through his hair, leaving it sticking up and making me want to run my fingers through it. Touch him. Hug him. Do mouth-to-mouth. I couldn't stand the awkwardness between us. I needed normal back, our new normal in particular, and both had sailed. I glanced back at the front door where Bailey had exited. Apparently normal had sailed on a lot of things.

"See you later, Allie," he said, brushing past me to the door as I breathed him in.

"Bash, what were you going to say earlier?" I blurted out. "Before,"—I gestured toward the air around us—"all that."

He forced a grin that didn't go very far. "It doesn't matter."

Then why did it feel like his leaving took all the air from the room.

* * *

It was a whirlwind afternoon. Business was hopping and so was my brain. Lange was gone—gone! Free of strings, free of everything. I could hardly wrap my mind around it. While the logical side of me said it was too good to be true, I was beginning to notice that when it came to certain things in Charmed, logic wasn't necessarily part of the equation.

The diner was mine again, and suddenly I felt full of ideas to make things better. Oddly, Lange's presence had created that. I'd just been going through the motions of what had always been done, before. Things were different now. I was different, now.

I'd had a taste of a tiny bit of freedom, of someone else taking on a few of the managerial responsibilities, and while I hated how it was done, some of those moments had been liberating. I had to recognize that. I wanted to relish being solo again for a bit, but I needed to make a plan for the future. I didn't see Angel following in my footsteps. She cared about it, but not in a career sort of way, whereas Nick… It was a thought to ponder on, taking on a *real* partner one day. Someone who would love the place like I did, that could split the responsibilities so that I could have a life outside of it.

I pulled up to Dad's trailer at dusk, chuckling as I saw him sitting outside in his robe and slippers, kicked back in his lawn chair and smoking on the tiny deck he'd built years ago that would kind of hold two chairs. I felt the need to check on him, knowing that Bailey had come by, and since Angel was at a sleepover tonight (at an actual girl's house, I checked with the mother), I had nowhere to be anytime soon. I took out my hair band and fluffed out my hair with my fingers.

"It's not time for you to visit," he said, attempting to put out the cigarette so that I wouldn't see it.

"I know," I said. "This day's crazy like that, so breathe through it." I held up a hand. "Quit stressing about the cigarette, it's not a secret, Dad."

"I take a shit every day, too," he said, grinding it out on a rock he'd set next to the chair. "Doesn't mean I want you watching me do it."

I lifted my eyebrows in agreement as I grabbed the extra fold-out chair leaning against the trailer and set it up next to him.

"I guess you have a point there, Confucius."

"I'm popular today," he said. "So what brings *you* here during my quiet time?"

I was always hesitant to bring up hot topics when he was being semi-lucid. I didn't like stirring him up.

"Remember the money?" I asked.

"From the trees," he said, his eyes going a little sad. "It's for you."

"I know," I said, patting his arm. "And it's legit. Bailey told me the story."

"Bailey came by today," he said, rubbing at his stubbly jaw.

"Yeah?" I said, playing innocent of that knowledge.

"Yeah," he said. "He told me that Landon Lange is out of the picture; that you didn't need to worry about him anymore."

I closed my eyes and blew out a breath. "That's the rumor." I looked at my dad. His stubble was white now, to match his hair. He looked so much older and more frail in the last year, it broke my heart. "Bailey was a good friend to you, wasn't he?"

"He was," he said. "He is." Dad gave me a sideways glance. "So, what did you do with that money?"

"Put it in my dryer," I said. "Where Angel then found it, and I had to tell her you won it gambling because she thought I was part of the mob."

My dad looked at me for a moment, and then started laughing. I got goose bumps at the sound. I hadn't heard him laugh in—I didn't know how long. I chuckled with him.

"And now?" he asked finally.

"It's in the bank, drawing interest." His expression changed to alarm. "I told them it was old family money, a gift from eccentric old people who hoarded cash and didn't trust banks," I said. "I'll pay some fees but it's fine. It's safer there than in my dryer. Or your drawer, or—trees."

I almost told him about the Honey Queen thing, but I figured that could be a discussion for another visit. This was about the most normal conversation we'd had in a long time, and I didn't want to push it.

Instead, I just enjoyed sitting with my dad, chatting about the squirrels he'd been feeding, Angel's life (minus the condoms and the night of the storm), the kids a row over who kept losing their Frisbee, and who was cheating on who three trailers down.

"It's entertaining, how much you witness when people think you're too crazy to notice," he said, a grin pulling at his lips.

I gave him an amused look. "Well, look at you."

He gave me a look right back, as clear as what was now a sky full of stars. "Say yes."

Chills covered my skin.

"What did you just say?" I breathed.

Your dad had his dreams...

"I said, say yes," he repeated.

I stared at him, blinking. This day was weird enough, I couldn't take much more.

"Yes to what, Dad," I managed.

"To all of it," he said. "For starters, go talk to him."

I laughed nervously. Possibly maniacally. "*Him.*"

Dad pushed up out of his chair with a grunt, and looked at me wearily. "What did I just tell you? My girl, you wear me out sometimes." He stretched his back. "Go on now, it's time for my chocolate pudding before my shows."

I just stared at him, unable to move. How could he possibly know—

"Or just sit there, then," he said, shrugging. "Makes me no difference. Just put the chair back where you got it. Night."

He shuffled in and shut the door, clicking it locked.

"Night," I whispered in stunned response.

I don't know how long I sat there on my dad's little porch, trying to make sense of yet one more thing that wasn't supposed to make sense. Eventually, I got up and folded my chair, put it back in its place against the side of the trailer, and got into my Jeep.

I started it, turned toward home, and kept driving.

CHAPTER TWENTY-THREE

Bash's house was on the same property as Anderson's Apiary. He'd built the business small to begin, and grew it into what it was now, never dreaming it would have come this far. He was on the edge of town, off the beaten path a little, and his home was even further tucked back. There was no traffic through here, so my headlights coming down his graveled street was a dead giveaway.

He was standing in his doorway in sweatpants and a T-shirt when I got out, and by the time I stood in front of him, even my insides were shaking.

"What's wrong?" he asked. "Angel?"

I shook my head. "She's at a sleepover."

I had no plan. No speech. No thoughts to lead with. No anything.

All I had was myself and my heart that was currently knocking around inside me like a rogue pinball on crack.

"I lied, today," I said, the last word coming out silently. "When I said I was okay. That things were okay." I took a deep, trembling breath and let it out slowly. "Nothing is okay without you, Bash. I miss you."

The last three words were barely spoken before he crossed the few feet between us and lifted my mouth to his.

All my worries, my stresses, my fears dissolved in a puddle at my feet as he kissed me. Soft and tender. Harder. Softer again. And again. And again.

I melted against him right there on his front porch, languishing in the feel of his body as my hands ran up his back and his tucked me tightly against him. One came up to my face and went into my hair, angling my head so that he could kiss me deeper, longer, more thoroughly. More lovingly. I never wanted to stop. Not this moment, this night, this man. Ever. That thought rocked me and I took a deep breath.

"Bash," I breathed.

"Sshhh," he said against my lips. "No words."

"But—"

"No arguing," he said, kissing my top lip. "No endless reasons not to do this," he said, running his tongue over my bottom lip. "I don't care." He kissed me softly. "Just shut up, because God, I need you."

He gave me a slow, deep, wet kiss that curled my toes and made me sigh with more wanting than I'd ever felt in my life. No one had ever kissed me like that. Unhurried, yet so full of desire it made my head swim.

Bash lifted me off my feet as we came up for air, carrying me inside and kicking the door closed, his mouth never leaving mine. He didn't set me down until we were in his bedroom, and by then I had his shirt off and he had my bra unhooked. It all came over my head in a lump, and he turned me around, palming my breasts as he wrapped his arms around me and dragged his mouth slowly down the side of my neck. Oh God, it was magic, his hands on my body, the addictive smell of him filling my senses. I stretched like a cat, arching my back, settling my ass against him while I reached up behind me to fill my fingers with his hair.

He made a seductive growling noise, his hands leaving my breasts to slide down my belly, pressing me back harder, teasing me with sliding below my jeans for just a moment then back out to unzip me and slide them over my hips. His hands followed them, as his mouth trailed kisses down my spine.

It was erotic and primal, concentrating on sensations without words. I turned and stepped out of my jeans, and let him kiss his way back up, unable to hold back the gasp as he ran his hands up my thighs and pressed a kiss to the tiny piece of fabric covering me.

I had barely recovered from that when I found myself lifted into his arms and placed in his bed. I opened my mouth to tell him there were things I wanted to do to him first, but he covered it with a finger, running it along my lips and looking at me with so much—oh my God, the words were bursting inside of me with that look. And my world changed.

Right then. Right there.

Tears burned the backs of my eyes as I pulled him to me and held his face in my hands as I kissed him with my unspoken words. As I tried to put every thought, every emotion, every feeling I had for him into my touch, my kiss. It physically hurt my chest as I looked into his eyes and knew. This was what it was like. The real thing. Our bodies tangled as we dove into one another, taking our time but yet needing, kissing like there was no tomorrow, caressing, touching, licking; bringing moans but no words. His pants were history as I made love to him with my mouth. My panties were tossed across the room somewhere as he tasted and sucked me to almost incoherency.

I was to the point of begging him to bury himself inside me when he did just that, groaning as he pushed deeper into me, and the feel of him stretching me to squeeze around him as he lifted my legs over his shoulders and pumped into me, harder and harder, sent me tumbling over the edge.

My whole body arched under him as the waves rocked me, and I cried his name out in ecstasy in my first broken rule of the night. He was right there with me, his fingers digging into my thighs, his eyes closed as the thunder rolled through him.

We collapsed together in a tangle of limbs and sheets, spent and so satisfied, the only thought coursing through my mind being *please keep up the silence.* Words ruined this the last time. I didn't want anything to ruin the amazing, over-the-top, beautiful thing we'd just experienced.

It was as if he heard me. He lifted his head and moved a wild lock hair from my eyes; that look burning through me. We stayed like that for several long moments, both of us realizing that may be the only way to do this.

Then he ran his thumb along my cheek.

"Stay," he said. "Stay the night."

The impact of those simple words—from this man—it brought tears to my eyes and they blinked free, tracking back into my hair.

"Okay."

* * *

Waking up sore and creaky, but with warm man solid against my back, his arms around me and one breast in his hand—it was something out of my fantasies.

It was real. It had happened. Bash Anderson, the perpetual bachelor who never let anyone sleep over, had asked me to stay. To make love all night, in every possible position, until we had nothing left, and fell asleep in each other's arms.

We didn't do the whole night in silence, obviously, but we kept it to sex and laughing banter. Only our eyes said other things, and that's when we'd go quiet.

I tried to disentangle myself without waking him, but he stirred when I nearly fell out of the bed and had to grab the nightstand.

"You okay?" he asked sleepily, rubbing at his eyes.

"Just a little rigor mortis," I said, wincing as I stretched. "I think you might have broken me."

Bash chuckled. "What a way to die." He balled up a pillow under his head and gazed at me. "What a sight to wake up to. Why are we awake, though?"

"I'm awake because I have to pee," I said. "And it's daylight, and non-vampires tend to move around at that time."

"That's assuming said non-vampires actually slept during the moonlight hours," he said.

"And I do have to be at the diner in a couple of hours," I said. "Nick can open, but I need to show up."

"You need a day off," he said.

"I'm—looking into plans for that," I said. "Right now, I just want to enjoy having my office back to myself again."

Bash got up and brushed his teeth, and I did the only thing I could do, which was to pop a piece of gum in my mouth so I didn't blow fire. I found all my clothes and put them back on, waiting for the dread to hit me. Waiting for that thing that was going to kill the wonderful.

When he padded back in, barefoot, wearing the sweatpants and a fresh T-shirt, I sighed.

"What?" he said.

"You can look that hot getting out of bed," I said. "It's not fair."

"You should be on my side," he said, pulling me into his arms playfully. "You have no idea how hot you are to wake up to. And how much I want to put you back in that bed right now." He took my hand and settled it against his rock hard dick. "Yeah," he said. "That much."

My thoughts went a little fuzzy as I moved my fingers along him.

"Hmmm."

"Keep that up, and there will be no work today," he said, his hand sliding down to my ass.

"Okay, okay," I said, shaking my head free of naughty thoughts and letting go of him amongst groans of protest. "I have to go be a grown-up now. Quit teasing me."

"I'll walk you out."

He kissed me before I shut my door, and I was just marveling at how well we'd managed the night and the morning without drama, without saying the things that were screaming to be said. Especially last night. Then he tapped on my window again as I went to back out.

I rolled the window down.

"You rang?"

He leaned in to drop another soft kiss on my lips, and then backed out slowly, locking eyes with me in that—

"I love you," he said.

He touched my cheek and backed up, a small smile pulling at his lips before he turned and walked back into the house, and shut the door.

"Holy shit," I whispered.

CHAPTER TWENTY-FOUR

Really?

You drop that on a girl and send her on her way to work with a kiss and a smile and just walk in the house like nothing happened?

Kerri had to nudge me four different times as I just stopped mid-activity and stared into space.

"Miss Greene, are you okay?" she asked, the last time. "You don't seem yourself."

I wasn't myself. *Myself* wasn't a person who normally got completely and thoroughly fucked all night and then told I love you the next morning. *Myself* didn't know what the hell to do with this person she was walking around in today.

Carmen called me.

"It's beautiful out, let's take the day off," she said. "I was going to work on some briefs today, but screw that. Let's grab Lanie and go play at the Lucky Charm and just have some fun. Bring Angel."

Normally, I would have laughed at everyone's attempt to get me playing hooky, knowing it was something I'd never do, but today I was—I was a looped out freak on a sex hangover. Maybe I did need to break away and clear the cobwebs. And when was the last time I brought Angel to do something that carefree?

That was the selling point.

I asked Nick to cover, Kerri to back him up on the floor (and crossed my fingers on that), called Angel that I was picking her up, and I was off.

I almost texted Bash, was so tempted, but no. This was a girl's day, and my stomach was already in knots from this morning. I needed to ponder that more. When I was alone. Because—I was an idiot.

We played for hours. Rode kiddie rides like fools, rode the bumper cars so everyone's brains could get knocked a little loose, and we all looked at the roller coaster construction going on. They could have that. I wouldn't be going up there.

We shopped at the little shops, went in Bash's only because his truck wasn't there, and ate pizza and chocolate-covered cheesecake and fried everything till we wanted to pop.

It was the best girls afternoon and evening, *ever*. I hadn't seen Angel laugh and have that much fun in a long time, and I found myself really looking at her and listening to her. She was almost sixteen. A young woman, with maturing facial features and a more maturing body. Her childhood was almost over, and it would be gone in a blink and she'd be off doing whatever she was going to do. It made me stick even more to my guns about the money I tucked away for us to start living a little.

"Y'all, we need to make this a thing," I said as we strolled slowly, all of us too full to make any sudden moves.

"I'm for that," Angel said, hope in her smile.

"I have a client in Cherrydale who co-owns a big antique trade-days thing once a month," Carmen said. "We should check it out. It's only maybe an hour away."

"Yeah, maybe y'all could do that one without me," Angel said, scrunching her nose.

"Oh come on," I said, poking her in the side. "Home décor and antiques don't get you giddy?"

"Hey, don't knock it," Carmen said. "They make some major bucks renting space for people to sell their crap. His son is getting married this spring and you wouldn't believe the kind of money they're dropping." She winced. "Did I just say that out loud?"

"Well, we'll check that out," I said, looping an arm around Angel's neck. "But we'll do some fun stuff too."

"How did it fare with Mr. Aaron at school this week?" Lanie asked Angel. She shrugged, and averted her eyes. I knew she was still embarrassed about that.

"He's been really quiet," she said. "I haven't hung around him, but one of his friends told me he's been weird. That he was going to start taking a *cooking* class?" She lifted an eyebrow in question. "What the heck?"

Sully brought Bailey to see my father and—*that other stop*. I clamped my lips together. No way. Wow.

"Someone else I haven't seen since that night is Kia," I said, half wondering if Bailey zapped her, too. Not really. But if there was one thing I'd learned, it was that nothing was out of the question.

"Sully said she's taken off for a while," Carmen said. "Headed down to the Gulf or something."

Was it bad that that really didn't hurt my feelings? Probably. I never saw any women try to be her friend, and a little poke in my side said I should have tried harder. For Bash's sake. Then again, Bash's old "benefits buddy" and I would most likely never be on a comfortable radar.

"Y'all," Carmen said, glancing at her phone when it buzzed. "It's almost dark. Let's go sit down by the water, or ride the Ferris wheel and check out the town lights."

"Or go in the rowboats!" Angel said.

"Unless there's a shirtless boat boy named Jorge willing to row it for me," said Lanie. "Then no thanks. I'm too full."

"So then the Ferris wheel," Carmen said. "It's right there."

"No thank you," I said. "I don't do Ferris wheels. But I'd be happy to watch y'all." I breathed in deep, and enjoyed the crisp air that smelled of popcorn. It was just what I needed, this day. I felt so invigorated.

"Doesn't look like it's working, anyway," Angel said. "It hasn't moved in the past thirty minutes."

"Well, I want to see," Carmen said, nudging Lanie, who suddenly wholeheartedly agreed.

We kept strolling, and I eyed them. "What are you two conspiring?"

"Nothing," they said in unison.

"You forget I have a teenager," I said, looping an arm around Angel's neck and laughing. "I live with a professional liar. I know the signs."

"Hey!" Angel protested.

"I'm just saying," I began, as we rounded a curve where a display wall hid the entrance. I didn't notice Carmen and Lanie slowing to transition behind us until I made the full curve. "I know sneaky when I—"

My feet faltered at the sight before me.

Angel laughed. "Uncle Bash? What are you doing?"

Someone pulled her from my arm and left me standing there by myself, looking at a scene that a movie couldn't have done better.

Bash sat in a Ferris wheel seat, arms draped across the back and rose petals on the seat around him, lit up by the flicker of tiny tealight candles *everywhere*. With his Honey King crown on his head.

"Oh—my—God—"

It was adorable and—amazing. And my feet felt glued to the concrete. I couldn't move. I didn't know what to do.

"Allie," Bash said. "My queen." He took off the crown and made a little mock bow. I laughed and clapped a hand over my mouth. "Would you care to join me?"

I turned to the girls behind me and laughed at Angel's oh-my-god mixed expression of gleeful delight and pure horror. Then something dawned in her face and she met my eyes.

"Mom," she whispered. "A gesture!"

My heart skipped a beat and I blinked back emotion as I looked back at Bash. Oh my God, this man.

I glanced upward at the totality of the beast. "I would love to, but I can't get on that thing, babe."

He got up and maneuvered his way to me. "If I said I'd made sure it's turned off, not moving, and locked down, would you change your mind?" he asked, holding out a hand.

I wanted to so badly, but the anxiety I knew so damned well squeezed at my chest and made my knees shake.

"What about me?" Sully said, appearing out of nowhere. "If I told you that I personally told the operator to leave, and turned off the motor myself, locked it myself, and Bash threatened my life if it moves, would you change your mind then?"

I laughed out loud, and Bash's eyes danced as Sully slapped him on the shoulder and disappeared off to places unseen by the rider.

"Well?" he asked. "Trust me?"

"Oh, that's so unfair," I said. "But I guess when lives are threatened and all that, I can't let that go to waste."

"That's my girl," Bash said, taking my hand and guiding me back.

It was shaky as I sat in the seat, just knowing what I was sitting in. I looked up—

"Nope, don't look up," he said, sitting sideways to face me. "Just look at me."

I turned sideways and focused on his face, smiling. Remembering this morning.

I love you.

My stomach flipped over and I pressed my hand against it. He did all this after saying that and letting me drive away, not knowing what I thought or what my reaction was? That was pretty friggin brave.

He pulled my bun free, letting my hair fall so he could let his hand play in it. Or distract me. Either way, it was good.

"Last night was amazing," he said.

"Yes it was."

"But now there are things to say," he said. "And since you and I together have the relationship skills of a tree, I figured we needed something a little extra special to set the tone."

I laughed out loud. "You may be right about that," I said. I swallowed to get my nerves under control. "And you already got a pretty good head start," I said.

He grinned but his eyes were serious. "I've never said those words before," he said, sending goose bumps over my body. "Not to anyone but that girl over there."

"Me either," I breathed. "Was it scary?"

"Terrifying."

I laughed and he smiled.

"But the second it was out there, I knew I wanted to do it again. And again," he said. "I told you the other day about my kind of business being such a risk, being at the mercy of nature?"

"Yeah."

"Well, so is this," he said. "It's a risk. It's a gamble. I used to think everything had to be a sure thing—like the service was. Nothing in my life had ever been a sure thing until then, and I guess I thought love had to be that way too. But it's not going to."

He took my hand from my stomach and wound our fingers together, looking at the union.

"It's a gamble," he said. "A harvest. You put it out there and then it's up to you to take care of it or let it go to shit, but my point is that we don't know for sure."

Bash's eyes lifted back to meet mine, and the look—the same one from last night and this morning—slammed into me, taking my breath.

"The thing I do know is that I never want another moment spent like this last week. Without you."

My image of his face swam with tears. "Me either."

"Dancing around words and worrying about what *might happen*," he said. "I'd rather chance that horrible maybe, than never love the woman I know better than anyone."

He let go of my hand and cradled my face in both of his.

"Nobody knows the real me like you do," he said. "And nobody knows Allie Greene like me: The you no one else sees. The one who's fearless and scared at the same time. Who has no earthly idea how beautiful she is with her hair all falling out of a bun. The girl with the foul mouth that picks up Mr. Wilson's napkin for him every day, who'll fight to the death for her family and makes no apologies for it. My best friend. I know *you*. You're the sure thing for me, Allie. The real deal. The rest is a leap of faith."

Take a leap of faith.

Holy crap.

My tears blinked free and fell to my cheeks, where he whisked them away with his thumbs.

Say yes.

Bash let go of me and looked deep into my eyes with something that looked like he was about to jump out of a plane with no parachute.

Take a leap.

Sliding out of the seat, he went to one knee in front of me.

A shriek came from the girls' direction, but I felt like my throat closed up.

"Oh my—what are you—"

"I had a talk with your dad," he said.

Tears fell freely down my face. "You—you did what?" I squeaked.

His hands shook as he took mine in his.

"You're it for me, Al," he said, his voice going rough with emotion. "We're messy. We're raw and rough and passionate, and we say the wrong things and stumble over each other, but there is no one I'd rather stumble through the rest of my life with than you. I don't want ordinary. I want mind-blowing."

In all my life, I'd never imagined a more messed up, perfect declaration of love. And it was being given to me. Mind-blowing? That was it.

"It doesn't get better than this," he said. "Better than us. So yeah, maybe it's fast, but is it? Hasn't it really always been—you and me and that little girl?"

He was right. It was freakish to admit that, but he was so right.

"So I went to see your dad," he said again, blowing out a breath slowly. "It was a bit of a carousel ride," he said, making me laugh through my tears. "But I'm ninety-nine percent sure he gave me his blessing."

Say yes. Oh my God. *Say yes.*

"He did," I said, my words choppy.

"How do you—"

"Trust me," I said on a laugh. "He did."

Bash reached into his pocket and drew out a satin pouch. Opening it, he reached in with shaking fingers and pulled out a ring.

I pulled my right hand free to press against my mouth, as full on ugly cry was about to happen. This couldn't be happening. Not to me. But this man was making damn sure I got the full-court press. All the grand gestures. The ring he held was beautiful. Simple with gorgeous lines and elegance. He put the ring to his lips and kissed it, and in that instance, my heart nearly burst from my chest. I knew what it was.

"I love you, Allie," he said, taking a breath to keep from breaking as he looked from the ring to me. "I love Angel—most of the time."

I laughed till the tears took over and he actually had tears tracking down his face, too. I wiped one away and looked at the man I'd always loved and never knew how to say it.

"I love you, Bash," I said, closing my eyes as he closed his. "Holy hell, that's what that sounds like."

He laughed and we opened our eyes.

"I told you," he said, two more tears falling. "It's terrifying. And forever is daunting, but I will love you forever if you'll spend it with me."

I didn't have to hear my dad's words again.

"Yes."

A huge breath came out of him. "Yes?"

"Was I supposed to wait for a question?" I asked. "Because I'm new at this."

"Marry me?" he asked, laughing and wiping tears away.

"Um—still yes."

Bash was up and I was in his arms in a rush of oh-my-Gods and laughter. He lifted me off my feet and I wrapped my arms around his head, kissing him with all I had, as the peanut gallery back there was jumping up and down and hugging each other.

"I love you," I whispered against his lips. "I love you so much."

He closed his eyes and kissed me. "You don't know how good that sounds."

There was the sound of running footsteps and we were tackled by a teenage girl with tears going down her face, too. Weren't we just the poster family for cheesy emotion.

"Ah yes, the girl child," Bash said, putting me back on my feet and including Angel in our embrace.

"I didn't know any of this," she said, wiping at her face. "How did y'all date and I never knew it?"

"Didn't date," I said.

"Leap of faith," Bash said.

"Don't ever think of doing that, by the way," I said.

Angel looked from Bash to me, and rolled her eyes. "Y'all are crazy."

"Maybe," I said, laughing. "Probably."

"Or we're just us," Bash said.

"And insane," she said. "But I love you anyway."

"Something I say about you every day," I said.

She ignored me.

"Do I have to call you Daddy?"

"Let's stick with the tried and true," he said.

"Oh thank God," she said, wrapping her arms around both of us. "That would be so weird."

Bash cleared his throat. "Mind if I finish, ladies?"

She pulled back. "What?"

He held up the ring and she jolted backward. "I'm so sorry. Carry on."

"This was my mother's," he said, lifting my hand. "I'd be honored if you wore it till we find what you want."

He slipped it on my finger, and I stopped breathing. To see a ring so beautiful there—it was just—unreal. I looked up at him, feeling all the feelings.

"It's perfect," I said.

"It's not fancy—"

"It's me," I said, touching his face. "It's us. It's perfect."

"I love you," he said, his eyes so happy it was overwhelming. "Want to ride this thing to celebrate?"

"Not even a little bit," I said.

"What do you want to do?" he asked.

I grinned, and Angel grimaced and put her hands over her face.

"La, la, la, I'm gonna head out with these ladies, kay?" she said, as Carmen and Sully and Lanie all came over to hug us.

"We've got Angel," Carmen said, swiping under her eyes and flitting her hands at us. "You just go—"

I looked up at Bash. My best friend. My fiancée.

"What do *you* want to do?" I asked.

He grinned and pulled me close. "Trust me?"

CHAPTER ONE

Why the hell didn't I go with the flats?
That thought would kick my ass later.
Shoes? Really? At a moment like that, my heart pounding in my ears,
sweating through fifteen miles of lace and silk and guilt, and picturing

everyone's appalled faces right about now—I was just wishing for good running shoes?

I was a selfish, horrible troll.

A troll that they'd be looking for any minute.

"Shit!" I huffed, weaving through the cars parked along the street, holding up a dress that cost more than my car—"My car!" I gasped, stopping short and spinning around. It was in the back of the church, waiting to take Jeremy and me to the reception…but no, my keys were in Jeremy's pants pocket, on his body, at the altar, waiting on the selfish and horrible troll. *Don't think about that.* "Damn it!"

I whirled back around and jogged into the street on my four-inch heels to make better time, knowing that at any minute someone would figure it out. Jeremy, my brothers, my friends—no, *Jeremy's* friends. Someone would come to see why the big heavy music that shook the floor so hard I felt it in my hoo-hah didn't come accompanied with a girl in a big white dress. My window was narrow at best.

I just had to make it to the signal light at the corner. Then I could— what? Call a cab? In Cherrydale, Texas? Right. And on what, my special holographic phone? Unlike my actual one still back in the dressing room.

*Breathe…run…breathe…run…*I chanted in my head to the rhythm of my feet hitting the pavement. Hopping really, like I was on stilts. *Breathe… run…* At the light I could duck into the old Smith's Drugstore, and pray that Mr. Dan, the pharmacist, would let me use his phone to call an Uber.

Breathlessly, I reached the drugstore door, the glass etched with time and dust and grimy fingers, and pulled. And nothing.

It was—

"It's two o'clock," I huffed. "Who closes at—" I closed my eyes and willed back the tears of panic I felt welling up in my eyes and throat. Mr. Dan was at the wedding, too. Of course he was. Because Jeremy's mother invited the whole damn town…

Plan B—what the hell was Plan B when there was never really a Plan A? I glanced upward. Really to drive back the tears, but I'd take any help at that moment.

What are you doing, Micah?

The unmistakable rumble of a Harley preceded an all-black machine straddled by an equally unmistakable male in jeans stretched to love him and a black t-shirt, his head and face completely covered in a black helmet as he rolled up to the light and set boots on the ground to balance the bike.

He turned his head my way, and goosebumps went down my back. I swear there was a question there. I couldn't see his face, but—no. *No. That's not Plan B*, little voices said in my head. *You're a responsible person now. You own—well, you sort of own a business. You have bills. Obligations. You're a Roman.*

Yeah. That one right there should have slapped me back down the street. But being a respectable Roman, always held to some invisible standard that only my oldest brother could pull off wasn't working for me today.

Harley-guy's right hand reached up and slid the mirrored visor up, revealing dark eyes that even from twenty feet away made my breath catch. In a good way.

Shit, double fuckwaffles! *No!* I didn't need breath-catching in *any* way. I just ran my dumb ass away from one man. But what the hell were my feet doing? I took two steps toward him, and I definitely saw the question that time. Curiosity. Puzzlement. Wariness? Yeah, *Harley-guy* should have that, because clearly I didn't have enough.

"You need help?" he called out over the idling rumble, his voice deep.

I caught a distorted reflection of myself in the dirty window. Hair falling out of the expensive ornate up-do, poking out in unruly frizzy corkscrews above the short veil. Black spreading under my eyes from sweat and tears. Standing on a steamy sidewalk in a mountain of blinding white. It was probably a logical question, but damn the guy had to have balls to jump off into that crazy.

All I could hear was my racing heart and my breathing, even over the motor.

No. This is lunacy. All of it is lunacy, but what you're thinking of doing here is the cherry on top of the—

"Micah!"

I gasped so hard it made me cough, as I jerked in the direction I'd come from, toward the familiar voice I'd known since I was twenty-four. In eight years, I'd heard every possible inflection and emotion in Jeremy Blankenship's voice. I'd heard every range of happy, sad, and controlled anger, but I'd never heard this. Even from all the way down the road, I heard the timbre of mortification in his yell, maybe mixed with a little hurt and *what-the-fuck*. I'd give him that. He deserved the what-the-fuckedness of this situation.

He was standing in the church parking lot alone, and then two other tuxedoed men appeared in the doorway behind him. Thatcher and Jackson. My eyes filled again as I turned away from them and stared back at Harley-guy. I couldn't face my brothers right now. I couldn't explain to them why—

"Micah!" Jeremy yelled again, this time in the tone I recognized. The one that said *how dare you embarrass me.* I glanced back to see him striding purposefully in my direction, and the panic seized my chest.

"Lady?" Harley-guy called out, yanking my attention back his way. "Light's green."

Fight or flight.

Fight or flight.

I looked into eyes I didn't know from Adam and felt the weirdest pull ever. My stilettoed feet made the decision for me, carrying me off the curb and into the street and hauling my weight in dress up to throw a leg over the seat and straddle his ass.

"You sure?" he said over his shoulder.

Fuck no.

"Are you?" I felt a laugh rumble through his body as he shook his head. "Yeah, touché. You aren't gonna kill me, are you?"

"Because if I was, I'd tell you?" he said, revving the engine. "Put on that helmet behind you and hold on."

Oh, sweet Jesus, what am I doing?

That was my last thought as I tugged the veil off, bobby pins flying in all directions, shoved the helmet on, shut my eyes tight and wrapped my arms around his middle the best I could around all that dress. Shut them against the reality of the world I'd just created. Against the sight of my veil lying in the street. Of Jeremy running down the street after me. My brothers running for Thatcher's truck.

All there was, was the bike moving under me and the man between my legs as we sped away, out of Cherrydale. Toward the highway. And to God knows where.

"Where are we going?" I yelled over the din as we hit the highway going south.

"I'm going to Charmed," he yelled back, turning his head slightly so I could hear him. The *I'm* in that sentence was stressed to let me know in no uncertain terms that anything after that was on me. "It's about an hour."

I nodded, trying to calm my heart rate and breathe like a normal person. I knew Charmed, or I knew of it. My family's flower farm rented beehives from Bash Anderson, the owner of an apiary there. That was fine. That'd be good. Not so far away that I'd totally lost my mind. Just maybe a little. Give me a minute to pull my shit together before the cavalry came. And it was good that the stranger I was straddling had a destination. Higher odds that he wasn't going to rape and kill me and leave me in a ditch.

My decision-making abilities needed an overhaul.

"Probably less than that, actually," he continued, making my heart skip in my chest as he upped the speed. "They are going to come after you and I don't feel like fighting today."

"You don't have to fight for me," I yelled.

"I'm not," he said. Well, so much for chivalry. "But that guy's gonna need to hit something, and it won't be you."

There was that.

"What are you going to Charmed for?" I asked.

He paused, and I wasn't sure if he'd heard me.

"Work," he finally tossed back.

"You work there?"

"I will shortly."

We sped along the road in silence for the rest of about forty-five minutes, me attempting to look over my shoulder with a giant ball on my head while maintaining my death grip on some really good abs. A few cars tapped their horns at us, probably thinking we'd just gotten married, but no little old Mustang of mine whipped up next to us with an angry Jeremy inside. No big four-wheel drive truck loomed, either. Which surprised me, because while Jeremy might give up, my older brother Thatcher wouldn't. They must have assumed I'd gone home first or was hiding in Cherrydale somewhere.

That would have been the logical thing to do. Well—if bolting for the door microseconds before walking down the aisle was the relative comparison. In that case, a logical person would have maybe just gone outside to calm her frayed nerves. Maybe walked around the block even. If *that* person had gone so off the rails as to climb onto a stranger's motorcycle and speed away, smart thinking would surely kick in after a block or two and she'd ask him to bring her back to the church. Or to Jeremy's house where we'd lived together for the past two years, to get some things. Somewhere that made sense.

They were looking for *that* person. The Micah Roman that had put away her spontaneous fly-by-the-seat-of-her-pants ways, along with her tendencies to ditch and run when things got too tough. The Micah that had stepped out of those immature shoes and into business ownership with her brother, channeling her spirited creativity into the flower farming instead. The woman who packed up her beloved funky hats and shoes to adorn herself like a responsible businesswoman and worthy future wife to the heir of the Blankenship Resale empire.

Empire, my ass.

They ruled over Cherrydale Trade Days, mostly, which was several square miles of booth space for people to buy and sell their damn junk. And that was awesome, in and of itself. It's where I'd *met* Jeremy, while I was digging through a box of old retro hats and jewelry. He'd stopped and smiled and teased me, and I'd found him delicious and adorable in that way a guy is when he's cutely making fun of your passion and you instantly think of fifteen ways you'll change him and you'll be picking out antique mosaic cabinet knobs together. Wearing matching plaid berets.

From that to now. In a ridiculous dress that was meant to say *I do* in, speeding down a highway with a nameless man to get as far away from Jeremy as I could—as quickly as possible.

So, it was just me and Harley-guy and speed. And it was insane. *I* was insane! I could just hear my brothers now. Well, not Jackson. Jackson knew me. He knew my soul, my heart, my endless need for nonconformity. He was my first shoplifting buddy when I was nine and he was eight, and I taught him how to pocket bubble gum from the corner store. He was the one who raised an eyebrow when I moved in with Jeremy and put all my cherished old record albums and crazy prints in Thatcher's attic and started wearing just one watch instead of four stacked up my arm. Jackson got me. He probably saw this coming like a volcano smoking in the distance. He'd just give me a look and then a hug and tell me he had my back. Thatcher—oh man. He was going to get all puffed up and probably pace and ask me, *"What woman in her right mind did this?"*

And he was right. I didn't know this dude I had my arms around. He could be fifteen kinds of psycho, but oddly enough I felt nothing but safe with him. It vibrated off him along with a primal intensity that was impossible not to feel. Okay, maybe that was the Harley's motor thrumming under my ass, but it felt like more than that.

Shit, yes, I was certifiable.

But the speed. It was awesome. It was like being out in the fields and the greenhouses with my hands in the dirt, textures and colors and aromas surrounding me, filling my senses. I loved being out there with the flowers, free and dirty and reaching for the sun. This was close. When I closed my eyes, it was like flying, free and unchained. Unshackled from expectations and the limitations of boxes. Boring, cream-colored Blankenship boxes. I felt like something freeze dried that had been dropped into water, or one of those vacuum sealed packages that explode to three times their size when introduced to air. I wanted to cry from the joy of it, but I wasn't about to add *hysterical female* to what this guy probably already thought.

The exit for Charmed appeared, touting a big sign with bees and flowers on it saying *Welcome To Charmed. Home of the World Famous Honey Festival.* We leaned into the curve of the exit and slowed, and I was surprised as disappointment washed over me and a new anxiety prickled my skin.

Exploding from my vacuum seal was great and all, but the adventure was ending. My fantasy was easy while adulting was put on hold and no words were exchanged, but shit was about to get real.

Another sign loomed before the turn, advertising a theme park called the Lucky Charm. I'd heard about it and the Honey Festival, but Jeremy never wanted to check them out, thinking it silly to drive an hour to buy bad food and ride a ride. Well, I'd done it now. Go me.

Rolling through Charmed, I was suddenly very aware of my attire. I felt every eye on us. Granted, I probably wouldn't have to be wearing a giant wedding dress for that. If Charmed was anything like Cherrydale, we'd get that same stare just for being out-of-towners.

Still, as we pulled to a stop in front of an old diner with a funky retro sign that said Blue Banana Grille, all I could think about was getting this thing off. This place looked like white bread and bologna and apple pie, like crazy didn't land here much, and I had crazy radiating off me. I could feel it. I needed normal, and I had a feeling that anything resembling it was back there with my cell phone and my keys. And—

"Oh, shit," I said, waiting while he grounded us.

"What?" he asked, his voice sounding preoccupied.

He pulled off his helmet and raked a hand back through short dark hair, while those dark eyes I'd seen earlier focused in hard on the diner door. I had the feeling the novelty of *me* had played out, and my new friend was ready to move on with his day.

"Nothing," I said, pulling my helmet off as well and hooking it back behind me, the reality of my situation rushing in on me from every direction.

I took a deep breath and smiled at a lady riding by on a giant tricycle, who waved and didn't miss a beat. Then again, maybe I could blend.

He held a hand out, supposedly for me, and when I paused, he blew out a breath.

"Well, I don't want to kick you in the face, so you need to get off first," he said, shoving the hand toward me again.

I gave the back of his head a look and resisted the urge to thump it. It was a good head, as heads go, but the part running his mouth was kind of a douche. Although what did I expect from my Harley-riding savior? For him to hold me while I had a good cry? Hell no. I'd pluck my head bald first.

"You should write Hallmark cards," I muttered.

Huffing a little, I tugged my dress up to almost my waist—at least high enough to catch sight of the blue glittery garter ribbon on my left thigh. So did he, I noticed, as the good head tilted downward. I grabbed his hand, expecting it to be for balance, but found myself nearly vaulted off the seat within a microsecond. I even forgot to let go of my dress, standing there with my girlie goods just about on display.

"You good?" he asked, letting go of me and swinging his leg over.

"S—sure," I managed, getting my balance and my first real look at him.

From the worn jeans to the black t-shirt to the really good arms rippling as he tucked his helmet under his arm. A little scruff peppered the hard lines of his face and balanced the sexiest full lips I'd ever seen on a man. Not to mention those soft, dark, haunted-looking eyes I'd already seen. Dear God, if I had to completely muck up my life today, at least it ended in this visual. This guy was jaw-dropping.

His gaze was dropping, too, sliding right down my bare legs.

"You might want to let go of that," he said, with a jut of his chin.

I dropped the fabric like it burned my fingers, and cursed under my breath. *Shit, get it together, Micah.*

"Okay, so thank you," I said, pressing my hands to my hot cheeks. "I'd pay you, but—"

"*Pay* me?"

I pointed at the bike. "For the ride? For the gas?"

"I was coming here already," he said. "You looked like you needed help. At least in those shoes."

I nodded as I glanced down at the spikes attached to my feet. "Something like that. But I don't have my wallet anyway, so…"

"Didn't think that through very well, did you?" he said.

I narrowed my eyes at him. "Thanks for clarifying that."

"Do you have a plan?" he asked.

"Didn't you just establish that I didn't?" I said, rubbing my temples and wishing for an entire bottle of extra strength something to dive into.

He blew out a breath and focused back on the door again, as if his attempt at polite small talk with the crazy lady had just run its course.

"I mean going forward," he said. "Obviously, you probably didn't start this day thinking this is where you'd end up, but I felt your mind spinning the whole way here. Do you know what you're going to do?"

I chuckled in spite of the barbs jabbing behind my skull. "That was survival prep you felt."

One eyebrow lifted in response. "Survival prep?"

"In case you were planning to chop me up and turn me into fertilizer, I had some defense going," I said.

Which wasn't total bullshit. I had thought of that for probably two minutes, before turning to the *what the hell do I do now* channel.

The dark eyes narrowed with amusement, and it warmed his whole face. Like—serious *push me backwards and hold on to my ovaries kind of warmth.*

"Oh?" he said, taking a step closer.

No. I refused to take a step back. He was either being intimidating or flirty and I had no room in my brain for either. I couldn't help that I looked like an idiot doing what I'd done today. It happened. I didn't need this guy to scare me into some sort of lesson about stranger danger. No matter how hot he was. Because if he was just being flirty—well, my body might react to that, but my heart said I'd just left one mostly-decent-mostly-sort-of-nice guy at an altar, and my head said I didn't any more alpha males. Period. I tugged at my dress to cover my boobs better, but it wasn't budging, so I crossed my arms. Which only drew his gaze to exactly there.

"And what was this defense plan of yours?"

His voice slid over my skin like butter, and my body needed its ass kicked.

"I—I'd tell you but—"

He held up a hand. "Yeah, I know how that one goes, but just so you know—"

He glanced past me as the door opened and an elderly man walked out, carrying with him the sounds of clinking silverware and chatter before the door closed behind him. Harley-guy's expression disappeared on me again, all caught up in that building.

"Hey, don't let me keep you," I said. "If you have to get to work or something—"

His gaze snapped back to me. "What?"

I widened mine. "You said you were coming here for work? And you can't get enough of the view of this diner, so—if you need to go in there, go ahead. I'll—figure out what I'm doing in a minute."

"Don't you want to go clean up?" he said.

Awesome.

Just kick me in the face, already.

I smiled and averted my focus down the street. To—more of the same. Another little town pretty much like mine, where everyone knows everyone and nothing is private or personal. I swiped under my eyes and mentally groaned at the black on my fingers.

"Sure," I said.

"And call someone?" he added.

I slid my raccoon eyes up to meet his. "No phone."

He sighed and rubbed at his neck. "Of course not," he muttered.

"I'm not asking to use yours," I said.

"And I'm not offering it," he quipped. "Again—I have my own shit to deal with, lady. I don't need a pissed off jilted lover tracking me down and making me have to hurt somebody."

I blinked and shook my head. Men.

"Let's just do this," I said, turning toward the door and then pivoting back and holding out a hand. "Thank you again if I don't see you when I come out of the bathroom."

Harley-guy looked down at my hand and took it in his. It was warm and protective and gave me all the good feelings I needed to run from.

"You gonna be okay?"

I took a deep breath and licked my dry lips. "I'll land on my feet."

"Do you have a name I can put with this story one day?" he asked, letting go of my hand to cross his arms over his chest. "Or do I just call you Miss Runaway?"

"Roman—" I began, automatically going into business mode, and too late thinking I needed to not tell anyone I was Micah Roman. "-off," I added.

His eyes narrowed slightly. "Roman-off? As in Romanov?"

I opened my mouth and then closed it, going with a nod.

"First name Anastasia?" he asked.

Cute.

No, not cute. Nothing was cute.

"Sure," I said.

"Well, *Anastasia*," he said. "In case I don't see *you* again, the next time you're plotting a defense, here's a tip. Start with what's on you."

"On me," I echoed.

"You have heels on those shoes that can put an eye out, and five hundred pins holding up your hair," he said. "With enough force, any one of those pins can puncture an eardrum and bring a man to his knees."

"Wow," I said as my eyebrows probably moved up there with the bobby pins. "That's—a lot of observation."

He didn't blink. "And that boulder on your finger?"

I glanced down at Jeremy's ring. Funny how I always thought of it that way. Jeremy's ring. Never mine.

"That thing could open a jugular," he said softly toward my ear, brushing against me as he headed toward the door.

"Okay," I said, turning with him, almost magnetically. As if being plastered to him for the last hour had bonded us and now there was this arc of electricity pulling at me. "And you, Mr. Scowling-Harley-guy? Do you have a name?"

"Leo," he said as he kept walking. "Leo McKane."

About the Author

Sharla Lovelace is the bestselling, award-winning author of sexy small-town love stories. Being a Texas girl through and through, she's proud to say she lives in Southeast Texas with her retired husband, a tricked-out golf cart, and two crazy dogs. She is the author of five stand-alone novels including the bestselling *Don't Let Go*, the exciting Heart Of The Storm series, and the fun and sexy new Charmed in Texas series. For more about Sharla's books, visit www.sharlalovelace.com, and keep up with all her new book releases easily by subscribing to her newsletter. She loves keeping up with her readers, and you can connect with her on Facebook, Twitter, and Instagram as @sharlalovelace.

CPSIA information can be obtained
at www.ICGtesting.com
Printed in the USA
BVHW07s0902010618
517924BV00001B/32/P